Damselfly

Jennie Bates Bozic

Printed in the United States of America
First Printing, 2013
ISBN 0-9897347-0-6

Published by Jennie Bates Bozic LLC
Cover Design by Jennie Bates Bozic
Copyedited by Rebecca Weston
Formatting by Polgarus Studio

For Gram, who taught me to love tiny things.

CHAPTER 1

IN TWENTY SECONDS, A FALCON will be released to hunt me down. Today I'm going up against Petunia. My trainer, George, has a thing for naming his birds after flowers, even though I can't think of anything less appropriate. Delicate and pretty they are not, unless you think talons and claws would look nice in a bouquet.

High up in the trees, I lean back against my preferred trunk, pinching my wings against the bark. Their usual vivid blue changes to the mossy brown of the pine until they are almost invisible. If only I could do the same thing with my blonde hair. The heat and humidity have frizzed it out to epic proportions.

I glance up at the counter that's barely visible through the leaves. Fifteen seconds.

My dart guns are strapped firmly to my forcarms. I press my thumbs against the triggers to test the pressure. Plenty of resistance, but still enough give to let me know nothing is jammed. The guns can't hit anything farther than two feet because the needle darts are too small. Longer-range darts are too big for me—in fact, they're taller than I am.

Ten seconds.

I crouch down and latch my gaze onto the goal: a piece of pipe wedged into the branches of the biggest beech tree. It's too small for the falcons, but large enough for me to squeeze inside. All I have to do is get from tree to tree without being spotted with as little flying as possible.

1

Five. Four. Three. Two. One. GO.

Petunia bursts out of the cage and instantly begins climbing above the canopy. I run along the branch toward the pine needles at the end, eyes fixed on each step. My wings cover my back and camouflage my scurrying legs.

I leap over a nub and feel my feet stick firmly to the branch when I land.

Sap. *Oh…crap.* I pick up my right foot with difficulty and wipe it against a clean patch of bark, but I can't get rid of all the stickiness. I should have worn socks today; I could have just slipped them off and kept going. Seconds are ticking away. Panicked, I look up at the sky. In the patches of blue, I can see Petunia circling overhead. Judging from her position, she's probably looking in my direction right now.

Walking is out of the question. She'll definitely see me if I fly.

So I wait. Sweat beads on my skin until my shirt is stuck firm to me, and a terrible itch makes me want to rub my back against the bark until it stops.

Then, out of the corner of my eye, I see a person running through the underbrush of the forest and my heart stands still. He looks just like…but he's not. I roll my eyes at myself. His hair is like Jack's—jet black and long enough to graze the tops of his cheekbones—but that's the only similarity. And Jack is not exactly close to the project seeing as he's on the other side of the world in South Dakota. Still, that hair is enough to get my heart racing and aching all at once. It's been a couple of days since Jack and I last talked. George has stepped up my training so that I'm out here several times a day, and when I'm finally free, the time difference gets in the way. Even without that, I don't know how much conversing we would be able to do after back-to-back training sessions. I've been so exhausted I've barely been able to eat before falling asleep at night. George still hasn't given me a good explanation for the extra workouts. He's just said that I need to be in fantastic shape before my birthday.

I'm trying not to get my hopes up, but maybe that means they're actually going to release me in a couple of days. I'll turn sixteen, become an adult, and get to go out into the real world where the falcons have sharp beaks and no one has seen a tiny girl like me before.

I don't recognize this Man-with-Jack's-Hair, and I'm pretty sure he isn't part of the Lilliput Project in any way since he's running toward me. He doesn't know that an invisible dome separates our worlds.

His face is about to find out.

He barrels into the dome and falls backward into the weeds, stunned. He's skinnier than the last straggler I saw, and his clothes are barely hanging on. He's only got one shoe; his left foot sports a holey sock. It's hard to tell how old he is through all that grimy facial hair, but the eyes say that he's in his thirties.

Mr. One Sock pulls himself up with difficulty, as though gravity has become too much for him.

He lets his head fall back, and he wails. I can't hear him, but I don't need to in order to sense his anguish. He pummels his fists against the wall until his knuckles leave oozing red marks.

That was the wrong move.

"Get out of here," I whisper under my breath. "Go before they catch you." The last time someone was found trespassing, Dr. Christiansen had her dragged out of sight, kicking and screaming and pleading for food. I don't know what happened to her after that.

As if on cue, he stops pounding and stares at me as if he can actually see through the thick fibers that are supposed to camouflage the Lilliput Project with light-wrapping technology.

Can he?

I flick my wings away from the branch so they return to their natural, brilliant blue color. The starving man gasps, steps back.

So he *can* see me. I make a shooing gesture. Get out of here. You don't want to be here.

But he just stands there, transfixed by the sight of a tiny teenaged girl. Then his eyes widen in horror, and he points at the branches above me.

Ever so slowly, I twist my head around, but it's too late for caution. Leaves and twigs rain down around me as Petunia crashes through the canopy.

I dive off the branch and snap my wings open so I can hide underneath the very spot where I was just standing. I hook my toes into the bark—

thank goodness for my sticky feet now—and extend both my arms out. My wings keep me hovering below the branch.

Now…which side is Petunia going to pick?

The branch bucks violently under her weight as she lands and bits of bark and dirt shower down around me. The impact dislodges my foot, and I flail around, trying to get my toes back into place. I fight to steady myself and keep my needle guns trained on both sides of the branch. If I'm a fraction of a second too late, I'll end up with a nasty bruise from Petunia's blunt beak. Maybe a broken bone.

Her head appears to my right. Before she can blink her beady eyes one more time, I fire a needle and it hits her on the cheek. For one terrifying moment, I wonder if it didn't manage to get through her feathers, but then her eyes lose their focus as the paralysis sets in. After one last, desperate beat of her wings, she falls into the net below.

I twist around and give her a little wave goodbye. Farewell, Petunia. I'm sure you'll sleep well.

I grab onto the bark, and with a few flutters, I vault back on top. I scan the fence, looking for my new friend. He smiles back at me and gives me a round of applause.

Then I see the guard. He's creeping up behind the man, gun already out of its holster. I wave my arms frantically. It's my turn to sound the warning.

I'm too late. The man turns his head and sees the guard, but he isn't strong enough to escape. The desperate look in his eyes belongs to someone who knows he is trapped.

"George!" I scream. "George, help him!" I fly as fast as I can to the wall and hover there, pounding the fibers with my fists.

The guard lifts his dart gun and fires it soundlessly. The man's eyes go blank, and he crumples into the weeds. There is no net to break his fall. The hawks of Lilliput are treated with more care than the people outside.

The guard signals his partner, and together they drag the man away. I wince as they tug his brittle form over roots and rocks. He looks like a bag of bones, and his face is so childlike…

How many others have there been? They come here looking for food, and they leave with a horrible headache. At least, I assume they leave that way. The last time I tried to ask, Dr. Christiansen shut me down. Then again, she does that regardless of the question.

My chest tightens, and it's not just because I'm upset. I flutter to the ground and double over, gasping for breath. Dang it, I'm wheezing already. It's not even noon, and my lungs are closing up.

"Lina! Where are you?" George stumbles through the underbrush and the ground shakes under my feet. I flick my wings so he'll see me. He crashes over as fast as his thick, middle-aged legs will allow. The falcon, now hooded, clings to his gloved arm and jerks her head side to side with quick movements. She senses me, but she can't do anything since George holds the tethers tied around her feet.

"Sorry she got so close," he says, kneeling beside me. I'm still doubled over, trying to breathe. "Asthma attack?"

A nod is all I can manage.

He reaches into his shirt pocket and pulls out a bag the size of his thumbnail. "Here you go. You'd better get it out yourself."

I grab the purse and rummage through it until I find my asthma medication. Opening the tin, I break apart one of the capsules and inhale as deeply as the vise grip of the attack will allow. I'm too small for a regular inhaler. At six-and-a-quarter-inches, I'm too small for a *lot* of things.

Within seconds, the feeling of drowning fades away, and I gulp down fresh air like a starving woman.

"Didn't you see him?" I ask George.

"See who?" He fiddles with Petunia's tethers without meeting my eyes. He's a terrible liar.

I roll my eyes. "Yeah, okay. I was just wondering why he was able to see me. And, you know, whether or not he's *alive*."

"No one who works for the Lilliput Project would hurt that man," George insists. Somehow his wording isn't all that reassuring and he can tell. He sighs. "The wall is transparent. It always has been."

"Then why did Dr. Christiansen—"

"I don't know why."

And that's all I'm going to get from him on the subject. I think George would rather be thrown into a shark tank than make Dr. Christiansen angry. Then again, I can't really blame George for hanging on to his job at all costs. I glance back toward the wall where my new friend stood only minutes ago.

"Do you want to try again? I'll keep a closer eye on Petunia this time," George offers hopefully. "No distractions."

I draw another ragged breath. The attack has gone, but my lungs feel like sandpaper.

"I think I need a break," I say.

"All right." He looks down at the leaf-strewn ground. The trees are beginning to change color and shed their summer gowns. Fall is here. The nights are going to get really cold for those who don't have a home anymore.

"Lina." He waits for me to look up at him. "I'm sorry about the man. I'll…ask about him."

"Thanks." I manage a smile. "I guess I'll go grab something to eat."

"I can carry you—"

"No." *Hell no.* He's not going to carry me anywhere. "I just need a little break, but I can fly on my own."

He chuckles and runs a hand across his stubbled chin. "All right. How long do you think you'll be?"

"Maybe an hour. I also need to stop by Mr. Coxworth's to get your tobacco. That is, if you've reconsidered my offer…" I raise a questioning eyebrow. "One last hurrah?"

He sighs. "Lina, I'll get fired. And there will be so many people there."

"It's my sixteenth birthday!"

"Exactly. All of your donors will be at the party. I saw the guest list."

"How about helping me leave early then?"

He knows it's a losing battle. "All right."

"One pouch of the world's finest tobacco coming right up!"

He cracks a smile, but it doesn't reach his eyes. "I suppose you don't become an adult every day."

"Nope. Free at last! Whatever that means."

George clears his throat and moves his mouth around as though it's full of pebbles and he can't get the words out. "What do you think will change? I mean, what are your plans?"

I hover above the ground and tug a pine needle off the bottom of my sticky foot. *I want to go outside. I want to see the sun without a transparent wall in between. I want to see Jack in person for the first time.*

I blush. "I don't know yet. I heard there are still a couple of colleges open. I want to finally get to use all the skills we've been training. Otherwise, what's the point, right?"

He nods half-heartedly. We've been over this before. I have to train in case animals break through a hole in the dome before it can be fixed. My life could someday depend on my ability to react and respond to the sorts of situations I would face practically every day if I were to live outside. I have to believe that's the goal—to make me ready to live on my own. Even if no one's talking about it, I need that hope. I cannot imagine living my life in this prison. It's just not possible.

"Maybe..." I begin, but my voice trails off.

George says nothing. I want him to finish the sentence. I want to know that someone else is dreaming on my behalf. I want to know I'm not the only person who envisions a life for me beyond this place.

Maybe I'll make friends. Maybe I'll get a degree. Maybe I'll finally be able to make clothes for other people the way I've always wanted.

"Maybe I can find a college without a lot of birds," I blurt out.

George laughs, but the worry creases in his forehead remain. "It's not so bad here, is it? What if you have to stay for a while?"

I give him a dirty look. "I'll see you later."

He nods and sighs as he flips open his wristpad to look at his calendar. "Dr. Christiansen has just now scheduled me to fix her computer in fifteen minutes."

I snort. "She probably forgot to turn it on." She doesn't enjoy looking stupid in front of the real IT guys, so she bothers George instead. As if he doesn't already have enough to do as my trainer and the resident veterinarian.

George kisses his index finger and brushes it against both of my cheeks in turn. His hands are rough and calloused, but he's so gentle he barely touches me at all. He devised this greeting and farewell because he can't kiss both of my cheeks according to his custom. It always makes me smile. I give his finger a big smooch, and he grins at me before taking himself and his falcon to the aviary.

I turn and face my forest. When I watch the sun filtering through the treetops, I almost forget I'm in a cage. My bars are transparent filaments that form a dome-shaped cocoon over the entire compound and forest. In 2065, the year I was born, the filaments were state-of-the-art, just like everything else in the Lilliput Project. Now, almost sixteen years later, the technology has yet to be updated. Sure, the fence has been mended, loose wall siding has been nailed back into place, and the software has been regularly patched, but the entire place suffers from the disease of shabbiness. I never noticed until I saw pictures on the internet of buildings with fresh paint, gleaming floors, and modern computers. Now, Lilliput reminds me of a dilapidated Gold Rush town in a Spaghetti Western.

Dr. Christiansen was the one who proposed the Lilliput Project to the Danish government when the energy crisis was causing infrastructure breakdowns across the planet. At that point, several civil wars had broken out in Europe, but no one knew how deep the societal cracks went. Governments were still hopeful that they might be able to find a solution before all hell broke loose. Global warming was really starting to get ugly, and farmers were fighting a losing battle to grow their crops. It was clear humanity was entering the worst crisis since the Black Death and when you're facing the threat of worldwide hunger, the idea of creating tiny people suddenly doesn't seem so crazy. The regulatory tape was thinner than ever, and since then, Dr. Christiansen has kept the project as small and close to the earth as possible.

Lilliput is sustainable, intimate, claustrophobic.

I was the only one created, and Dr. Christiansen treats me as though the world depends on her raising me perfectly. She calls herself my mother; I call her my jailer. She controls the vast majority of my life, and I'm sure she'd keep me here forever if she could.

I think she was born with a soul full of bleach. She looks like it, too.

That's why her silence over my upcoming emancipation is making me more than a little nervous. I've seen the articles online hinting that there will be some big reveal. I can only assume they're talking about my photograph, which the world has never seen before. Every detail about my sequestered life in this compound has remained a closely guarded secret.

I pull my bush of tangled hair away from my face. It makes me look like a rock-and-roll princess and there's nothing I can do about it. Hair ties won't stay in because of how fast I fly, and no one makes rubber bands for someone my size.

I unfold my wings and take off through the trees. Mr. Coxworth, the resident botanist, lives in a cottage along the forest path. To the uninitiated, it's a dilapidated wooden shack that's only one strong wind away from extinction. To Dr. Christiansen, it's an accident waiting to happen. To me, it's a cozy wonderland of plants and odd smells. While all of the buildings on the grounds are environmentally friendly, Mr. Coxworth's house manages to be *part* of the environment.

I slip through the crack under the door, along with several ants, and fly up to sit on the pincushion Mr. Coxworth has always reserved for me. Then I wait for him to notice I'm here.

The cottage only has one room. The glassless windows are partially rotted, and the door is designed to keep out people but not small animals and insects. It looks more like an old gardening shed than someone's home. It's a mash-up of sinks, flower pots, dirty dishes, broken jars, and dusty books. Some of the volumes are rare editions, but Mr. Coxworth does not discriminate. They are all piled haphazardly, each of them only as valuable as its usefulness. Dried and drying plants hang from the ceiling rafters by thin wires so the mice can't climb down and chew them.

A rickety twin bed sits squeezed into the narrow alcove. Right now, Mr. Coxworth is stretched out on top, hands folded on his chest, eyes closed. His gray dreadlocks are squashed against the pillow. His two pet mice scurry up his arm to his face.

"No, Disney," he murmurs in his British accent. The white one runs along Mr. Coxworth's arm and collides with the other mouse, Munch. They chitter and roll together onto the mattress and then scramble to the floor before disappearing into the shadows under the bed.

Mr. Coxworth opens one eye and then the other. "Fee fie fo fum, I smell a girl as tall as two thumbs."

I laugh and fly over to his nightstand. He's greeted me this way since I was the size of one thumb. He's had to adjust his rhyme over the years.

"Good morning," I say with a smile.

"Is it?" He scratches his head. "Seems a rather average morning to me."

"Fine. Be ornery then."

"Well, now that I have her majesty's permission…" He sits with a grimace, then swings his legs over the edge of the bed, resting his wrinkled feet on the floorboards. He smells of old sweat, garlic, and lemon soap. "I suppose you're here for your pay." He nods at the nightstand drawer.

"Yep. You're going to make me work even harder for it, aren't you?"

He grunts and grabs his water glass from the nightstand. There's a leaf floating in it, but he doesn't seem to notice as he gulps down the liquid.

I fly to the knob, wrap my arms around it and push against the nightstand frame with my feet until the drawer pulls open a couple of inches. Inside, I find a drawstring pouch just small enough to fit in my arms. It's full of the best tobacco money can buy on the black market. While George has always been my friend and protector, Mr. Coxworth is more like a partner in crime, and I've never been completely confident he wouldn't squeal on me if it would benefit him.

Mr. Coxworth raises his eyebrow. "Don't smoke it all at once. Your head will explode."

"Oh, it's not for me."

"As far as I know, it's you who smokes it. But I can't judge. Smoked worse stuff myself when I was your age and it didn't hurt me a bit." He looks at the glass in his hand then fishes inside it for the leaf. He pulls the limp bit of green out with a flourish and holds it up. "How did this get in there?"

"I guess it was thirsty."

He flicks it onto the packed dirt floor.

"The tobacco really isn't for me, though. Gotta buy a favor!"

"Good. Don't tell me what it is. If you're up for it later, I'm going to need more moss."

This is our trade-off. I fetch him samples of the moss that grows at the top of the trees, and he gives me tobacco. Then I bribe George with the tobacco whenever I want something I'm not allowed to have. I have an online date with Jack on my birthday. It might even be our last one. I push that thought out of my head.

"Mr. Coxworth?"

He's pulling on his socks. "Yes?"

"What happens to the people who come here for food? Isn't there anywhere else they can go?"

"My. my, Lina. I haven't even had my coffee yet," he says, but he sets his half-socked foot back down on the ground. "That isn't part of my research."

"That isn't really an answer."

He laughs, but it has a brittle edge to it. "You're very perceptive. My best answer is that I don't know for sure, but you needn't worry about it. Lilliput is committed to the wellbeing of the world." He gestures vaguely in the air, as if the world is a pesky fly to be swatted.

I try really hard to be comforted by that explanation, but the starving man's expression when he realized he had been caught isn't an image I can easily dismiss. Still, I know I'm not going to squeeze out any more info today.

He points to the pouch I'm holding. "Don't get caught with that, love. Although there's more where it came from if you want to scavenge for me again soon."

I blow Mr. Coxworth a kiss and wave goodbye as I fly toward the door. "Maybe later!"

I look furtively in all directions before flying out into the open. I have no intention of getting caught today. All of the workers are busy at the main buildings at this hour, so I hold my bag of contraband snug against my chest and take off toward my house.

I stare at the forest floor below me as I fly, looking for exceptionally colorful leaves to use for decoration. Summer has only recently rolled into autumn, but some of the trees have already begun to turn orange and red and yellow. Not many have shed their leaves yet, but there are still a few gems littering the ground.

Green, muted yellow, pale orange, brown. White tennis shoes.

Oh crap.

CHAPTER 2

I DART TO HIDE BEHIND a tree and lose my grip on the pouch. It plops right on top of a pair of brilliant red leaves. Just my luck.

"Good morning, Lina." Dr. Christiansen's tone is laced with ice, per usual. She's a snow queen in a lab coat, all white and blonde and pale. She could have been pretty if she'd ever cared about such things.

I desperately want to retrieve the tobacco, but I'm hoping she didn't notice it and the last thing I want is to draw attention to my precious stash.

No such luck. She walks over and kneels to retrieve the pouch. Her fingers give it an exploratory pinch.

"Now, what is this?" She holds it to her nose and frowns. "Tobacco? Where did you get this?"

I clamp my mouth shut.

A blizzard forms behind her eyes. "Lina, did one of the interns give this to you? I won't allow this on the grounds. The chemicals interfere with natural development and impede my observations."

Her voice is like plastic scraping against packed snow. Why does she always have to talk to me as though I'm utterly stupid?

I fold my arms. There's no way I'm giving her any information. She won't be returning my bag, and I worked almost every day for a month to get that stupid pouch.

She cocks her eyebrow at me. I cock mine right back. We're locked in yet another nonverbal gun-slinging contest. First one to speak loses, and it's not going to be me.

"Well." She flares her nostrils triumphantly. "I'll confiscate this, take it to the lab, and run the fingerprints. I'm sure that will reveal your accomplice."

And I'm sure Mr. Coxworth already thought of that and used gloves, but nice try!

"We'll speak later, Lina. After I determine which of your privileges to take away."

I try to think of something snarky and clever to say but decide against it. Best not to push my luck any further today. She walks past me, clearly not expecting an answer. I take a deep breath and continue on toward my house.

Now I'm going to have to think of some other way to get out of that party. In a perfect world, I would be able to just ask George for favors, but since I've already put his job into jeopardy several times, I can't keep a clear conscience and continue asking without giving him something in return. Something he really wants.

Something that is now in the doctor's pocket.

I dive down until I'm gliding along the ground so I can give the leaves several good kicks. And then the path opens into the clearing which surrounds my little home.

My treehouse is at the center of the woods, far from the other living quarters. The house itself wraps around the trunk of one of the oldest trees—a gnarled beech, but you probably wouldn't even notice it at first glance because it's covered in moss and tree bark. It's my own forest refuge.

I fly through the garden below the house to check on my herbs. They don't get a lot of sunlight here, so I have to give them extra love to help them survive. The beech's roots serve as handy section dividers between my basil, lemon balm, and spinach. I also grow blackberries, even though they tend to choke out the other plants and their thorns are a pain. But nothing's better than a blackberry for dessert, so I think they're worth the hassle.

I also have a little landscaped section with lily of the valley, mushrooms, moss, and…weeds. When I first planted the garden, weeds didn't last a day if I could help it, but I have grown to appreciate their unruly wildness. It's nice to have some part of my life not under strict control. I love to sit in my flower garden on the stone bench George carved for me and watch the weedy stems curl around the flowers until the whole thing is a big bed of green and white and purple.

I dig my hand into the rich brown to inspect the soil underneath my basil. It rained last night and everything is still damp. That's a good sign. I pat one of the beech's roots.

"Don't hog all the water," I whisper before flying up to my porch, which resembles an alien mushroom landing pad. I unlock the door and step inside.

Quiet.

I stand there, listening. I hear nothing but the wind tugging at the branches of my tree. The wood floor rocks with gentle motion under my feet, and I breathe in deeply. The asthma attack has passed, and my lungs feel brand-new.

I wipe my bare feet off on the rug. I rarely ever wear shoes because no one makes decent ones this small. In fact, I sew the majority of my clothes, but I can't get the shoes right quite yet. Instead, I wear several layers of stockings when it's cold. Dr. Christiansen says they considered engineering me with insect legs instead of human ones but decided against it in the end. Thank goodness.

The thought of Dr. Christiansen reminds me of the tobacco, and I fling myself onto my couch in frustration. What am I going to do? I've had this date planned with Jack for weeks now, and I can't postpone it. As soon as I step outside the compound the day after my birthday, the press will have my picture, and everyone in the entire world will find out what "Thumbelina" looks like for the first time. Everyone, including Jack.

I run my finger along the edge of the upholstery. The couch is a little overstuffed since it's actually for dolls, but I can't complain. George finds collectible doll furniture for me from all sorts of exotic places, even though Dr. Christiansen disapproves. She would prefer I weave my own bed out of grass to increase my survival skills. Too bad for her. The outside of my house might belong in the forest, but the interior is a castle. Silk curtains, handmade rugs, carved wooden furniture. I even have a canopy bed.

I just wish I could show it off or have someone over. Anybody. And not only through the Internet.

At the other end of my living room sits my computer desk and halojector. The halojector is a fancy pair of goggles that allows me to enter virtual online worlds and chat rooms. It can read your facial expressions, and it uses sensors to determine how you would move, walk, talk, etc., without you having to do any of those things in the real world. The result is an almost perfect avatar of yourself. I'm not supposed to have it, but George (once again) came to my rescue when I guilted him into it three years ago. I still remember that conversation.

"But Dr. Christiansen said…" George protested.

"This is the only way I can have friends. Do you want me to not have any friends?"

"I'm your friend."

"No, you're like a nice uncle. And you're old enough to be my dad, so you don't count."

"You are going to get me fired one day, Lina."

"That's what the Germans would have said in Nazi Germany. Do you want to be like a Nazi?"

That settled it. He adapted a halojector to my scale and even gave me a webcam so I can talk to people with my regular face instead of an avatar if I want.

Right after George installed it, I got involved in Internet games and chat parlors. I experimented with all sorts of different haircuts and skin colors and fashions in order to meet people of all stripes. Sure, their voices still had to come over the speakers and occasionally someone would disconnect and vanish into thin air, but it was the closest I'd come to having real friends my own age.

After a while, I got tired of playing someone so different from myself, so now my avatar is authentically me…sans wings. I started going into chat parlors—big virtual living rooms. Some have themes; some are run-of-the-mill meeting spaces with nothing fancy in terms of decorations. I always find a place along the edge so I can watch the comings and goings. There I wait, stuck closer to the wall than its last coat of paint, and hope someone comes over to strike up a conversation.

That's how I met Jack one year ago.

He sat sprawled in his chair in a chat parlor, tracing his finger around the rim of a glass. Jet black hair dangled in his eyes and grazed the tops of his tanned cheekbones. He was alone but didn't seem to be in a hurry to be sociable. A couple of teenaged guys walked past him, gave him high-fives, but didn't stay long. He was friendly with them but didn't look desperate to get anyone's attention.

I started plotting how I could inch my way along the room's perimeter, but then two girls giggled their way over to him. He smiled and leaned forward with casual interest.

One of them was pretty. Prettier than me, anyway. She had hair to die for—smooth sheets of spun gold. I patted at my frizz ball, but taming it was impossible. Why oh why did I scan in with my real hair?

Those girls laughed and talked too easily, as though they'd popped out of the womb with a bachelor's degree in flirtation. Goldilocks sat down next to him (really close, practically on his lap) and started working the space between them as though there was a rubber band of desire pulling her close, then easing up, then pulling her toward him again. But he was an immovable object, firmly friendly and unaffected by her advances. He didn't flirt back the way I'd seen other guys respond.

Goldilocks must have realized her mating display wasn't getting her anywhere, so she and her friend stood with little waves of farewell. He smiled but didn't get up.

Then he turned his head and caught me staring at him.

I have never averted my eyes so quickly in all my life. Unfortunately, I also averted my neck in the real world and gave myself a horrible cramp. After massaging the resulting knot for a few painful moments, I worked up the courage to look at him again.

He was hiding his mouth behind his hand, laughter in his eyes. He had totally seen my contortionist impression.

Then he stood up. I'm used to people towering over me, but I couldn't help noticing how tall he was, even with my adjusted height.

He breached the space between us far too quickly for comfort. I needed time to figure out what do with him, how to meet those eyes without blushing. But there he was, standing in my space, *looking* at me. Looking at *me*.

A grin spread across his face, easy as breathing. I didn't want to look too eager. Then again, I didn't want to turn him off either. I certainly didn't want him to go away.

"Hi," he said. White teeth, crinkling eyes. "You must be Thumbelina."

The words wrapped around my throat, choking me. How did he know? "What?"

"Thumbelina1847? I really thought I'd guessed it right."

"Oh. *Oh.*" I held the relief from my face as much as possible. "How did you figure it out?"

"Well, let's see here. You don't look like an 'aragornnn20' or a 'woodchuckman' or a 'nosteroids.' Shall I continue?"

"So which one are you?"

"I'm Jack."

"Jacknostalk?"

"That's me."

"Kinda creepy name."

"Yeah. I didn't realize it until it was too late to change it. I should have made it 'beanstalk' instead. Do you mind if I park my chair here?"

"I guess. Since you left your stalk at home." Oh, me of little wit.

I slid down along the wall and stared at the floor as he scraped his chair into place.

"I've seen you in here before," he said. How come I'd never noticed him? "You always stay by the wall with this look on your face like you're thinking really hard about something."

"Oh." What could I say to that?

"So where are you from?" he asked.

"Um." I decided to tell the truth. "Denmark."

"Really? I don't think I've met anyone from there before. Where is that exactly?"

"Northern Europe, right on top of Germany."

"Oh, okay. You speak English really well."

"Thanks. I mean, it's my first language. One of my moms is American."

He raised his eyebrow. "Two moms? That's cool."

I blurted out a nervous laugh. "No. Not that. I mean, I have step-parents. How about you?"

"No step-parents here. Not anymore, anyway. Just a mom."

"Oh, I'm sorry."

He shook his head, his dark hair scattering from his forehead. "My dad died years ago in the civil war. I live in South Dakota now. On a reservation."

"I'm so sorry."

"The reservation isn't *that* bad."

I threw my head back and laughed. My nervousness evaporated when I saw the delighted look on his face.

Jack leaned forward in his chair, his eyes locked on mine. I held my breath and returned his gaze. It was easier than I thought.

"So, Thumbelina, do you have a name?"

"Lina."

"How old are you?"

Shoot, what if he thought I was too young? "I'm almost fifteen. You?"

"Sixteen. When's your birthday?"

"In two days."

There was that gorgeous smile again. "Happy birthday. Any big plans?"

"I really hope not." Visions of a Dr.-Christiansen-orchestrated-debacle paraded through my mind.

"Not much of a party animal, are you?"

"No," I said a little too defensively. "I guess I'm not."

"Me neither. Unless it's a tribe thing. Even then…"

"I don't really know anything about those."

"We don't have them very often anymore. Usually there's some traditional dancing, and that part's all right. But then people start drinking and that's when I leave."

"Oh."

"I seem to have a knack for bringing up depressing topics today. Sorry about that."

"No, it's fine." I fidgeted with the hem of my skirt. I had made it myself out of a taffeta that folds and wrinkles like raffia paper, but it looked smoother in its digital incarnation. I looked up to find him watching me with a sort of perplexed curiosity.

"So…what do you do for fun?" he asked.

Escape from falcons? Tend my garden? Read?

"I design and sew my own clothes. I make my own dyes, too."

His eyebrows shot toward his forehead. "Wow, that's awesome. I'm not very creative. I can't draw anything except stick figures. But I do play a mean harmonica."

I giggled but then tried to grab it back in case he was seriously proud of his harmonica skills. "What songs can you play?"

"Hmm, well, 'Twinkle, Twinkle Little Star' and 'Twinkle, Twinkle Little Star.' I tried to learn 'Mary Had a Little Lamb,' but it was a bit too complex for me."

I laughed again, and his face lit up.

"If it makes you feel any better, I don't play anything at all," I said.

"Awesome! I win this round."

"Oh, are we having a competition?"

"It's a contest for who can play the most ridiculous, useless instrument. Clearly I am the champion." He leaned into his chair, his shoulders easily as broad and strong as the wooden back. I had to wrench my eyes away from them.

"Well then, I'll just have to accept defeat."

"Don't give up so easily now."

His eyes traced over my facial features. I blushed and scratched a non-existent itch on my forehead. He seemed to recede into himself, and the open, happy guy was replaced with the cool and confident Jack I saw talking to those girls.

"That seriously is amazing though," he said.

"What is?"

"That you make your own clothes. You do a good job. I'm not good with style, but yours are cool. That shawl thing is really colorful."

It was a scarf, but whatever. "Thank you. That's a…a really nice compliment." No one had said anything about my clothes before.

"Maybe you could come over and stitch up this hole in my sock…"

"Oh, no, you didn't. You did not go there."

"I think you're learning how to be the perfect little housewife."

"Sure. Too bad you're not training to be Prince Charming."

"Ha." It came out like a bark. His face scrunched up under the sting of my words, and I instantly felt bad. When would I ever stop putting my foot in my mouth?

"I'm sorry," we both said at the same time. Then we laughed in unison.

"Don't bother," he said. "I probably deserved it. And I think I should make it up to you."

My heart stopped for a moment. I tried to think of something clever to say but all that came out was, "No, really, you don't have to." Mentally, I kicked myself. Hard.

"I know I don't have to, but I'd like to. Unless *you* don't want me to."

"No, I would." It came out way too quickly.

"Do you play Pixelsgarden?"

Pixelsgarden was a game or, really, a digital world where players constructed their own environments. You projected yourself into the world with an avatar. Most people used their regular scanned selves, but you could alter almost anything about your appearance.

"I have an avatar for it, yes."

"Why don't you meet me there on your birthday?"

"What time? And what construct?"

"If you give me your email address, I'll send you an invitation."

"Oh, that's very smooth of you."

"Getting your email? That's nothing. I just got you to agree to go on a date with me on your birthday."

My cheeks started burning at the word "date." It was getting hard to meet his eyes again. Instead, I focused on typing my email address out for him in the chat box.

"Thanks," he said. "You'll hear from me soon. I've gotta go—Mom needs me."

"Okay. It was really nice to meet you." Wow, was that the best goodbye I could manage?

He returned my smile. "Likewise. See you soon."

I grinned awkwardly at the screen as he vanished and his sign-on blinked off.

And that's how Jack and I began.

CHAPTER 3

AFTER JACK SIGNED OFF, I had tried to go about the rest of my day as normal. I'd read about those girls who pined by the phone (even though I didn't have one), and I was determined not to be like them. I would be confident. I would continue on with my life.

Instead I chewed down all my fingernails and refreshed my email every ten minutes. And every hour I logged into Pixelsgarden to check out my avatar and tweak the outfit, fix the makeup, or primp the hair.

But I didn't get an email that day. By the time bedtime rolled around, I had worked myself into despair over the absolute *surety* Jack had forgotten me. Even though I really, really hoped I was wrong.

There was no email the next morning either. I had kicked myself for checking and gave myself a long lecture on the way to morning practice with George about how stupid I was being over this strange boy I did not even know and how could I have a crush on someone I had just met? But then I would convince myself it wasn't really a crush, that I was only extremely curious about this handsome guy and we were going to have a nice, friendly chat together if he ever got around to emailing me about this date he had proposed.

I was in such a mood by the time I arrived at the aviary that George hadn't known what to do with me. When I asked to practice with the poisoned needle darts, he handed them over with more trepidation than was really warranted.

I continued to practice with George until lunchtime. I'd hoped the flight speed drills would distract me from thoughts of Jack, but he stayed there in my mind the whole time like a shadow.

We stopped for lunch and I returned to my house to eat. I mixed a nut and herb salad for myself and ate the entire thing before I gave in to the siren call of my computer.

There, in my inbox, was an email, its subject letters bold and new. It read: "So…about tomorrow." With my breath stuck in my throat, I clicked on it, half-afraid he was writing me to cancel.

Hey Thumbelina,
Meet me tomorrow at 9 p.m. your time in the construct called 'Linasbirthday.' It's case-sensitive. The password is your screenname.
Looking forward to it! Let me know if that time doesn't work for you.
– Jack

I reread it too many times to count, even though he didn't give me much to analyze. All I knew was that he was "looking forward to it!" and he'd gone to the extra trouble of creating a construct specifically for my birthday. Those two observations alone gave me a high unlike anything I'd experienced before. I was completely useless during my afternoon tutor session. I could not wipe the smile from my face for the rest of the day, not even when I accidentally stabbed my palm with my sewing needle.

The next evening, I resolved I would not change clothes ten times. My hair was a complete disaster. I had put it into pin curls the night before because I'd envisioned tight, well-defined ringlets that would, of course, become looser and sexier as date time approached. But when I took the pins out, my hair became an even more enormous puffball than usual. I looked like someone had attached a rabbit tail to my head. Or a porcupine. Or a blowfish.

There was only one thing I could do: wet it down and put it into a ponytail. I tied a lace ribbon as tight as I could to keep it all in place.

By the time my watch clock beeped to tell me it was 9:00, I was presentable. I logged myself into Pixelsgarden, loaded my avatar, and checked it one final time. It looked better than I did. As long as he didn't want to chat afterward over webcam, I was good to go.

I clicked on the construct and held my breath as it loaded.

Stark pine trees came into focus against a cloudless blue sky. The ground below them ended at the sky, and it took me a moment to realize I was on a mountain, staring off a steep ledge.

I was also alone. Five minutes late and he wasn't there yet. Unease settled into me, stealing my excitement. Where was he?

I turned around to take in the scenery behind me and was instantly blinded by the sun. It definitely wasn't 9 p.m. in this world. A dirt path wound up the mountain, mostly obscured by dry shrubs. All of the evergreens gave me the impression they needed a good meal.

While the view from the ledge was of a beautiful mountain vista, that was the only exceptional thing about the location. Large masses of rock erupted out of the thick, endless forest below. Not a drop of haze appeared even when the blue sky dipped behind the horizon.

I could not, for the life of me, figure out why he would bring me there. Or why he hadn't already arrived himself.

At 9:16, as I was about to log off, Jack's avatar loaded right next to mine. He looked around, worried, and then let out a sigh of relief when he saw me.

"I'm really sorry," he said.

"It's okay." Except it wasn't.

A strained smile forced its way onto his face. "Happy birthday."

"Thanks."

Awkward silence.

A lump started to grow in my throat, and no amount of reason would make it go away. I was too disappointed. This was all a mistake. I told myself I should give up and log off.

I wiped my hands on my shirt, pretending to iron out any wrinkles.

He cleared his throat. "So how was your day?"

I swallowed a sigh. I did not want to play the small talk game. Especially with someone who was not at all enthusiastic to be with me.

"It was fine. Just had some chocolate cake with friends."

"That sounds really nice." He kept looking away, out at the view.

Another awkward pause. I drew lines on the ground with my toe as the silence grew stifling. Finally, with a sick feeling in my stomach, I decided it just wasn't worth it. I'd clearly gotten my hopes up for no reason.

"Look," I said, "we don't have to do this. I'm not sure if something is wrong or what, but it doesn't seem like you want to be here."

"No, I do."

I folded my arms. "Is something wrong?" I braced myself for the answer.

He sighed and rubbed his eyes. "My mom drinks too much sometimes. Today she…she started early." When he took his hand away, he was blinking rapidly.

I closed my own eyes for a moment. "I'm so sorry, Jack. Can I…can I do anything? To help?"

His voice was shaky. "No. Not really."

"We can hang out a different time if you want."

He seemed to think about this for a moment, but then he drew himself up and cleared his throat. "No, today's your birthday. And I'd rather be here. So let's make it a good one."

"Okay." I tried to think of a conversation topic that would distract him and get us on track for a more pleasant evening. "So what is this place?"

His face brightened. "This is my mountain. Harney Peak. It's the tallest point in South Dakota."

"*Your* mountain?"

"Well, not mine exactly, but I come here a lot." He pointed toward the east. "I live over there on the Pineridge Reservation. Come on, there's a better view at the top."

I'd never climbed a mountain before. Actually, I'd rarely climbed anything at all since I could fly instead. The whole process was rather tedious, but I humored him anyway and we were rewarded with a clear view of what seemed to be all of South Dakota. Trees and strange outcroppings of rocks stretched out for miles. I stepped to the edge of the lookout point and had to fight the urge to jump and test my wings at such a tremendous height.

"Happy birthday." He sat on a log and patted the spot beside him.

I joined him but didn't get too close. Since it wasn't "real," I couldn't feel his body heat, but I could still sense his intent. He leaned forward and rested his elbows on his knees. He asked me about my friends. I described their personalities to him but skipped their ages and the fact that they're all scientists and janitors and cooks and housekeepers. He asked about my house, my school. I didn't lie about a single thing; I just didn't tell the whole truth. As the half-truths piled up, I grew more and more uncomfortable, so I started asking him questions instead.

I learned he lives in a two-bedroom house where nothing works exactly right but there's not enough money to make repairs. I learned he has a stepfather who walked out when he was sixteen but still lives on the reservation. Whenever they run across each other, they pretend the other doesn't exist. His favorite book is *Moby Dick*. He has a horse and goes riding bareback and barefooted out in the Badlands to get away from everything.

That is still my favorite mental image of him—riding out into those windswept wilds wearing his worn white t-shirt and jeans and no shoes. I asked him once to take a photo of himself out there, but he's never gotten around to it, so I've contented myself with the picture in my mind.

We talked for four hours. It was early morning when I signed off, eyes drooping and heart full.

Since then, we haven't always met in constructs. Sometimes we set up our webcams, and he watches me sew. I've told him I don't get along with my "step-mother." I've told him about her clinical coldness, how she pushes me to participate in more "sports" than I'm really comfortable with, how she doesn't allow me to have any friends over. He told me how his mother's drunken loose lips say more than he has ever wanted to hear but how she's a good woman when she's sober. She makes a mean Reuben sandwich and tells him often she is proud of him.

I've told him everything. Well, everything except the fact that I'm small enough to fit inside his heart.

In two days, he'll know.

CHAPTER 4

EVEN NOW, AFTER NEARLY ONE whole year, I feel the weight of the half-truths as a heavy woolen cloak I am forced to wear every day. I have tried to tell him in a dozen different ways that I am only six inches tall. I've told him I am as tall as his heart, that he could hold all of me in his hand, that I am shorter than I appear. Every time, he's acted as though I'm saying something romantic or poetic.

And it's my fault I've never driven the truth home. I've never forced him to see it. I've never told him in words he would understand.

Now I don't know how I ever could. In the beginning, I convinced myself our friendship wouldn't last long anyway. I thought he would get tired of talking to a girl who lived on the other side of the world, who went to bed at inconvenient times and had no experience talking to boys. But he didn't.

He actually likes me. Or, rather, he likes the girl he thinks is me. The version of Lina that is normal-sized and doesn't live in a scientific compound.

I can't tell him yet. I just can't. No one has ever liked me who wasn't paid to be around me. I can't give that up.

In two days, I won't have a choice. I'll turn sixteen, my picture will be released, and Jack will know I've been lying all along.

The clock on the wall beeps noon, dragging me back to the present. Half an hour until I have to go back for the rest of my daily training. I look down at my hands. I've twisted my skirt into wrinkled rope.

How am I going to tell him? Anxiety squeezes and twists my stomach as tightly as my skirt. Maybe if I just talk to him, the words will come and I'll know what to say. I fumble under the desk to click the power switch, but it's not there.

It's gone.

My computer is gone. I shove aside everything on my desk, searching for my halojector. It's not here either. Panic claws at my throat as I look at the ceiling. A thin line of light pushes through a crack that wasn't there before. *Someone opened my house.*

I explode from the floor, my wings knocking over a chair and a potted plant. I run my hands along the edges of the roof. I'm not sure what I'm looking for, but I have to do something.

I know who did this. There's only one person who would take my things…

Dr. Christiansen took my computer. And all of the video files of Jack.

I hover there, horror racing through my veins. I don't want to know what she will do if she finds those files.

Then I remember what George said just before I headed back for lunch. Dr. Christiansen had scheduled him to fix her computer fifteen minutes from then. It wasn't *her* computer that needed work. No one but George would have given me something she'd forbidden, especially a computer, so I'm sure this is just her way of cornering him in her office to confront him with the evidence. I close my eyes and hope against hope he doesn't get fired. It would be all my fault.

Jack's face presses to the forefront of my thoughts, and my heart aches so deeply I struggle to breathe. If I don't get that computer back…

I have to find Dr. Christiansen.

I blast out the door without stopping to close it. Fears of invading rodents trashing my place fall behind me and are beaten apart by my furiously fluttering wings.

Five minutes later, I hover outside the door to the main office. Dr. Christiansen is talking to someone—I can only presume it's George—but I can't tell what's she's saying because she's "quiet yelling." Getting scolded by Dr. Christiansen is worse than being screamed at. I learned pretty quickly not to throw tantrums as a child because it was impossible to get her to care. I remember one time, when I was about five years old, I nearly passed out from screaming because I was trying so hard to get some sort of reaction from her. But she only took out her notebook and wrote down observations. That's when I realized she sees me as nothing more than her pet science experiment.

I pick at my already raw cuticles. Without my computer, I won't be able to talk to Jack one last time before he finds out about me through the press. However, now that I'm here, I have no idea what I'm going to say. *Oh, hi, Dr. Christiansen, did you steal the computer I'm not allowed to have? Could you give it back so I can talk to my secret crush?*

Yeah, *that* will go over well.

I float to the floor where a cat door is installed for me. I can see the bottoms of Dr. Christiansen's pleated white pants. They're slightly frayed, which is unusual.

I push open the clear plastic flap and fly to their eye level behind Dr. Christiansen's head. George cowers in the corner, and he gives me a grim look.

Dr. Christiansen continues her quiet diatribe, neatly enunciating every syllable. "…and I expect you will lay aside your own personal insecurities in the future so you will not be manipulated next time. I realize you are the resident veterinarian here, but I do not think your skill set puts you in a position to decide what is best for her. She is part-human after all. I suggest you stick to caring for animals." Dr. Christiansen slams her clipboard on the desk. It sounds like a gun going off.

I hover there with my mouth open. Did she really refer to me as *part*-human? Only *part*-human?

George stands a little taller. "Pardon me, *ma'am*, but she is completely human. She just happens to have other parts added in."

Dr. Christiansen hates being called "ma'am." I've never heard George say that to her before.

She sighs in her condescending way. "I do not expect you to understand."

31

I find my voice and project it as strongly as I can. "I understand."

Dr. Christiansen comes as close to whirling as I've ever seen. She smiles at me as if we're strangers.

"It is impolite to intrude, Lina. It's also impolite to eavesdrop and interrupt a conversation you are not a part of."

"You gave me an open invitation to come in anytime."

"Did I?" She picks up her clipboard and jots down a couple of notes. "Consider that invitation withdrawn."

Blood pounds in my ears. *Part-human. Only part-human.* What exactly does that mean? I know that if I ask her, she won't answer because I was eavesdropping. Why did I come in here again?

"I want my computer," I blurt out.

George covers his face with his hand. Dr. Christiansen picks something up off her desk and holds it up for me to see.

"You mean this?"

"You had no right to take it." I can't think of a better argument. I'm trying, but all that comes to me is pure anger.

"You had no right to have it in the first place. I have already reviewed some of the contents of your files this morning."

I hold my breath.

She continues. "It seems you have forged an adolescent romantic relationship with a young man named Jack. Is that correct?"

I lick my lips and look to George for help, but he's staring at the floor.

"I have viewed several of the videos and plan to watch the rest for research purposes, so unfortunately I cannot return the computer to you. Your relationship with this young man must come to an end now. Do you have any questions?"

"You...you can't watch those. They're private! They're none of your business! Give them back!" I veer off to the left. My trembling affects my ability to control my movements, and I sink to the floor. I hate that I'm at her feet.

She looks down at me with a calculated smile. "I am afraid that is not possible."

I stare at her, numb. Leaden despair threatens to crush me into the floorboards.

"On the other hand, I have some good news for you." Her voice is too high, almost hysterical. It's as though she's mimicking someone who possesses the ability to be genuinely excited about something. I prepare myself to hate whatever she's about to say.

"I have arranged a birthday party for you where you will be introduced to six companions who are your own size and species. I am sure one of them will make a much more suitable mate."

Six companions… Own size and species… "What?"

"Six males, called 'Toms,' were created shortly after you, but they are the property of Lilliput's sister project. We deemed it appropriate to raise you separately from one another to keep any familial bonds from forming. They are your surprise sixteenth birthday present, and you may choose one of them to mate with."

Countless invisible bugs of panic crawl along my skin, raising every hair on my body. My lungs have stopped working, like the time I got socked in the stomach with an intern's golf ball. *"What?!"*

"Lina, do you not understand your purpose? The entire goal of this experiment?"

My breaths are coming so fast I'm beginning to get dizzy. Purpose? Experiment? I've always been told my purpose is simply to survive.

"You are the answer to humanity's problems. It is your duty to choose a mate and reproduce." She smiles. *Oh my god, how can she smile?*

I shake my head. "No. You can't make me marry someone. I'm leaving when I turn sixteen. I'll be legal then, and there's nothing you can do about it."

She taps her pen against her chin. "That is a very interesting assumption, but it is incorrect. You will not be leaving."

"Excuse me?"

"Scientifically speaking, you are not actually a human, so those laws do not apply to you."

I snort. "Then what am I?"

"Your species is categorized as a type of damselfly. We took special care to make sure there would be no legal difficulties when you came of age. So you will remain the property of the Lilliput Project. Do not worry. I will do everything in my power to provide you with a comfortable life in a controlled and safe environment."

My throat tightens, but I force out my question. "When were you planning on letting me in on this little secret? You knew I was looking forward to leaving."

"It would not have been productive to tell you. For research purposes."

I back up toward the door, shaking my head all the way.

"You can't keep me here," I whisper. She can't hear me. "I won't let you."

I take off out of the room, my wings burning into a dead sprint. The door opens behind me, and Dr. Christiansen calls my name before hitting the lockdown button, which triggers an eardrum-piercing alarm. I know that button well, and I already have my escape route planned. There's a little mouse hole in the corner of the rear chemistry block leading to the underside of the porch.

I fly up along the ceiling, my wings scraping layers of dust and cobwebs from the exposed rafters.

Dr. Christiansen's assistant, Jane, bursts out of Chemistry Block #2, and I meet her eye as I fly right over her head. Her lab coat is covered in a foul-smelling solution, her face wearing her normal confused expression. The screeching alarm hasn't registered in her head yet.

"Lina? Oh! Lockdown! Lina, come here!"

Too late. I fly into the room she just left, and I'm almost to the open door between the blocks when I see what she's been experimenting on. A simple lab table sits in the middle of the room. A cat lies on top, soaked in blood. It looks as though someone's ripped out all of its fur and its bones are poking out at unnatural angles. It can barely move because of its wounds and bonds, but it blinks and opens its mouth ever so slightly to cry to me through its muzzle. The sound is so familiar somehow. Then I realize the cat didn't make any noise—it was me.

I hover there, unable to move. What are they *doing* to that poor animal? And why? Tears fill my eyes, and I stretch my hand out to it without thinking, as if I could take its pain onto myself. Jane's voice catches me by surprise.

"Lina! You're not supposed to be in here!"

I can't look at her. My stomach decides it can't hold anything anymore, and I throw up just as Jane reaches out to grab me. It startles her enough to give me time to escape, but I don't have any anger left to propel me. It's been replaced by the cold grip of fear.

I feel her fingertips on my feet, but she's not as fast as I am. As I get close to my escape hole, I realize I can't use it while anyone is looking. I can't have them blocking me on the other side.

Jane smacks the block's lockdown alert button to tell everyone where I am. She doesn't take her eyes off of me.

"Lina, what's going on? You can talk to me." Catlike, she steps forward, hands at the ready, looking for the right moment to pounce on me. "Let's have a nice chat, you and me."

I glance over at the cat on the table as I formulate a plan, and a fresh surge of terror floods my veins. Panic has become my new life force.

That's it. Panic. Break things.

I hurtle myself toward the cabinet and steel myself for impact. I strike the large glass flask on the end which clatters into the rest, sending them airborne. Jane forgets all about me and tries to catch one of the bottles, but it shatters when it hits her hands and she screams and runs to stick her hand into a chemical neutralizer.

I feel guilty she's hurt, but there's no time to stop. I head straight for the hole and crawl inside, praying I don't actually run into a mouse or some other rodent or large insect. Inside of the hole is half-eaten sheep's wool insulation and dust. I stifle a sneeze and wade through the thick stuff until I reach the wood of the outer wall. Crawling along a stud beam, I search for a way out.

There it is—a splintered gash in the wall.

And it's surrounded in mouse droppings.

Really? It had to be this? I grit my teeth and hold my hands up and away from the disgusting little turds as I pick my way through to the exit. I suck in my breath and squeeze through to the outside, but the underside of my shirt catches on the splinters on my way through and I don't notice it until I'm somersaulting into the large pile of droppings on the other side. I bolt up from the ground, shaking my arms and legs and head. Even when I'm pretty sure I've gotten it all off, I can't get rid of the feeling of lingering filth.

The alarm screams that I don't have much time to figure out my next move. I have to get out of the commons and into my forest. But then what?

A half-hearted voice in my head suggests I turn myself in, but it's only telling me what should be logical in every other situation. Every fraction of my heart and mind tell me it doesn't make sense to give in this time. A rush of adrenaline brings a huge grin to my face. I've fantasized about running away since I was old enough to fly. It feels good to have complete conviction on my side for once.

Now I have to get out of here.

Little nagging thoughts asking, "Where will you go?" and "What will you do?" and "How will you even survive?" are pushed aside. I call upon all of my training to assess my surroundings.

The porch is nothing more than a glorified doorstep with stairs. The sides are wooden lattice, and I can see hurrying feet outside.

I carefully poke my head out through one of the lattices. Two security guards run by, but they don't look at the porch. Everyone seems to be running toward the supply gate. I guess I won't be escaping that way.

Darn it. There's no other way out of the compound. The dome fence surrounding the project doesn't end at the ground; it goes deep a few dozen feet. But then I remember the hole I crawled through. It wasn't supposed to be there. Maybe the fence has a hole somewhere, too.

I wait a few seconds to see if anyone else runs by, but everyone seems to be gone. I pull myself through the lattice and climb up to the step. I can't hear anything except for the alarms.

Then the screen door opens and almost squashes me against the wall. The door stop saves my life, and I jump off of the porch in the nick of time to avoid being seen. I float down to the ground and listen hard. Dr. Christiansen's steely voice cuts through the alarms.

"...and I want you to alert Dr. Lee and Lilliput II. We are about to release the drones on autopilot until I can get home to control them."

I freeze. The drones. I haven't heard them mentioned in years. I didn't know they existed outside of my nightmares.

The drones are round, flying robots specifically designed to do one thing: find and capture me. When I was a kid, Dr. Christiansen told me they were rescue drones and they would save me if I was ever kidnapped, but when I asked her how they would fight off a bad man, she didn't have an answer. To make them more child-friendly, she had them painted to resemble bumblebees. Somewhere in her sick, twisted mind, she thought that would make it more fun for me. We would run drills where she would tell me to fly as fast as I could so the drones could practice chasing me and swallowing me up in their metal bellies.

I still have nightmares about them. And now I'm going to have to escape them—something I've never managed to do before.

Dr. Christiansen puts her phone away. She walks down the steps, pauses at the bottom, and pulls a pair of tiny scissors out of her pocket. She stands on one foot, draws the other foot up to her knee, and snips off the single stray thread on the hem of her pants. Then she puts the thread and scissors into her pocket and walks toward my forest, though not directly toward my house.

I flutter up to the step, avoiding the door this time, and run to the end of the porch so I can get a good look at the other side of the building.

Nothing. Everyone's gone.

Unease sweeps over me. Why did they all leave so quickly? Wouldn't they want to search inside a little longer?

Then a sickly sweet smell hits my nose, and my fingers lose all feeling. I hold them up in front of my face and try to move them, but they hang limply from my hand.

The smell is a paralyzing agent.

I hold my breath and take to flight, racing for a nearby tree. My lungs are burning, but I don't dare inhale. A cardinal tumbles through the branches and lands on the ground with a soft thud. The chemical's reach is spreading, so I turn to fly upwind. When I can't bear to hold my breath any longer, I stop, lie down on a tree branch, and suck in breath after breath.

Immediately, movement and sensation return to my fingers. I shake off the residual dullness and leap off of the branch into flight. I clear the tops of the highest trees and race along them, keeping as much of the forest between myself and the ground as possible to avoid being seen. My lungs are starting to feel tight, but so far my asthma has decided to cooperate. I cross my fingers and hope it stays that way.

There is no sign of any of the Lilliput Project's employees. I glance behind me in time to see five small yellow-striped discs pop up above the trees.

Damn it.

All five of them head in my direction without the slightest hesitation. How on earth have they already tracked me down?

I fly backward, not wanting to take my eyes off of my pursuers, until I run straight into a branch. Blunt pain knocks out all light and sound for a split second, and I scramble to grab onto a twig. A flock of startled sparrows bursts from the leaves and scatters into the sky. I squint, but they remain blurry blobs to me and my head lolls to the side.

The drones get closer and closer. They separate from one another, and each goes after a different bird, swallowing the terrified creatures up inside their metal bellies.

Then it hits me. They're heat-seeking drones, and there are only a few creatures in this entire compound close enough to my size to be mistaken for me.

My vision gradually returns to normal as the machines turn tail and head to the main buildings. I rub my head, my stomach still roiling within me. I can't move too quickly otherwise the world starts to spin. But I can't stay here. They'll be after me again once someone realizes they only captured birds. I need to be out of the compound before that happens.

I take off at half-speed, fighting to stay upright through my dizziness. I can make out the edge of the trees from here. The forest will end, and I will hit the invisible wall. Then I have to find another mouse hole.

And then? Waves of uncertainty push the nausea back into motion, and I struggle not to dry-heave. The adrenaline recedes, leaving me with the exhausting sensation that I am alone. There is no one to help me—not even George.

My hands reach the fence first, fingers exploring the strange fibers. Up close, it isn't transparent; it resembles glowing silver threads all tightly woven. But when I fly backward, the world outside snaps into focus. The only way I'm going to find a hole is to fly close to the wall so I can see any breaks or gaps.

I glance upward at the gently curving slope, and discouragement overwhelms me. Even if there is a hole, it will probably take me days to find it unless I'm very lucky. I wipe my eyes and blink hard to fight the tears. I can't cry now. I *will not* cry now.

But my tears are not interested in obeying me. They run down my cheeks as I flutter along the wall, testing the strength of the fibers, trying to determine what or who could get through this fence. When I try to slip my fingers under one of the fibers, I'm met with failure. They are so tight, so strong, I can't see any way I could ever pull a hole apart myself. Maybe a rodent could. I'm not sure. I'm probably better off checking along the ground.

I look over my shoulder to check for drones and spot several flying in formation in the distance. A sparrow bursts from the trees, and the drones give chase for a moment before something else corrects them. They're not on auto-pilot anymore.

"No," I whisper. I kick the wall in frustration and fly downwards with my hand on the wall the whole way. Gleaming silver meets ground and I run along the edge searching for somewhere to hide. Maybe if I can find a molehill, the coolness of the earth will mask my body heat and confuse their sensors just enough that whoever controls the drones won't realize I'm here.

I race across the weeds. Blades of grass switch at my feet as I look for any sign of an opening.

The crack of breaking twigs and leaves breaks the silence, and I look above in time to see the drones crashing through the canopy and heading right toward me. A shower of debris falls onto the leaves, and I have to make a decision. Run or hide?

Now. Make a decision now, Lina.

I dive headfirst toward the intersection of wall and ground. I fold my wings behind me and unfurl them just before hitting the ground. The impact knocks the wind out of me. Gasping, I roll as close to the wall as possible with my wings against the fence. I wedge myself into the dirt, then lie as flat as I can so the drones won't have much to grab on to.

Four of the them fan out to block off all possible escape routes while the remaining one draws closer. I can almost hear its mechanical little brain trying to process the situation and determine the best way to get me out of my half-dug grave.

I close my eyes and bury my face in the dirt. I try to ignore the strange metallic noises as they hover like a band of children encircling a frightened animal, ready to poke me with sticks.

Jack's face appears inside my head. I grab onto him with all my strength, and my gaze holds his without apology. *I need you now!* I yell at him. He understands. He smiles as though nothing is wrong, as if his existence can make all the bad go away. We fool each other that way sometimes.

Something cold touches my foot, and I scream so hard Jack fades away into blackness. The sound crushes out everything but me and the drones. I pick up my head to see the closest one prodding at me with a long, mechanical arm.

"Stop touching me," I hiss at Dr. Christiansen. I know she can hear me.

The drone doesn't care about respecting my personal space. It prods my calves, the back of my knees, my thighs…

That is going too far. My rage overpowers my fear, and I spring up from the ground and seize hold of the plastic "hand" that was violating me. I wrap my legs around the arm and snap the hand off. The drone tries to pull away with stuttering movements, but I am too angry to be beaten. I crawl up the arm to the gaping belly, but I don't go inside. The other arm snatches at me, but I am invincible now. If it grabs me, I will tear it apart with pure willpower.

I scramble up the side, its heat burning my legs and palms as I struggle to find handholds beneath the peeling yellow and black paint. I can't just fly over because it might out-maneuver me and then I'll really be screwed.

On top, a red light glows at the very center of its dome—the heat sensor. I crawl over to it and dig my fingers into the screws.

And I sit on it.

The drone whirrs in circles, confused. It pulls its arms inside its belly and then it does something I don't expect.

It flips. And we're not talking about a graceful aerial move; it tosses me into the air and then the other end spanks me toward the earth.

I get a quick face-full of grass before the ground punches my lights out.

CHAPTER 5

THE WORLD IS WATERCOLORS ALL mixing together, as though the artist put too much water in the paint. Blues and greens and browns swim lazily out of the black canvas. Then the blackness pushes through again with glints of yellow.

The glints are coming for me.

I try to stand, but my head is so heavy. I can only remember snippets of the last few hours. Words like paralyze, drones, cat, Jack.

Drones. Black color, black sounds. They're pushing out all of the greens and blues. Their heat presses toward me.

Something crashes through the forest, shattering twigs and dried-up leaves. The drones hesitate, then float away.

Now George's face is far too close to mine. My eyes are working better, and I almost wish they weren't.

"Lina!" His voice is a knife in my skull. My whole body winces as he scoops me up with gentle hands. His callouses are sandpaper against my skin, and I feel their every ridge.

This time he whispers when he speaks. "Hold on. I'll get you to the compound so we can fix you up."

His words remind me why I'm out here, why the drones were chasing me. I sit up straight in his hand. "No."

"What?"

"I won't go back there."

He sighs. For the first time, I notice gray in his whiskers. "But where would you go, pixie? Hmm?"

"Does it matter? Anywhere is better than here. You heard her—she won't even let me out when I'm an adult! This place is a prison." The leaves are turning into swimming paints again. I lie down again to give the world a chance to return to normal.

"Maybe it won't be so bad…?" George's voice trails off into a question. He doesn't believe his own words.

"Yes. It will. It's not going to get better. And now my computer's gone, too, and that's the only thing that was…keeping me going." My admission shocks me. I didn't realize it was true until I said it.

George's mouth pinches into a line, and pain radiates in his eyes. He's bent over backward to make life pleasant for me all these years. I've hurt his feelings, but I can't unsay those words. We both know I meant it.

"I will get you another computer," he says. He starts walking again. "I will hide it better this time."

I bite on my finger to distract myself from the tears. A new computer won't fix everything that's gone wrong.

"I promise," George says. "After your birthday, I'll get you another one. Now will you let me take you to get fixed up?"

He looks down at me, and I nod. His fingers curl gently around me to keep me from falling out of his hand.

Sun splits the trees and slices into my eyes. I cover my face with my hands and will myself to sleep. Exhaustion and nausea take over, and I fade away into dreams.

***

When I wake, the world is fluorescent and dirt-tinged white. I'm still groggy, but my head no longer hurts.

"You slept for twenty hours," says Dr. Christiansen. Her face steps into view. "I trust you will not do that again."

"What—sleep for a whole day?" It's hard to talk around the cotton dryness in my mouth. "Can I have some water?"

She nods her head toward a small bottle next to me. I grab it and suck down its contents. The cold gives me an instant headache.

"Fortunately for all of us, there was no permanent damage done. I've now inserted a tracking microchip under your skin so the insubordination of yesterday will not be repeated. Stand up please."

I stand, but I glare as I do so. I rub my hands over my arms, trying to find the "bug" they put into me. Without my permission.

"Your special birthday dinner is this evening. In—" She checks her watch. "—five hours. All of the Toms will be there to meet you. Your biological donors will make an appearance as well. As for your...clothing, I have placed some items for you to wear in your home. Please make sure you shut your door next time. Jane spent half an hour cleaning the bugs out."

"Fine."

"Do not be late," she warns as I fly out the door.

Or what? Will you cook me and eat me?

Once I'm outside, the fatigue forces me to slow down. I must have hit my head harder than I thought. I bring my fingers to my face; my cheeks are still hot and tender to the touch. I imagine Dr. Christiansen pulled out all of the medical stops to fix me up as much as possible for the dinner so I won't embarrass her. She's probably selected some ridiculously frothy dress for me to wear.

Whatever.

My stomach churns out rage, filling me with heat and fury. My anger gives me fuel to fly. I reach my house without returning any of the greetings of the workers. They're part of all of this...this trap. I check on my garden only to find it's been trampled by Jane. Stupid Jane who doesn't know the first thing about beauty. Jane who experiments on helpless cats. Jane who thought I was dumb enough to fall for her pretend concern. And to think I used to like her.

I fling open my front door. The inside is tidy, but the wallpaper—from Italy!—below the ceiling crack is warped and crinkled from water damage. I kick the front door shut as hard as I can. It doesn't slam hard enough to satisfy me, so I reopen it and kick it shut again. And again. And again.

Open, kick, slam. My vision drowns in tears. Open, kick, slam. *Stupid, stupid, stupid.* Open, kick, slam. *I hate her. I do.* An angry sob burbles out, complete with spit strings. I slip down to the floor, exhausted.

The irritating, saner part of me reminds me I don't really hate anyone, not even Dr. Christiansen. *Yes, I do!* my angry part shouts back. But they're fading now, disintegrating into despair and leaving me nothing to hang onto except this unworkable, horrid situation that has no solution. What sort of human being forces someone else to pick a spouse out of a lineup? And it's not even fair to the Toms. I mean, there are six of them.

Now that I think about it, why are there six of them and only one of me? That doesn't make any sense.

I stare at the floor, my mind numb.

"What do I do?"

The silence doesn't answer. A squirrel chitters in the distance.

I pull my knees up and drop my forehead against them. I have to think of something. I can't give in so easily.

After a few quiet moments, I stand. My head is clearer, my emotions more balanced, but I still feel fragile as glass.

Might as well check out the outfit I have to wear tonight. I sigh and walk into my bedroom, an explosion of reds and purples and oranges with twisty pieces of furniture made of grapevines. Normally the cheerful decor makes me happy. Today it's almost offensive.

The puffy, white abomination of a dress lies across my bed. It looks like a cheap wedding gown that was hacked off at the knees. The beads are almost as big as my head, and the fabric so stiff the dress won't even lie flat.

The only way I will ever wear this is if I'm dead.

I toss it on the floor and step back with arms folded. I'm so tired of dealing with Dr. Christiansen, but I can't let her win this one. I have to think of something else to wear or some way to alter…

My eyes flit up to the vibrant shades on the wall. That's it! I run out to the kitchen, grab one of my razor knives and return to my bedroom where my full-length mirror hangs. I grab a chunk of blond frizz and hold it out.

Do I really want to do this? I'm one snip from the point of no return. One snip from a considerably shorter mane.

With a deep breath, I slice off a two-inch lock and wait for the feeling of panic to come. It doesn't. Instead, relief and excitement wash over me in a giddy mix. I make quick work of the rest and then survey the damage.

In the mirror, a teenaged girl with chin-length hair smiles back at me. I add some inexpert and probably uneven layers to it, and I've got myself a brand-new hairstyle. My neck feels deliciously bare and cool. I wish I'd done this much sooner.

Next, I dig out my homemade dyes from the craft stash in the living room. I keep them in old perfume sample bottles. Green, orange, brown...*there's* the purple! I take the bottle to the bathroom, put the stopper in the sink and apply the entire batch of dye to my freshly cropped hair.

I leave it in for a solid hour then wash it out in my stone bathtub. Rivulets of lavender run down my arms and create a pool on the floor that seems as though it was touched by the sunset. After a good scrub and towel dry, I check out my dye job in the mirror.

My hair is a vivid candy purple. I blurt out a laugh and then stand there staring at it with a huge smile on my face. One giant drop of watery dye heads straight for my eyes, but I whisk it away just in time. My skin looks almost white next to the brightness of the purple.

Oh, Dr. Christiansen is going to *love* this.

Now for the dress. I pick it up gingerly with two fingers. The beads have to go. So do all of the petticoats underneath. Where did she get this—a doll shop?

I get my sewing scissors, the ones I made with George's help. They're small enough to fit in my hand, and they could slice through a grape without even denting it first. I snip a few threads, and the beads tumble to the floor. Several more snips later, the petticoats are lying in a discarded pile.

Now for the color. Dr. Christiansen must have chosen white to symbolize my supposed upcoming nuptials with one of the clowns I'll be meeting tonight. I'm supposed to look girlish and sweet and innocent. Positively bridal. I have nothing against being any of those things, but I won't be them just because it's what the doctor ordered.

This calls for black dye. I gather all I have and mix it with the remaining purple in the tub before submerging the dress in my concoction. When I pull the dress out an hour later, it's a dark gray. Not quite black, but a far cry from bridal white.

It'll do.

CHAPTER 6

I WAIT UNTIL 6:05 P.M. to make sure I'm late enough to further annoy Dr. Christiansen, and then I take off for the party. My new haircut is surprisingly easy to style. I've got a silver headband in it, and I'm wearing makeup—bright pink lipstick and a smidge of eyeliner. Black slippers on my feet. My dress is still damp, but I don't even care. I'm actually excited.

The main buildings of the compound circle the planetarium/dining hall. Tonight, three limousines are lined up outside while several photographers snap pictures of the gathering guests. I freeze at the edge of the forest. There's no way I'm flying through that crowd. Best to go through the back door.

I find an open window into the kitchen. The chef and her staff are milling around like angry bees, setting up dishes, chopping ingredients, and generally getting into each other's way. They don't even see me as I cross the ceiling and slip into the dining hall.

The hall is almost unrecognizable. The wood plank walls are draped with white, and hundreds of candles hang from the ceiling, along with white streamers and gold hearts. White and gold cloths cover all of the tables. The planetarium dome is all lit up with stars and planets.

It's beautiful. It's also nothing close to what I would have picked myself. But tonight is not really about me, is it?

I take a deep breath to equalize my rising frustration levels as the front doors open and guests begin to mill into the room. A confused-looking reporter and cameraman step inside and search along the walls. They must be looking for me. Too bad for them. I wait until they turn away, and then I fly up into the dark ceiling. There's a lip around the edge of the planetarium's dome and that's where I intend to hang out until I decide how to make my entrance. I get up there without being spotted, then sit cross-legged, with my arms and chin resting on the smooth wood. It's a good vantage point. I can see everything from up here.

I spot some of my parents. The last time I saw them I was ten years old. They came to see "how I'd turned out." I guess they're not so much my parents as they are my biological donors, but I still like to think of them as my folks. It makes me feel a little more normal, as if I'm a kid whose parents got divorced and remarried several times and now they have this big, weird family. I've even separated them into "real" parents and "step" parents.

Norbert Eisler is my "real dad." I picked him mostly because his last name is the best. "Lina Eisler" has a nice ring to it. I'm told I got half of my looks, including my hair, from him. He's a famous Germanic composer. I would never listen to any of his music for fun, but he's got great blond hair (or did before he lost it all) and he's talented. I guess.

I picked Natalia Chislova to be my "real mom." She's a Russian ballerina, and she had a miniature cross necklace made especially for me that I wear it all the time. She writes me letters now and then, but my Russian isn't so good. When we met, she actually spoke to me like I was a human, a real person. The others treated me like a science experiment. I suppose I am both of those things.

There, by the lemonade fountain, is "step-mom" Corinne Albertson. She won a Nobel Prize for something math-related and boring. Well, boring to me anyway. Next to her is another "step"—Jimema Lopez, the daughter of the first female president of the South American Republic.

I scan the room for my favorite "step," Philip Ford, and find him hanging out by the door to the men's room. He has the world's highest IQ and has won two Pulitzer Prizes. I caught him picking his nose around the corner during the speeches at my tenth birthday. I nearly flew right into his face, so I got a nice close-up of his clandestine activities. He was horrified, but at the time, I thought it was pretty cool I'd busted an adult for doing something gross. Four of the "steps" are already seated at the head table and ignoring each other. They're all from the United European Republic, but I can't remember all of their names. They were probably famous sixteen years ago but have since fallen into obscurity. One's an Italian chef, another is a Greek Olympian, and Lord Anthony is the descendant of three separate defunct European thrones. Then there's Hassad Jabir, who solved the Israeli-Palestinian crisis the year before I was created. Unfortunately it unsolved itself shortly after that.

I don't see Dr. Lee anywhere. He's an entomologist from China. We don't really get along because I hate insects with a passion. I was terrified of them as a kid. Most children are afraid of monsters or lions or something. Those never frightened me as much because all I had to do was fly away from them. But you can't fly away from a bee—those darn things chase you.

It was Dr. Lee who created the Azure Megaloprepus Caerulatus Damselfly, the largest, most colorful damselfly in existence. He messed with its genetics so its wings have the blue coloring. Then he combined the resulting DNA with everybody else's to create me: the first successfully engineered six-inch human with a twelve-inch wingspan. He picked the damselfly instead of the dragonfly because the damselfly folds its wings behind its back when it's not using them. It makes it a lot easier to walk through the doors in my house.

Dr. Christiansen comes in through the side door wearing her pinched smile. Her eyes scour every inch of the place, but she still doesn't see me. She snaps her fingers at Jane, who leans in like an obedient dog to receive her instructions before scampering away. I half-expect her to crawl on the floor and look under all of the tablecloths, but she slips out the side door that leads into the hall.

She's probably going to my house. If she tramples my garden again, I will personally… Well, I don't know what I'll do. But I'll think of something.

The flutter of small wings catches my eye, and I spot two of the Toms. They sit down at the tiny table on the center platform. I can't make out any of their features other than their hair—pitch black and blond—but I'm suddenly curious. I lean forward to get a better look.

Light pierces through my retinas and blinds me. I shield my eyes, furiously blinking. I've been spotted. Literally.

The room breaks out in scattered applause. As my eyes adjust, I squint out into the audience. Dr. Christiansen's got her arms tightly folded across her chest, and her nostrils are flaring like an angry bull's at the sight of my hair and dress. Score one for me.

Jane's voice echoes across the dome. "And…here's Lina!" I guess she didn't head to my house after all. There's another smattering of polite clapping. A string quartet begins to play in the corner, and Jane starts singing "Happy Birthday" completely off-key. The room joins in gradually. I think it's safe to say we don't have any vocal superstars here tonight.

The song tapers off as Jane's microphone picks up some reverb, screeching everyone into silence. A dozen camera flashes go off, blinding me yet again.

Dr. Christiansen's voice replaces Jane's. "Lina, please come down and blow out your candles."

The guests remain quiet. You could hear a pin drop.

I hesitate, but I can't resist her without looking petty. She wins this round. I descend onto the cake—a three-tiered wedding cake with a platform on top. I tuck my dress in around me and blow out each candle in turn. I'm so winded by the time I'm done that I can only stand there, dazed and seeing stars, as everyone claps.

Now Dr. Christiansen stands beside the cake wearing her constipated smile. In a painfully high voice she says, "And now there are some young men I would like you to meet!" She gestures toward the center platform where all of the Toms are standing in a line. I guess that's my cue.

With a sigh, I fly over. The photogs follow after me, snapping pictures all the way. I'm going to have to meet them one by one while everyone watches. I come closer and their faces grow clearer. They all seem generically handsome. It's so strange to have six guys near me who are the same size as I am. I've talked to people online with my scales adjusted to theirs, but these are flesh-and-blood young men and there's really no comparison. Their features look sharper, and the entire effect is more immediate. I'm me, in the real world, in my own body, about to talk to six guys who don't tower over me. It's *weird*.

I land right in front of the first one. He reminds me of a piece of overstretched taffy. When I shake his hand, he grips mine sincerely. His eyes are earnest, serious, and nothing like Jack's. Tom2 has strawberry-blond hair, and he smiles so hard I think his face will break. Next. Toms3, 4, and 5 are forgettable and go by in a blur. However, when I get to Tom6, I'm completely startled by his vivid blue eyes. His hair is completely black and his features suggest his DNA is primarily Asian, but his eyes... Then I realize I'm not taken aback so much by their color, but the intensity that reminds me of Jack. Except Jack is not as serious. Jack would have me laughing by now.

"I'm very pleased to meet you," he says as he lifts my hand to kiss it.

"Um."

He turns his eyes to my hand, breaking the spell. I give my head a little shake to clear the fog and then I focus on his jet black hair. It's only hair. He's just a guy. He's not Jack. Still, I'm a little unnerved by my reaction. Maybe I should just avoid staring into his eyes for the rest of the evening.

The Toms turn to their seats, and I'm about to follow suit when I spot George hovering nearby. He's got a guilty expression on his face which can mean only one thing: a new computer. The rest of the room has gone back to their conversations, so I shouldn't draw too much attention to myself if I go and talk to him now.

"One moment, guys. I'll be right back." I fly over to George and hover right in front of his face.

"You're quick," I say.

He shrugs sheepishly. "Happy birthday."

"You're a peach, George. Thank you!"

"Shhhhh." He ducks his head, sticks his finger into the black olive in his drink and then lifts the empty glass. "Time for more."

"Enjoy." I return to the table and suppress a groan when I see the Toms are all watching me eagerly, waiting for me to come and sit with them. There's only one seat open and it's at the head of the table. When is this party over? When do they all go home?

As I approach the table, they all stand up, and two of them reach out at the same time to pull out my chair for me. I bite my lip as a wave of guilt sweeps over me. This isn't their fault. It's not their fault that they're not

Jack, that I'm the only girl their size, or that Dr. Christiansen has put us all into this room together.

I take a deep breath. I can be polite and friendly and charming for one evening. I'm pretty sure that's all I have in me right now. So I put on my game face and take a seat.

"Thanks for coming," I offer.

"I bet we had as much of a choice as you did," Tom4 says without looking up. Well, at least he's honest.

Tom1, Overstretched Taffy Boy, clears his throat. "Shut up, Shrike."

"Shrike?" I ask.

"Only the staff call us by our numbers," Tom2 says cheerfully. "We've come up with names for each other."

"That makes sense. What are they?"

"We picked the names of birds, and they've gotten shortened down over the years. Let's see if you can guess what they stand for." Tom2's smile nearly cracks his face in two again.

Tom5 runs a hand through his fiery red hair and rubs his eyes. "Are we really going to do this?"

I ignore him and nod at Tom2. "Okay, you start."

"My nickname is Row."

I squeeze my lips together while I think. "Short for Sparrow?"

"Excellent!"

I can't help but smile at his enthusiasm. I turn to Tom1. "How about you?"

He unwraps himself from his dinner plate. "Sorry, but it's Crane. I don't have a nickname other than that."

"Oh, well, at least it suits you."

He stops chewing and gives me a sideways glance.

"I mean, you're really tall. And sorta thin?" *Oh my gosh, Lina, stop talking now!*

"I'm called Blue." The deep voice snaps my head around. The blue eyes are staring through my skull again, but this time I manage to grab hold of my composure as it tries to flee the room.

"Hmm… Not Bluebird. That doesn't quite fit. Bluejay?"

He nods but says nothing. Man of few words, that one.

"Well, you've got him pegged already!" Row says. "Very perceptive!"

I'm beginning to wonder if Row should be renamed Mark. Short for Exclamation Mark.

Shrike tosses his napkin onto the table and leans back in his chair. "My turn."

"I don't think I'm familiar with—"

"Tiger Shrike," he interrupts. "It's a small bird of prey. Eats butterflies."

I raise an eyebrow. I suppose there has to be one bad apple in every group. Shrike would be attractive if his default facial expression wasn't a scowl. He's got medium brown hair, and he's smaller than the others. Maybe he has something to prove.

"Charmed," I say.

"Your turn." Row elbows Tom6, a hulking boy-man with midnight skin.

"You can call me Al," he says after swallowing his food. He would be a lot of fun to sculpt with his incredible inky skin and toned muscles.

"Al is for...Albatross? Let me guess—you fly the fastest."

Shrike snorts. "Nah, just the longest. He floats like a feather. Perry's the fastest."

"And that must be you?" I turn to Tom5. He's the one with the bright red hair.

"Short for Peregrine. Peregrine Falcon."

"Does that mean you're twice as fast as the rest of us?"

He winks at me. It is not a friendly wink. "Sure."

Row leans forward, breaking the unpleasant connection between myself and Perry. "I have to say that I love your hair. I—we—were so worried you wouldn't be, you know, normal. It's very refreshing. Says a lot about you." He takes a breath. "I'm sorry I'm so talkative. I'm not normally this talkative. I guess I'm nervous!"

He blurts out an awkward laugh, and I can't help but join him. They're all watching me, and every single one except for Row resembles a rapidly deflating balloon. Row made me laugh, and they didn't. Their disappointment seeps into my own heart. I have to say or do something funny. I need to turn this ship around, and I need to do it fast.

"I'm glad you like the hair. This is actually my natural color."

"No, it's not," Shrike says. "They told us you were blonde."

Crane sighs. "Which donor did you get your tactlessness from, Shrike?"

"At least *I* don't look like a limp noodle. I don't have one either." He laughs at his own joke, but no one joins in. Crane's face turns bright red, and he reabsorbs himself with the thrilling activity of pushing bits of food around on his plate.

"Did you dye it yourself?" This time it's Blue talking to me. I'm getting whiplash from turning my head so often.

"Yes. Earlier today." My head begins to pound. I rest my elbows on the table and close my eyes for a moment while I rub my temples. I want this to end so I can go home, boot up my new computer, and have my *real* birthday with Jack. I'm sure he's wondering where I've been for the past day and a half. Last time we spoke, he told me he was planning something special, and I have no idea what it is. I can't wait to find out.

The quartet stops playing. I open my eyes again to see Dr. Christiansen step up onto a small stage erected during dinner. She's allowed her hair out of its ponytail prison for the night, and she actually looks pretty in the spotlight. She blinks into the glare and holds her microphone up to her mouth.

"Greetings, honored guests. Happy birthday, Lina." She could not sound more dismal if she was announcing our impending demise. "I have a very special announcement to make on this historic occasion. Today Lina has reached adulthood, and it is time for her to move on to the next stage of her life: marriage and family. Please direct your attention to the video we are about to play. Thank you."

Marriage and family? Excuse me?

The video image pops up out of the projector and unrolls itself along the wall in full-color, then snaps into focus. It's just a green background. Some cheesy pop piano blasts over the speakers, and flowers and hearts begin to "bloom" over the green. Then words write themselves in cursive white lettering as the deep voice of a male narrator booms, *"Little Love: A Tom and Thumbelina Story."*

My mouth drops open, and one of the photographers snaps a flash in my eyes.

The narrator continues: *"Deep in the forests of Denmark, the land of fairy tales, lives a young woman who is only six inches tall."*

The green background dissolves into some footage of me flying around the flower gardens, then video of me doing drills with George. At least, I think that's what I'm doing. When did they start taping me without telling me?

"Meanwhile, six young men of the same size are preparing to fight for her heart."

Footage of the Toms parades past. They all look handsome and strange as they race each other across a course and then practice wrestling bare-chested. It's more than a little over-the-top.

"There is only one woman in the entire world whose heart is the perfect match for theirs. And now, Thumbelina will choose her true love, her husband, from among them as you watch from your very own living room."

I get the vague impression music is playing, but all sound has turned to sludge in my ears. Jane bounces onto the stage as the video ends. Her voice pierces through everything.

"Thank you so much for watching! We're so pleased to announce that Lina and the Toms are going to have their very own reality show to find true love!"

CHAPTER 7

SHOCK PARALYZES ME. EVEN MY thoughts seem unable to move forward in any logical fashion. I stare open-mouthed at the empty wall where the video just played. The crowd finishes their applause. How can they possibly clap for that?

Fingers touch my hand, and I jump and pull away. They were Blue's fingers.

"They didn't tell you?" he asks, his voice low and tender.

I stare at him, then look at each of the other Toms in turn. They're all watching me with strange expressions.

"We thought you knew," Row says, his eyes darting to his brothers for help.

I stumble to my feet, knocking my chair over in the process. Al rushes to grab it and set it aright and takes my arm to steady me. His strong grip holds me up, but his hands are too warm. Everything feels much too warm. Another flash goes off in my face, and I press my hand to my stomach. My dinner threatens to make another appearance, and I've broken out into a cold sweat.

All eyes are on me. One or two guests wear furious expressions along with their formalwear. A couple more people look concerned. Everyone else smiles as if forcing a girl to pick a husband on international television is the best idea they've heard in their entire lives.

I can feel my heartbeat pulsing through my head. The world goes silent, even though people are still talking. I can see their mouths moving, but all I can hear is pulse, pulse, pulse and a faint ringing.

The spotlight centers on me yet again, and the light hurts so badly I close my eyes.

"I…I'm sorry. I don't feel well." I back up, then head for the back door.

"Lina, please sit down at the table," says Dr. Christiansen's voice behind me. It's not a request, but I don't care. The door is all that matters right now.

Get through the door, then worry about the rest.

Chairs are scraping, footsteps coming from every direction. I grab hold of the door's edge and pull myself into the kitchen. Just like before, none of the staff notice me. They're too busy cleaning up.

Get to the window. Window, window, window. As my fingers touch the cold pane of glass, the door opens behind me and slams into the wall.

"Lina! Get back in there now!" It's Dr. Christiansen. I've never heard her yell before.

Window, window. Get through the window. Someone's left it open a crack to let the fresh air in. To let me out.

"Shut that!" the doctor screams as I slip through. She's all blonde rage and limp curls.

I head for home. I won't have much time. She won't ever let this one go, but there's one more thing I need to do and I direct all of my focus, all of my energy, toward that one goal.

I hurl through my living room window, exploding the glass into chunks. My shoulder hurts from the impact, but that doesn't matter.

I fumble for the power switch to my new computer, a converted old cell phone with built-in camera.

Bless you, George.

Everything whirs to life. Jack's video chat invitation pops on the screen, and with shaky fingers, I push "accept." Moments later, Jack's face appears on the screen.

"Happy birthday! Nice hair. Are you all right?"

A sob bursts out of me before I can stop it. No, not a sob. A wail that cannot stand to be contained any longer. I crumple in on myself and cry into my hands.

"Lina! What's wrong?" His palms are pressed against the camera. He looks like he's about to push into my living room.

They can't be far now. I force myself to catch my breath. To slow down so I can speed up. I try not to think too hard about what I have to say. "I'm...I'm so sorry," I manage before another wave of tears overwhelms me.

"What?! Tell me what is going on. Do you need me to call someone? I will."

"No." There's no one to call. "I'm sorry, Jack. I can't explain. But I won't...be able to see you anymore. It will all make sense...very soon."

He pushes himself away from his computer as if I've punched him in the face. "What are you talking about, Lina? What is going on? What happened yesterday?" He keeps going on and on with questions I have no time to answer. I can't get a word in.

Fresh tears. Footsteps running toward me outside.

"Jack, I need to tell you something, so stop talking."

He stops, cold and motionless. I do not recognize this Jack.

I inhale hard and deep. "I love you."

He blinks. His mouth opens to say something, but I can't bear to hear what it is.

"Goodbye," I whisper, and I pull the plug.

He's gone.

A raw sob tears its way through my throat and mouth. I force myself to get up, grab my razor knife, and open the cell phone. I will not allow Dr. Christiansen to have this piece of me. I scrape the blade over the motherboard, popping off dozens of tiny pieces. Then I dig through until I find the memory card. I unscrew the cover and stab the inside over and over again until the metal is a mess of dents and punctures. Panic overtakes me. Look at what I've done! I run my fingers across my broken memories as tears drip down onto the unforgiving metal and plastic.

The ceiling opens. Jane's face enters my house like an unwelcome ogre. Her flashlight gives her features a gruesome appearance as she shouts to Dr. Christiansen that she's found me.

I stand, still holding the destroyed bits of my computer. My fingers explore the holes, wrapping themselves into twisted places, becoming one with the last tie to Jack I still have.

I don't resist when Jane picks me up and gently clips my wings together, nor when I am placed in an animal carrier that still has tufts of fur from its last occupant.

As I am transported to the main buildings, the deadening realization that Jack and I are truly over hits me full force. It isn't until I am locked securely into Dr. Christiansen's spare bedroom that I notice I left the computer pieces in the carrier. I don't even remember when I let them go.

CHAPTER 8

I WAKE UP WITH A stiff back, still clothed in the awful dress. Dim light seeps through cracks in the blinds.

Where am I?

My hand stretches out across the bedding. It isn't mine; it's cheap and ugly and smells of bleach. I sit bolt upright and my surroundings come into focus.

I'm in a strange bedroom in Dr. Christiansen's house. I push off the mattress—a small pillow wrapped in a shirt—and smooth down my hair. A tangle of purple comes loose in my hand, and I stare at it as the events of the previous night replay in my head and heart.

Jack is gone. I wait for the tears to come, but instead my heart comes up dry. I just feel flat, with a dash of panic under the surface.

Where is everyone? I fly up to the window and try to crack it, but it's nailed shut. The door can only be opened with a keypad, so I won't be getting out that way. The white walls and ceiling stare down at me like jailers.

"Hey!" I shout. "Let me out of here!" Silence answers me, and after several more tries, I retreat to the shabby pillow bed and curl up into a ball. The clock on the wall reads 8:43 a.m., and I watch the neon numbers advance for the next hour and fourteen minutes.

A click. The door opens, and Dr. Christiansen appears with her clipboard. An assistant I've never seen before pushes in a cart holding a projector and some other equipment I can't identify.

"Shut the door," she says. I disentangle my limbs and wings from the pillow and hug my arms around myself.

"What's this all about?" I ask, trying to sound brave. But all my courage from yesterday vanished with the remains of my computer.

"We're going to discuss your participation in the upcoming show and the consequences you will face if you choose to be difficult again."

I sigh. What more could she possibly do to me at this point?

"Shooting will begin in two weeks. You are expected to show up on time, participate in every date with a smile, and at the end of the show, you will select one of the Toms."

"I don't think so." The words are heavy on my tongue, but I can't just roll over and let her win.

"I thought you might say that. You seem to have no concern for your own wellbeing, but I think you might be interested in keeping your online friend safe."

"What are you talking about? If you think I'll believe for one second that you are big and powerful enough to hurt him all the way in another country…you've got a screw loose." I fold my arms, incredulous that she would stoop to such ridiculous blackmail.

Dr. Christiansen grabs the cart, aims the projector at the wall, and hits the power button. Footage of a dilapidated shop materializes on the wall. A young Native American man leans against the porch post, looking nervously from side to side. My heart quickens at the sight of him, but it isn't Jack— just a guy that could be his doppelganger. He stuffs his hand into his coat pocket and grips something inside.

It's a gun.

"Do you understand what you are seeing?" Dr. Christiansen asks. "Or do I have to break it down into small words for you?"

I pry open my dry lips. "You're going to frame him."

"Very good. The civil war was hard on the Americas. So many impoverished and desperate people willing to work for whatever the pay. All I need to do is send him one simple text and our friend will walk into that store in broad daylight and rob it. Then he will disappear, and the police will look for a young man who looks just like Jack. Unless, of course, you agree to cooperate."

The feeling has drained out of me onto the floor. All I can do is nod.

"Perfect." She holds up her phone and hits send.

The young man on the screen jumps and fishes his own phone out of his pocket. With trembling hands, he reads the message, and his shoulders droop in relief. He lets out a cracked laugh and, with a smile, stands up straighter and walks away.

The projector flicks off, and the assistant backs out of the room.

I stare at Dr. Christiansen. I've always thought of her as a cold-hearted woman, but I've never seen her this ruthless. A spear of terror pierces my heart as she smoothes her coat, smiling.

"I'm so glad we've been able to work this out," she says. Then she's gone.

***

Later, Jane brings food, a bowl of hot water, and all of my clothes in a squashed bundle. If it didn't take all of my energy to eat and get myself clean, I would be upset over the mess of wrinkles she's made of my clothing. I've always taken good care of those things, and now there they are in a heap. I tug on my pajamas and curl up on the pillow.

When I was a little girl, about five or six years old, Mr. Coxworth gave me several pop-up children's books. He propped them up on the kitchen counter in his house, and I would play in the paper castles and oceans. I'd never heard the stories my "forts" belonged to, so I made up my own instead.

Cinderella's castle became the home of my "real parents," who would come and rescue me someday and break the curse keeping me so tiny. We would ride away in a gilded carriage, and I would never have to return to Lilliput ever again.

Hansel and Gretel became my brother and sister. Together we would bury the evil witch in candy and then live in her gingerbread house forever. In my reimagining, Hansel was my protective older brother and Gretel much younger, the baby of the family. And I was smack in the middle. Normal. And I didn't have to go to school or have tutors or learn old, dead languages.

The Snow Queen looked so very much like Dr. Christiansen in the illustrations that I imagined they were one and the same. Hansel and Gretel would come and spring me from her icy castle, and we would escape to our gingerbread house on the next page.

As I grew out of the pop-up books, I began to write my own stories in a little notebook. I called them my "True Tales," and they were my dreams for what my life would have been if I'd been born under different circumstances. Tales of my first day at school, getting a poor grade in English, first crush, first kiss…

When I met Jack, I stopped writing them.

Today I write a new one. Not on paper. Not for anyone to find. I write it on my soul.

The heat of the morning sun and the man lying next to me draw me from slumber. Light wraps around his bare arm, setting the tiny hairs aglow, then comes to rest on the sheet as a perfect triangle of white.

The man is Jack, but he's a few years older now, as am I. We have both grown into our faces and wear them with confidence. We know the landscape of the other's body better than our own.

Still, I hesitate to touch him. The featherweight blanket of quiet has settled upon us. I watch him sleeping, but staring and even touching is an intrusion into his space, a violation of his trust. And his trust is my most priceless treasure. I have fought to keep it with sweat and tears.

Somehow, now, we are nearly the same size. I'm not sure how it happened. I don't know how he forgave me for lying to him or what he said when he discovered the truth. I don't know why he loves me, why he stays.

But he does. And I do. I always will.

I seal up my story within myself. I seal up my body, heart, and soul so they will remain safe. I seal myself inside of my bedcovers to block it all out.

CHAPTER 9

IT'S ALMOST THREE O'CLOCK IN the morning, and I still haven't fallen asleep. The glowing numbers on the clock cast a pale blue on the white wall. This is not my room, but I live here now. The only way I'm allowed to leave it is in a cage. They call it a "carrier trailer," but it's a cage.

A seamless white pillow and a small metal chamber pot are the only pieces of furniture. The pillow is far too big, and I wake up in pain every morning from the lack of support. I have a small pile of my things on the floor that Jane took from my house: a few books, my toothbrush, and some pens and paper. That's it.

I alternate between blind rage and hopelessness. It's an exhausting cocktail. Since that first day, my life has been an endless parade of photo shoots, costumes, and the Toms whom I've grown to resent. I have become the master of the fake smile. All Dr. Christiansen has to do is mouth the name "Jack" to me and I become the picture of happiness on the outside.

I have an entourage now. They're all former doll-makers, puppet costumers, and doll repair specialists. They come in each morning to stuff me into whatever "look" the show's chief stylist has decided I should sport that day.

The first thing they did was bleach out the purple dye from my hair. I was too tired to protest. If I'd realized I would be a Barbie when they were done, I would have made more of a fuss. Not that it would have done any good. They pull out their magnifying glasses to paint my face with makeup.

They strip off my clothes without any thought for my privacy. I have learned to go silent, to hang on to my memories inside so I don't go crazy. Then again, maybe insanity wouldn't be so bad. I'm already locked in a white room with no means of killing myself. Why not go the extra mile and give them an actual, logical reason to keep me here?

I stare up at the ceiling, eying the edges of the recessed lights. I haven't been sleeping well since my birthday, and all of the days run together in my mind in one confusing blur. It actually seems surreal. I'm not sure all of this is happening to me. Except there, on the wall, is the shooting schedule for the show.

I have two weeks to figure out what to do before they start taping me live and putting me on international television.

Some small remnant of me in the corner of my mind keeps asking, *Why? Why does Dr. Christiansen want this so badly? Why are there six of them and one of me?* They are questions I should pursue. I should figure it out. But the rest of my soul is so very tired. It turns out apathy is stronger than life itself.

I close my eyes. The little remnant keeps poking at me. *Why?*

"Shut up," I whisper to myself. "I want to go to sleep."

Why?

My eyelids flutter open, and I scan the room as I search for answers inside my head. Dr. Christiansen has never been a pleasant woman, but she's not one to do something without a reason. It might not be a reason I'd agree with, but there'd still be a reason. What logical explanation could she possibly have for putting me on the international stage and forcing me to pick a husband? What reason does she have for thinking it would actually work?

She has to realize she can't threaten me every step along the way without some negative consequences. She's observed me for too long to think that would be possible, even with drugs.

What is it I'm missing?

The clock on the wall changes to 3:01, and the door swings open and my hairdresser (can't remember her name) flicks on the light. I fling my arm over my eyes and groan. The rest of the entourage follows the hairstylist inside, and they shut the door. Not a single one of them apologizes for waking me up. What on earth are they doing in here so early?

They've each dragged in their personal workstations, and now they're lining them up along the walls. Buttons are pushed and the stations unfold themselves into things resembling desks.

The hairstylist clasps her hands together, bends over at the waist, and scurries over to me as if she's about to have a conversation with a small child or a dog. Her hair is a mass of wiry gray-streaked brown curls; her face is a lesson in how *not* to apply makeup.

"Helloooooo, peeeexieeeee!"

I have never met a more distasteful person in my life other than Dr. Christiansen. I open one eye and fantasize about shooting needle darts into her flaring nostrils.

She claps her hands again. I grit my teeth.

"Rise and shine! Up up up! It's time to get you ready for your romantic sunrise pictures!"

So that's what this is about.

I clear my throat. "What's your name again?"

"Tina! We have rhyming names—isn't that so exciting?" She nearly hyperventilates from all the "excitement" as her gold eye shadow sparkles in the fluorescent light. If Tina were ever to slice open a vein, I'm pretty sure she would bleed glitter.

The makeup artist pokes her head to the side of Tina's hair. Her name is Susanna, and she's the only person in the entire entourage I like. "We've got breakfast for you, Lina. Are you hungry?"

If anyone else had asked me that question, I would have said "no," but Susanna treats me like I'm one of her girlfriends and we're getting ready for a normal day. Somehow she manages to do it without diminishing the situation or being condescending. It's a breath of fresh air and enough to make me realize I'm ravenously hungry.

"Yeah, what do you have?" I stand up cautiously, the cotton in the pillow shifting under my feet.

"One sec—I'll bring you the tray." She disappears behind Tina's hair and then returns with a breakfast tray nearly overflowing with sliced berries, cracked grains, mini-omelets, and me-sized pancakes. I grab a plate and load it up with a little bit of everything before sitting down on the edge of the tray and eating as much as I can stomach. Susanna brings me some freshly squeezed orange juice and sits on the floor in front of me, cross-legged. She's not much older than me—probably in her early twenties. She's got shoulder-length dark brown hair that's ridiculously shiny, and the rest of her is very pretty as well. If I was to ever pick an older sister, I think it would be someone like Susanna.

"So," she says, "did anyone explain to you what's happening today?"

I shove another bite of pancake into my mouth and give her a look that says, *What do you think?*

"Sorry. I thought—" She stops and sighs. "I should have known better. Next time, I'll make sure I brief you every night if I hear something has changed."

I swallow a too-large lump of pancake with a grimace. "Thanks. It's not your fault."

"No, but still." She rearranges her feet. "So today we have two hours to get you all ready, and then we're doing sunrise photos on the hill with the Toms."

"What hill?"

"The hill they built at the west end for this photo shoot. It's actually a mound of dirt with some sod on top. I didn't get a good look at it."

"Fabulous. Do you have any coffee?"

"Faye! Bring me that thermos!"

Faye obeys and hands me a miniature stoneware mug that is still too big for me. But I manage to gulp down some coffee out of it anyway, and ten minutes later, I'm trembling like a kite in a hurricane.

"What *is* that stuff?" I ask Susanna. I can barely stand still.

"Coffee with espresso and a couple caffeine pills. We need all the help we can get to stay awake. Hey, are you feeling okay?"

"Yes. Aside from the permanent seizure, I feel absolutely fantastic."

"Okay." She gives me a half-smile as she studies me. "How about other than the coffee? How are you doing?"

"I guess I'm all right. I haven't really been sleeping." I wonder if she knows about Jack, but I don't want to ask. I almost trust Susanna but not quite. She's not exactly George or Mr. Coxworth. Doesn't it bother her she's working for a company that thinks it's cool to force people to get married? And I still have no idea why Dr. Christiansen is doing this.

And that gives me an idea.

"Hey Susanna? Do you think you could do me a favor?" I have to word this just right. "This caffeine is really messing me up. There's this stuff called guarana that our botanist grows. It's all-natural and has caffeine in it, but it doesn't make me all jittery. Do you think you could get some?"

"I don't know, Lina…"

"Please? I'm not sure how many more of these early mornings I can take. I'll even give you a note for him."

I can see her wavering. "Who is it?"

I've already won. "Mr. Coxworth. He lives in a shack between the dining hall and my house. Does that sound familiar?"

"I think I've seen it. What do I tell him? And what do I tell the staff if they catch me?"

"I'll give you a note for him. You can just leave it in his mailbox and then pick the stuff up later. If the staff ask what you're doing, tell them you're running an errand for the cook and getting some herbs."

She wrinkles her nose up in worry, but she pulls a little pad of paper from her pocket. "Here, do you need this?"

"That and a regular-sized pen."

"Okay. Why the bigger pen?"

"Because Mr. Coxworth is mostly blind, so I have to write it in braille. If I use my pen, it will cut through the paper instead of making a dot impression." I feel bad for lying to Susanna, but I can't have her reading my note.

When I'm done, it reads "Help. Why the show? Guarana" in heavy-handed Morse code. I can't make it any longer or it might look suspicious. I almost forget to add "guarana" at the end. I'm sure Susanna would suspect something was up if she went to see Mr. Coxworth and he didn't hand her something to bring back to me.

I run my hand over the little dots I've created to make sure they're enough to convince Susanna it's braille, and then I fold up the note and hand it to her. "Thanks," I say. "I really appreciate this."

"Ready for some makeup?"

"I guess. Can I brush my teeth first?"

"Please do."

I take care of my business, and Susanna paints my face on. I'm a little glad for the makeup today since the dark circles under my eyes seem to extend all the way down to my boobs. Still, it feels heavy and unnatural.

When Susanna is finished with me, my costumer takes over and carefully seals me up in a fuchsia dress not unlike the awful one Dr. Christiansen picked out for my birthday party. Thankfully, this one does not have beads or petticoats, but the fabric is so stiff I have to keep pushing down the skirt to keep from flashing everybody. Tina the Terrible curls my hair with the world's smallest curling iron and then gives me a gold headband. When everyone is finished, I am a miniature, and slightly older, Shirley Temple.

"It's five o'clock, laaaaaaaadies!" Tina screeches. "Let's get ready to go! Chop chop!" She claps her hands. Workstations are collapsed into carts; brushes and clothing and makeup kits are all tucked away.

Dr. Christiansen walks through the door with my cage. I fold my arms but force myself not to scowl.

"Get inside, Lina," she says. "We have no time to waste."

Sounds like someone woke up on the wrong side of the bed this morning. Every one of my instincts screams at me to resist, but all I can think about is Jack. I can trade a few minutes in a cage for his safety. I exhale and fly inside. She shuts the door and locks it.

I plop down on the cushion padding the entire floor of the carrier, and fatigue nearly overwhelms me. The only windows are the narrow air slits lining the walls and the ceiling, so it's dark and stuffy in here. Not a great recipe for staying awake, despite the fact that I'm still shaking all over from the coffee. Even when we start moving, the constant banging of the carrier against Dr. Christiansen's leg isn't enough to keep me from falling asleep.

***

The first crack of sunlight poking through the slits wakes me. The carrier is motionless, so I can only assume we've stopped. I stand up and peek out through the small opening in the door.

I have no idea where we are. The carrier sits on the ground in front of a mound of dirt that is the spitting image of an out-of-control anthill. They must have erected a smaller dome fence over the photo shoot area because it's magnifying all of the sunrise colors from the sky. The dirt and grass are painted with electric oranges and pinks. Several crew members mill about, adjusting lighting and reflectors.

Someone picks up my carrier again, and I lose my balance, flying backward onto the cushion. When the door opens, I get up but then stand there, confused. Why does this setting look so familiar?

Then it dawns on me. The mound of dirt is a replica of Harney Peak.

Dr. Christiansen has recreated my first date with Jack.

CHAPTER 10

UP UNTIL TODAY, I'VE MANAGED to be a good sport to make sure Jack remains unharmed. I've had my picture taken in trees, on a lily pad in a pond, and in the midst of an artificial cloud made with a fog machine that gave me several asthma attacks. I've also had about ten billion portraits taken, and I smiled dutifully for each one.

But this...this is too much. I press the backs of my hands against my cheeks to cool them. Hot tears of embarrassment and violation escape before I can sniff them away.

Dr. Christiansen's face appears in the doorway, and her expression shocks me to the core. She looks *hopeful*, as if she expects me to be enjoying this set-up.

"What the hell?" I whisper.

She sees my tears, and her demeanor instantly reverts to its default coldness. "Come out," she says in her clipped tone. Do I actually hear disappointment in her voice? "Stand next to Tom2." She disappears from my view. Stunned, I walk out of the cage into the sunlight.

Did that really happen? Did I see a look of sadness in her eyes? I take my place next to Row without even really looking at him. The doctor stares off into the distance, but her face is pulled into a blank mask. Whatever I thought I saw definitely isn't there now.

A shoulder gently bumps mine, and I look up into Row's face. "Hey, Lina," he says with a weak smile. "Good morning."

I try to pull up the corners of my mouth into something resembling a happy face, but I can't. "Hey," I reply. "How are you?"

"Sleepy." His eyes are all puffy. Poor guy.

"Yeah, me too."

He takes a deep breath. "I just want to say I'm sorry about all of this."

"What?"

"You get that this wasn't our idea, right? We don't have a choice either. I'm sorry it's so unpleasant for you. I mean, we grew up with each other and we're friends—well, most of us—and you don't anyone and now you're stuck with a bunch of strange guys."

I bite down hard on the inside of my cheek. I wish I could tell him it has nothing to do with him or any of the other Toms, although it would still be a terrible situation even if I'd never met Jack. Deep, ragged breath. Get a handle on yourself, Lina!

I eke out a smile for him. "Well, let's make the best of it, shall we?"

"When life gives you lemons, make lemonade?"

"No, no, it should go like this: When life gives you lemons, squirt the juice in your enemy's eyes."

He looks confused for a moment and then bursts out laughing. His laugh is a little squeaky and high-pitched, but real. It cracks my sadness, and I can't help but join in.

A flash goes off in our faces, shattering the brief moment of happiness, and I immediately cringe.

"Lovely, absolutely lovely, darlings," the photographer mumbles as he gets into position for another shot. "Let's do that again. Lots of laughter! Happy thoughts!"

But the joy has already leaked out of me.

***

By the end of the morning, my face hurts from smiling. We wrap right before lunch, and food is served on a folding table right next to the "mountain." Another tiny table sits at the end, and I join the Toms. It's the first time we've sat together for a meal since my birthday.

This time I end up between Blue and Shrike. Lunch is macaroni and cheese. In our case, a single macaroni with a drop of cheese.

I hate macaroni and cheese.

With a sigh, I slice off a quivering chunk of noodle with my spoon. Al has already eaten half of his. Blue sits there, chin in his hand, staring off into space. Row is happily going on and on about something to Crane, who listens without a word. Shrike and Perry are deep in their own conversation.

It occurs to me that, if circumstances were different, I wouldn't mind hanging out with these guys. Most of them have been kind to me. I look over at Blue again, and he turns and meets my eye. He smiles, although his expression remains serious.

"So…" I say.

"So here we are," he replies.

"It's a nice day."

"For Denmark, sure."

"I never did hear where you guys live."

He pauses as though he's carefully planning each word. "The Lilliput II Project is in New Zealand. We live right near the beach. I wake up every morning to the sound of the surf. It's weird being here and not hearing or seeing the ocean every day. I miss it. I even miss the salt."

Embarrassingly, until now, it hasn't occurred to me they might miss their home. I certainly didn't know they'd come all the way from Down Under.

"So you all live in one house," I said. "Do you share a room?"

"No, not all of us. And I'd say 'house' should be used pretty loosely. We have little shelters built along the beach, but whenever a storm comes along, they don't hold up. We had to build them ourselves. Row and I teamed up to make ours, so we share. Al and Crane share one, and Perry and Shrike share another. Perry and Shrike have the best spot; theirs is up in a tree. We couldn't find another tree that was suitable, so ours butts up against a rock."

"Did they give you the materials to build it?"

He nods. "Well, some of them. We never did get any glass for the windows. It gets interesting when it rains."

I shake my head, grateful for George. "Do you at least have beds?"

He grins. "We have sand beds. They're really comfortable. We had normal beds when we were kids, but I definitely prefer the sand ones."

"What exactly is that?"

"It's a wooden box full of sand. You put your sheets and blankets right on top, and it molds to you while you're sleeping."

I laugh. "I'll take your word for it. So are you and Row good friends?"

He nods. "Row and I are pretty different, but he's solid. I trust him." He pokes at his macaroni. "You should get to know him."

I'm not sure what to make of that comment, so I shove a spoonful of food into my mouth. It's not as bad as I remembered. Maybe they hired a better chef for the show. I glance over at Blue. He's watching me, waiting for an answer.

"I'm serious," he says. "You won't find a better guy than Row."

Well, I guess you're *not interested in me.*

"Okay, okay," I say. "Now you have to tell me why you're pushing me toward him."

"He's a great guy, and he deserves to be happy."

"What about you?"

Blue stares over Al's head at the sky and shrugs. "I'll get my chance."

And now I'm annoyed. What the hell is that supposed to even mean? Is that all I am—a chance at happiness and they're all lining up to get their turn? Well, I guess I'll give him what he wants then.

"You're right," I say as I stand. "I *will* get to know him." I fly over the table and wiggle in between Row and Crane. They quickly make room for me, and Row catches me up on their conversation.

"...and then we pushed the paper plane off the top of the house and Crane rode it all the way down to the beach without even cracking his wings open."

Crane grunts and smiles. "The tongue depressors were the trick."

Row leans in, practically lighting up the table. "Yeah, we used them as a frame to make it more sturdy! Crane was only what—seven years old?"

Crane directs his shy grin at the tablecloth. "Yeah, around there."

"*Nobody* else could do it. We all crashed into the bushes or had to start flying."

I can almost see sunbeams shooting from Crane's face. Now I understand Row's magic; he finds a way to make everyone feel like a superhero.

As Crane floats on cloud nine, I turn toward Row. I can see it in his eyes; he knows exactly what he's doing, but he's still completely sincere.

"How come you're always so happy?" I ask him.

His glory fades a little. "I have my down days, too. I don't know... I prefer to stay optimistic."

"Okay, okay, I have a question for you. My stylists have been reading magazine articles to me with questions to ask potential dates."

"That's not fair—we're not even shooting yet!"

"Consider it practice," I say with a smirk.

"All right, go ahead." Row reaches around me and taps Crane on the shoulder. "Hey, you have to answer this, too."

"When was the last time you cried?"

Row goes white, then flushes bright red. Crane chews his food thoughtfully.

"I can't remember when," Crane says. "I don't cry very often. It's probably been a few years."

"I think it was about a month ago for me," Row says quietly. I'm suddenly sorry I asked, and I don't dare push him to find out why.

"I beat both of you," I say.

An awkward silence descends on our corner of the table. Nice going, me. Time to change the subject.

"Okay, I have one more question."

They're both wearing wary expressions, but Crane says, "Okay."

"Who has been your biggest crush to date? Models, actresses, and made-up characters count."

"Elsa Ridek," Crane says without the slightest hesitation.

"Who is that?" I ask.

"She's a Polish movie star from the 2030s. Really pretty." He turns red and stares down at his food again.

"Um, I had a crush on our gardener's daughter," Row admits. "When I was a kid."

"Daphne?" Crane asks.

"Yeah. How about you, Lina?"

Shoot, I forgot I would have to answer, too. I have to think of something, some movie star.

"Clark Gable," I blurt out.

Row puzzles over the name as though he's trying to place it. "From *Gone with the Wind*?"

"Yeah, that's him."

"Frankly, my dear, I don't give a damn," Row says in an absolutely terrible imitation.

I crack up laughing and give him a round of applause. "Very nice."

"I'm sorry. I didn't mean to direct that at you."

"I know, Row. Don't worry about it. It was funny."

One of the production assistants comes and hovers over us. "I have some updates for you all, so listen up."

The guys set down their silverware, and we all pay close attention as she reads off of her notes.

"First two individual dates are coming up. You'll go in order of your names. So that's Crane, then Row. Then there's a group date followed by dates with Al and Shrike. Then another group date, then Perry and Blue. After that, Lina will get to pick who she wants for the last two dates."

"Where are the dates taking place?" I ask. "Is it going to be more stuff like this?" I wave toward the fake Harney Peak.

"That's a surprise."

"Of course it is."

***

After the shoot wraps, I'm only in my prison cell of a bedroom for five minutes before Susanna slips through the door.

"I only have a minute," she says before setting her paper bundle on my bed. "Hope this helps. He didn't seem to have any problem seeing me when I picked it up."

"Yeah, well, he can see shapes and stuff, so he fools most people." I hope she never mentions this to anyone else. "Thanks so much."

"You're welcome. I'll see you tomorrow. First date!"

"Yeah." I pump my fist weakly into the air. "Whoopee."

She gives me her concerned look once more and then leaves. As soon as the door clicks closed, I take a giant winged leap toward the package and flip it over. Mr. Coxworth's wax seal is still intact so I tear the paper carefully around it and then unfold everything. Inside is a tiny bag full of the requested guarana, but I don't care about that. The note inside the bag is all that matters to me. It's written in hastily scrawled English.

My dear Thumbelina,

Can't begin to fathom what goes through the white witch's head. Might be motivated by money. I think the project has lost funding over the years. I'll see what I can find. So sorry. Next time, ask for peppermint for the terrible stomachache you have.

– Mr. C

I fold up the note into a miniscule sliver before sliding it inside a hole I've made in my giant pillow bed.

Money. I've been sold out for money. I'm not sure what she's planning to do with more funds because Lilliput is largely self-sustaining now. She must have something else up her sleeve. Something to do with Jane's ugly experiment with the cat. I suck in my breath and sit down on my pillow.

I have to figure out what she has in mind. In order to do that, I need to get into her office and the only way out of this room is through that giant locked door.

Come on, Lina! You can figure this out. You can get out of here.

And like a jolt of electricity, an idea lands in my head.

A devilish grin spreads across my face as a plan formulates in my head— a plan involving lightning bugs.

CHAPTER 11

I SLEEP LIKE A BABY for the first time in weeks. When the hair and makeup crew rolls in at 7 a.m., I'm already up and waiting.

"Wow, that stuff must work well," says Susanna as she sets her makeup kit next to me.

"Like a charm."

"I've never seen you looking so…awake."

"It's pretty powerful. Only thing is, and I forgot this earlier, it gives me a nasty stomachache."

She grimaces. "I'm sorry. I think I have some medicine in my purse."

"I can't take that stuff. It's not meant for people my size. But Mr. Coxworth makes an amazing peppermint concoction that works like a dream."

She unlatches her box and sets out her brushes. "So you want me to go and ask him for it, right?"

"I'm sorry, I know it's a lot."

She sighs. "Lina, if I get caught, I'll be fired. I was really lucky to get this job. I was unemployed for six months before I started working here. You don't know what it's like…"

"You're right. I don't. Because no one lets me out of here." I gather my anger and try to stuff it down. I do feel bad for her, but I still need this favor. "I don't want you to lose your job, Susanna. If you go during the date tonight, I'm sure no one will see you. Everyone important will be at the shoot."

She nods slowly. "I guess so. All right."

"Can I borrow your pen and paper again?"

"Sure."

I write "Lightning Bug Juice" in Morse code and hand the note to her. She acts as though I'm handing her a venomous snake.

Two hours later, I'm fed, washed, dressed, and made up for my date with Crane. If Dr. Christiansen plans on recycling all of my construct dates with Jack, then I'm pretty sure what the next scenario will be.

The pyramids of Egypt.

CHAPTER 12

OUR SECOND CONSTRUCT DATE HAPPENED after a few more weeks of long talks in chat parlors and over instant messenger.

The sand swirled up from our feet when Jack and I loaded into the desert. I took one look at his mummy costume and burst out laughing. He put out his arms all stiff-like and shambled in my direction with a moan.

I took off running in the opposite direction and promptly tripped on a stone. I face-planted into the sand, and Jack started laughing so hard he collapsed onto the ground next to me.

"I'm not normally a klutz," I insisted as he unwound his bandages.

"I know. That's why it's hilarious when your clumsy side makes an appearance."

"I think you put some sort of mummy curse on me."

"I think you've got no one to blame but yourself."

I flung a handful of sand at him, but he dodged it with an elegant roll.

"Oh, look at you! Do you do martial arts or something?"

"Maybe," he said with a grin. "It's been a while though."

"You're just one surprise after another."

"You too, Thumbelina."

That name sobered me instantly, and he noticed.

"What's wrong?"

"Nothing. Let's go see some pyramids!"

"I'll race you." He jetted off, and I quickly followed. Since fatigue and muscle aren't a real factor in constructs, I won.

"Let's go up!" I shouted back to him. We ran around the perimeter until we found a trail up the southwest side of the Great Pyramid. After twenty minutes of climbing, we weren't anywhere close to the top so we decided to come down.

"We could just load at the top," he said.

"Let's go check out the inside first."

We circled around until we found the entrance. The wind picked up as we crept inside the silent pyramid.

"I bet it would be really hot in here if this was real," I said as we descended into the tunnel.

"Just turn off your air conditioning so you can imagine it better."

"I don't have any. Besides, it's kind of cold here right now."

"Really? We're getting some record-breaking heat for October. I've been drinking water non-stop, and I haven't had to piss all day because I'm sweating so much."

"Wow, thanks for telling me, Jack!"

"You're welcome." He paused. *"I can't believe I just said that."*

"Yeah, I haven't noticed you be quite so...open before."

"I guess you bring it out of me."

"Great," I said, but I was smiling into the darkness.

I followed him down the tunnel into the Queen's Chamber. *"How do you know where you're going?"* I called after him.

"I've been to this construct before. I dig exploring old, historical places. Especially ones that are a little creepy."

"How long did it take you to put together the mummy costume?" I asked with a snort.

"Not telling! Anyway, here we are."

The Queen's Chamber was a compact, stony cube.

"It's really small," I said.

"The King's Chamber is bigger."

"Typical."

"Yeah, it seems odd to me though. If I believed I could have access to all my stuff and my wife after I died, I think I would want her buried in the same

chamber. The way they have it now, they might as well be sleeping in separate bedrooms."

It gave my stomach a bit of a flip to hear him talk that way. He'd never hinted he'd thought about having a wife in the future before. I rubbed my arms and focused my gaze on the empty stone container in the middle of the room.

"How come it's empty?" I wondered aloud. "Was anyone ever buried here?"

"No one knows. Some people think Cheops and his wife were buried here and robbers plundered everything."

"Plundered. That makes them sound like pirates."

"Mummies, pirates, treasure… Pretty good movie material."

"I think that's already been done," I said.

"Yeah, but all those things together?"

"Yep. Several times."

"Well, shoot, there goes my career in screenwriting."

We walked up to the King's Chamber, which was not as large I'd expected. Its sarcophagus also sat empty. The room held nothing but sand and cobwebs.

"What a waste," I said. "Hoarding all of those supplies in here, only to have them taken by robbers instead of going to someone who could have used them."

Jack shrugged. "Yeah, but they believed they would need all that stuff."

"I guess they were wrong."

"Maybe."

"Well, obviously they didn't use it because it was here for the taking. Like Tutankhamen's tomb where they found everything still intact. All the food—everything."

Jack shrugged. "Maybe you use things differently in the afterlife."

"If there even is one."

He studied my face. "I think it's real. Maybe not the way they imagined it, though. Did your parents raise you in any religion?"

I laughed. "No, not really." I remembered my Russian mom and the cross she gave me. "A couple of my family members are Christians, but I think that's it. Science is king where I live."

"Would it bother you if someone you dated had their own faith?"

The question took me aback. Was he asking for a reason or to find out how I felt in general? "I guess it depends on the faith. I don't think I could date someone who believed in Santa Claus…"

"I was raised as a traditional Lakota."

"What does that mean?"

"We believe in a Great Spirit and in respecting nature. It also means I went to the dances and ceremonies."

"That sounds kind of cool." I lapsed into silence, thinking about it. "I don't know if I believe in a god or not. Or a goddess. No one here really talks about it." I shrugged.

"Honestly, sometimes I'm not sure either."

"Maybe we're not that different, after all," I said with a smile. His worry melted into a boyish grin.

"I guess not," he said. "I just wanted to ask."

So now you can ask me to be your girlfriend? I held my breath and half-hoped he would.

"Want to see the grotto?"

I bit back my disappointment and smiled. "Sure."

I followed him down the winding tunnels to a small room full of strange round formations. Minerals crusted the walls.

"There's a well right over there, so watch your step," Jack said as he pointed to a hole in the floor. "But this here is what I want to show you." He jerked his head toward a tunnel.

"Where does it go?"

"Absolutely nowhere."

"I don't believe it. This is a pyramid! It has to go somewhere." I wished I could transform to my real size and fly along the passageway. Then I noticed the mischievous grin on Jack's face.

"I thought you might say that," he said. He handed me a spare flashlight and a chisel. "Want to do some exploring? You're not claustrophobic, are you?"

"I definitely want to check it out. But will it work to chisel through since this is just, you know, a construct?"

"I'm not sure. Let's find out." He bent down and began to squeeze into the narrow space. "You coming?"

I was already close behind him. We crawled for what felt like miles before we hit a dead-end. Jack ran his fingers along the edges of the wall. "Anything look funny to you?"

"I see light coming through," I said. "Hammer your chisel right there."

He wedged the chisel into the crack and brought the hammer back. "Might want to scoot away. I don't want to accidentally clock you in the head with this thing."

I obliged, and he drove the hammer into the chisel. The stone along the edge cracked and splintered before crumbling into sand. He pressed his hand against the remaining piece and pushed.

An avalanche of bricks tumbled into the next room.

A room. I held my breath as we crawled through the entrance and stood up.

"Am I really seeing this?" I asked, turning in circles. The chamber was small but lined with elaborately painted sarcophagi. "No way."

Jack chuckled and ruffled the dust out of his hair. "You can say that again."

"How can this be here? Without being discovered? Or, since it's in the construct, maybe it's been discovered? I don't get it."

"I don't know, but I want to check out the coffins. Can you give me a hand lifting this lid?"

"Should we really look inside? I feel kind of weird about doing that."

"It's just a construct, remember?"

"I know, but still…" I slid my fingertips into the groove where the lid and the base of the sarcophagus came together.

"One…two…three!" We lifted together and liberated enough dust to suffocate ourselves. I coughed out of habit as we set the lid on the ground, even though I obviously wasn't breathing anything but perfectly dust-free air.

As the dust cleared, we crept up to the edge of the coffin. A shriveled, human-shaped mass of cloth lay in the shadows.

"Is that what I think it is?" I whispered.

"I'm going to check the lid for an inscription. Should have done that first." He panned his flashlight across the top and found some faded hieroglyphics. "I wish I could read those."

I was still staring at the face. The features were intact, although they reminded me more of burnt leather than human skin.

Jack made a faint moaning sound, and I whirled around. "Jack, are you okay?"

He looked completely fine. "What do you mean?"

"You made a noise."

"No, I didn't." Then his mouth dropped open, and he pointed over my shoulder.

I already knew what I was going to see, and I couldn't breathe or move. After several agonizing seconds, I forced myself to face the mummy. It was slowly unfolding its arms and starting to sit up.

"Oh, no, you don't," I hissed. I sprang backward and grabbed one of the bricks we'd knocked out of the door and threw it at the mummy's head as hard as I could. The mummy shuddered as its head snapped to the side, then it fell into the coffin in a soft shuffle of bone and skin and cloth.

"How the hell did that just happen?!" I stared at Jack, fully expecting to see him wearing the same panicked expression.

Instead, his mouth was twisted into an I'm-trying-really-hard-not-to-smile sort of face.

"You!" I squealed at him. "This was your idea, wasn't it?!" The adrenaline was draining away, leaving me with a bad case of the shakes.

A short laugh escaped. "I'm sorry, Lina. Don't hate me!"

The mummy costume, the fake room… I groaned. I should have known. "You stinker!"

His eyes crinkled up as the laughter took over. "You—you should have seen yourself! You almost took its head off!"

My breaths were coming in short gasps, and I started hiccoughing. My chest began to tighten, and the familiar drowning sensation of an asthma attack expelled all of my anger.

"Jack," I gasped. I wanted to tell him I would be right back, but I couldn't speak. My hands fumbled up to my face and I pulled off my halojector. Medicine. Where was my medicine?

I spotted my handbag sitting next to the front door and flew over to it, knocking several pictures off of the wall in the process. I opened the tin, broke the capsule, inhaled.

I sank against the wall, breathing hard as the vise around my chest began to loosen. My pulse increased as the medicine entered my bloodstream, and I trembled all over, exhausted from the rush.

I could hear Jack's muffled voice through my halojector, but it took me a few minutes to steady my breathing enough so I would be able to tell him what happened.

When I put the halojector back on, I found that Jack had loaded us just outside the pyramid.

"I'm so sorry," he said as soon as he saw my avatar moving again. "I'm so, so sorry. I had no idea it would make you so upset."

"I'm not upset, Jack. It was my asthma. Sometimes the adrenaline makes me breathe extra-hard and that can trigger an attack. It wasn't your fault."

He exhaled. "I really thought you were furious. Are you okay?"

"My lungs are a little sore, but I'm good." I forced a smile to make him feel better. "I really can't believe I fell for your prank."

"I didn't think you would," he admitted. "Your reaction was pretty impressive. You really held it together."

"Yeah, up until my lungs rebelled."

"I won't do that again, I promise."

"Go ahead and try! I'm not falling for any more tricks after that one!"

His gentle smile sent shivers down my arms, and I blushed and looked away. I was used to George's concerned looks, but this was different. In Jack's eyes, I wasn't a child to be protected—I was a whole person with feelings and weaknesses and emotions I couldn't share with anyone. He saw through my brave face and my jokes, and we both knew it.

"Are you really okay?"

I frowned. I suddenly had the urge to cry, and I wasn't exactly sure why. "Yeah," I said. "I'll be fine."

He stepped closer. "You sure?"

"Yeah, but I think I need to go lie down for a little while. Can we talk later?"

"Definitely."

"Okay, great. Thanks for the date. It was fun." I needed to log off. The tears were threatening to push their way out.

"Right. Next time I'll try not to give you an asthma attack. I really am sorry."

"I know, Jack. It's okay. Goodnight!"

I ripped off my halojector before I'd completely logged off. I cleared my throat several times in a vain attempt to stymie the tears. Why was I crying? I couldn't even remember the last time I'd cried. I saw Jack's eyes, full of compassion, over and over again in my head, and that broke me.

I ran to my room and jumped on my bed. I would not cry into my pillow. That would be stupid and cliché and I wasn't that sort of girl.

Tears dripped onto my satin bedspread with whispered splashes. Are you really okay? *he had asked me. I'd thought I was. But I knew he wasn't just asking about the asthma attack. Unlike everyone else in my life, he wanted to see if I was okay with everything that was happening to me. And even though Jack didn't know about half of what I was forced to put up with, the question felt like it applied to everything. Was I okay with the prank he'd pulled? Was I okay with being chased by huge falcons? Was I okay with having no friends my age, no freedom, no real parents?*

No. I was not okay, and I'd never given myself permission to think that. Sure, I would whine and complain when I didn't like the things I had to do, but I'd always prided myself in keeping a stiff upper lip and meeting the challenges head-on. But what if I didn't have to do that? What if I could live a life where my being okay actually mattered to someone?

It felt like a lost part of my heart had ripped open at the seams and out of it poured sob after sob. I don't remember when I stopped crying and fell asleep.

CHAPTER 13

THE PRODUCTION ASSISTANT SETS DOWN the carrier inside my room and opens the door so I can fly out.

"Need anything?"

"I could use some dinner," I say as I buzz over to my bed and belly-flop onto it.

She grimaces. "Yeah, the catering tonight was…different."

That's one word for quivering blocks of overcooked tofu and soggy veggies. Another word I might choose would be "horrifying."

"I'll be right back." She keys her code into the door's opening mechanism, and it swings open to reveal Susanna.

"Oh! Are you leaving? I just came by to help her get ready for bed."

"Yeah, getting food. Do you want any?"

"No, I'm fine. Thanks, though." Susanna steps inside, and the door closes behind her. "I have your stuff."

"Awesome. I think I might need it after the horrible food. I only took one bite, but it's already doing a number on me. Go ahead and toss it."

"It's kind of heavy."

"And I'm kind of used to that."

She tosses it hesitantly, lightly, and I fly up to catch it. It socks me full force in the chest, but I swallow my surprise at its weight. Mr. Coxworth sent more than I thought he would.

"How was the date?" Susanna asks.

I tear open the packaging and set aside the paper so I can read the note later. "It was interesting. Sort of what I expected. The art department made a really uninspired miniature version of the pyramids, and we pretended we were enjoying ourselves running across glued-on sand."

"Who was this one with?"

"Crane." I tug out the tiny vial that is, mercifully, not labeled. "Check this out."

She squats next to me, and I pull out the cork and sniff the clear, gel-like substance in the bottle. Smells of grass and alcohol. Reaching my hand into the bottle's neck, I poke at the gel, and it instantly sticks to my finger in long strings.

"Give me your finger," I say.

"What for?"

"You have to feel this."

"Is that peppermint jelly or something?"

"No, it's essence of lightning bug," I say, my voice dripping with sarcasm. She won't believe me because the truth is just too weird to accept. I tip the bottle onto her index finger until several drops of the goop are quivering against her skin.

"This reminds me of when I dissected a cow's eye in school," she says. "It feels like the clear stuff that comes out."

I nod, even though I've never dissected anything larger than an earthworm and that was hard enough. She squishes her thumb against her finger and rubs the stuff in a circle.

I hop from one foot to another. "Pretty gross, huh? But if you really rub it in, it makes a great moisturizer." Lies.

"Really?"

No.

She follows my suggestion and stares down at her finger. "I guess that's why they put peppermint into lotions. I have that ingredient in a lot of the makeup I use."

"Of course."

She sniffs at her finger. "Doesn't smell very pepperminty. How does it taste?"

"Well, this stuff is really, you know, distilled. Probably doesn't taste like anything."

"Oh." A frown creases her forehead, and she stares at me as though she's trying to figure out if I'm pulling her leg. "So tell me more about the date."

I shrug. "There's not much to tell. Crane was really, really nervous, and I had a hard time talking to him. They kept stopping the shoot to give us topics to discuss, and then they taped us walking through the desert a lot."

"I wonder why they started with Crane. He's not the cutest one in the bunch."

"He's Tom1, that's why. Dr. Christiansen has a weird thing for numbers and going in order."

"Well, now you've got a few days before the next date."

"Yeah." I sigh. I have a feeling this whole show is going to drag on forever.

The door opens, and the production assistant comes in bearing dinner.

"I had the kitchen make you some wheat salad. I figured it would be easy to eat?" She sets a thimble-sized bowl into my hands.

"It's perfect, thank you." And it really is. The grains are toasted just right, and the tomato bits look fresh. It's something I would have made for myself in my old house.

She turns pink at the compliment. "Great! Well, see you tomorrow. Sleep well!"

"I'll leave you to your eating," Susanna says as she stands and stretches. "More promo pictures tomorrow."

"Joy. I'm sure I'll see you in the morning."

"Bright and early. Goodnight!"

I watch as she keys in her code for the door. It swings open, and she gives me a little wave as she walks out.

I wait a minute to make sure Susanna is well out of the building, and then I set my dinner carefully onto the floor and fly over to the light switch. I kick it off, and the room falls into darkness.

And there, on the keypad, are four glowing fingerprints.

CHAPTER 14

I ZOOM UP TO THE keypad, listening for footsteps in the hall, but I can't hear anything other than the pounding of my own heart and the fluttering of my wings. There are Susanna's fingerprints, plain as a lightning bug's butt. I wonder how many of them had to die to make that gel. I'll have to start my own lightning bug farm when I get out of here to make up for it.

I can't hear anyone outside my room, so I take a deep breath and push my hand firmly against the fingerprints one at a time. One, two, three, four. Nothing happens. Must not have been the right order. I try it again and still nothing happens.

I groan. This could take a while.

On the fifteenth try, the door clicks open and I almost squeal with excitement. I quickly memorize the order of the code so I'll be able to get back inside without any problems.

The hall is dark and far too clean for a home that's supposedly lived-in. I fly down to the ground and peek around the corner. A single dim sconce casts a dull yellow circle of light at the end of the hall. Across from my room is another closed door, but this one doesn't have a keypad.

Now all I have to do is try and turn the handle. I fly up and wedge myself between the door jamb and the handle and push up with my butt. The handle turns with a creak, and I shove as hard as I can. "As hard as I can" only gives me a crack that's a couple of inches, but it will work. I slip through into a library without a single comfortable place to curl up with a book. Plain wooden bookshelves line the walls. The books are probably all sorted and alphabetized.

I bet there's not a single work of fiction in this entire room. Curiosity gets the best of me and I fly along the shelves. There are books on ecology, psychology, and biology. Entire dictionaries on insects and birds. I have no idea why Dr. Christiansen insists on having books in paper form. Everyone else in Lilliput reads digital books. But then again, her best friend is a clipboard. Seriously, who uses a clipboard anymore?

I come to an entire bookshelf dedicated to specific psychological disorders. There's one row full of books about the autism spectrum. The blood rushes to my face. Does she seriously think I have autism? For a woman with such brilliance, Dr. Christiansen can be real stupid sometimes.

There's another door on the far side of the library, and I bet it leads to her office. I return to the door I came from to double-check the hallway. It's still empty.

The naked quiet works its way down into my soul, making me uneasy. Back across the library, I press my ear to what I hope is the office door and listen.

Nothing.

I try the handle. It's unlocked, and the door swings open easily. I peek inside.

Score.

There's her gigantic monitor. I'm surprised it's so big. I almost expected her to have something ancient, but this appears to be state-of-the-art. I just have to find the power switch.

I turn on the computer, and gray-blue light washes across the room. Simple desk chair, plain wooden cabinets, an extra set of clothes on hangers. Pretty much what I expected.

Now where does she keep her records?

I scroll through the programs on her computer, searching for folders that contain financial documents or anything related to the future of Lilliput. Anything about the TV show or cats or…

"Journal," I whisper. I double-tap on the monitor, and the folder opens to reveal hundreds of documents, one for each week of the last several years.

I'm not sure I should read these, but they're my best bet in my quest to figure out why Dr. Christiansen is trying to ruin my life.

My guilt evaporates when I think about it that way, and I double-tap the most recent entry. It's handwritten. She must pen all her journal entries by hand and then scan them in. And her writing is the only thing about her that isn't very organized or neat. I scroll through the page.

There are notes about the show, mostly insignificant details such as uniforms, supply lists, contacts, and advertising plans. I flick my finger against the screen to scroll it again.

Show budget. There we go.

But even this is disappointing. There's a list of major sponsors and the amounts they're paying (pounds upon pounds of gold—eek), but nothing indicates where all of this money is going to go. The only clue is a payout to an animal shelter in Copenhagen. They could be buying animals for testing, or it could be for some future episode where one of the guys rescues me from the jaws of a pit bull. I have no idea.

Then I find a folder inside called *Cancelled Sale.* What does that mean? I tap the section open and skim. Looks like Dr. Christiansen arranged to sell Lilliput to some American company but changed her mind. Sell it? Lilliput is her whole life—her baby. Why would she ever do that?

Okay, *this* is interesting. About six months ago, the same American company withdrew their funding from Lilliput. Dr. Christiansen cancelled the sale two months after that. I never knew we were being funded by an American company, but I guess that makes sense since Dr. Christiansen is originally from New York. But which part of the former United States is this company from and why on earth are they interested in Lilliput?

I scroll down some more and come to a far more intriguing section: "Thumbelina Case and Lawyers." Below the title, Dr. Christiansen has pasted in a letter from the European Union 12th district court of Denmark. I scan through it and stop when I read this:

The first hearing for case entitled "People vs. Lilliput Project 1 Inc." is scheduled for December 15, 2081 at the Copenhagen Courthouse.

Complaint: That the defendant did knowingly and willingly conduct biological experimentation that resulted in the deaths of the six "Thumbelinas" that died on an unknown date in 2066.

Oh my god. I sink down onto the desk, my fingers pressed so hard against my lower lip that I can feel my teeth biting into skin. How could… How is this even…

I cover my face with my hands, but I'm unable to tear my eyes away from the words on the screen. If I stop watching them, they will come to life and kill me, too.

I suddenly want to be back inside my room, safe behind the door and not here where Dr. Christiansen might find me and become angry. I don't know what that letter means, what the "biological experimentation" was, or who the other Thumbelinas were. If they died in 2066 and they were born at the same time as me, then they were possibly less than a year old.

Six Toms. Seven Thumbelinas. There should be thirteen of us total now. I close my eyes and sink down to the keyboard. So that's why I'm alone. She killed them. She kept the Toms away from me because she didn't want me to figure all of this out. It would have destroyed how her little science experiment interacted with her and developed.

I glance down at the clock. The date today is November 5. Only about five weeks left until the hearing.

My stomach heaves, and I dart down to the power switch. Just as I turn off the computer, I hear the click and drag of the front door opening and snagging the carpet. Someone's inside the house.

CHAPTER 15

KEYS SHUFFLE AND CLINK; SHOES are removed. I can hear it all from my frozen position near the computer.

I force myself into motion and fly out of the office to the library door where I crouch in the shadow. Heavy footsteps halt before the light at the end of the hallway as if deciding whether or not to proceed. Then the figure steps into the orange glow. Long, tangled hair, but too tall to be Dr. Christiansen.

It's Mr. Coxworth.

I let out the buildup of breath in my lungs in one big whoosh. Why is he here?

He pads down the hallway in his stocking feet and whistles low and long when he sees me hiding.

"So it worked," he says. "I do not have much time because the production meeting is ending soon, so we need to hurry. I had a feeling I might find you out here, although I'm not quite sure how you escaped."

I fly up close to his face and wave my fingers at him. "The keypad."

"Of course. And what have you found?"

I've always liked this about Mr. Coxworth; he gets down to business. "Journal entries and something about a court case. Did you know about the other Thumbelinas?"

"Not until recently. I started working here when you were three years old, and no one outside the project knew about the other girls then. Dr. Christiansen kept her research a well-guarded secret."

"Then who outed her?"

"That remains a mystery."

"And why isn't she getting arrested?"

"Because, legally, you are not a human, so there is no precedent for dealing with this sort of case. She cannot be charged with murder until the court determines the Thumbelinas were similar enough to humans for their killing to be considered immoral. And that will be difficult to do since Dr. Christiansen is the leading expert on tiny people."

"Why don't they ask me? I bet I know a little bit more about how it feels to be a tiny person than she does."

"That just might happen. I wouldn't rule it out. I also wouldn't be surprised if some of your next dates are in other countries."

There's one question nagging at me. "How did they die?"

"I'm sorry, Lina, I really don't know."

"Does anyone know other than her?"

"Perhaps Dr. Lee, but he is in the Western United States."

I cross my arms. It feels like there's something he's holding back. "Why didn't you tell me before?"

"Because I did not get the news until last week."

"Is that why she's keeping me locked up? She doesn't want me to find out?"

"I'm sure that is part her reason, but I think she was already planning the show before this blew up. There's something else she's trying to do. Did you find anything about her future plans or experiments?"

"No, not yet. I didn't have a lot of time though, and the letter about the court case really threw me."

"I understand. It might be best if you go to your room and let me look for a while. That way, if I get caught, you won't suffer any consequences. No use in both of us facing the wrath of the white witch. I'll find a way to inform you if I find anything."

"But what will happen to you if she finds you?"

"Let me worry about that."

"Okay." I give him a grateful smile. "Don't get caught. I don't want to come out tomorrow and discover you're an ice sculpture."

He tips an imaginary hat and waves me toward my room. "Goodnight, Thumbelina."

CHAPTER 16

I LIE ON MY SIDE, staring out the window. Rain sways against the glass in sheets, and every so often, lightning illuminates the tops of the trees with a crack.

I wonder how it happened. How did those six girls die and how old were they? I assume we were born at the same time. It only makes sense that the project tried to make an even number of girls and boys. What did Dr. Christiansen do to them?

Horror chokes me, and I gasp for breath. Did she do the same thing to me? Is there something about myself I don't know? I hold my hand up in front of my face and study it, then my wrist, then my arm. I don't look any different than Susanna except for my size. If there is something wrong with me, how would I ever be able to tell?

Why am I the only one who lived? Tears creep up into my eyes as I imagine what it would have been like to grow up with sisters. With friends. Would we have gotten along? Maybe, like Row and Blue, I would have only been close to one or two of them. We could have shared a room or my treehouse. I would have had someone to tell about Jack. Or maybe I never would have met him at all since I wouldn't have been so lonely. I don't particularly relish that possibility.

What would the other girls look like now if they'd survived? All of the Toms have separate biological donors and look completely different from each other. I'd wondered before why some races weren't represented between the Toms and myself. None of us look Hispanic or Indian. Al is the only one with dark skin. Maybe one of the other Thumbelinas looked Polynesian or Ethiopian.

I remember the cat Jane was experimenting on and shudder. Dr. Christiansen's restraint is non-existent when it comes to experimentation and "progress," but was it always that way?

Maybe the Thumbelinas died by accident or caught some sort of sickness and it was all a fluke.

But my heart seems to think otherwise. I can't get it to calm down. It seems intent on beating its way up into my throat to suffocate me.

"What do I do?" I whisper.

The pounding of the rain swallows up my voice, and the room feels as though it's filling up with darkness.

Helplessness presses me down against the bed. Even if I find out what Dr. Christiansen has planned, how on earth will I stop her? Mr. Coxworth might help, but it feels like something is already in motion that's much larger than the two of us.

For the first time in my life, I feel small. Not only physically small but small-souled. I think about each person in my entourage. Not a single one of them cares I'm my own person. We are all swept up into Dr. Christiansen's machine. Everyone does their job and doesn't stop to think about the consequences. How can I get any of them to listen to me when they don't respect me in the slightest? Even George has always obeyed her almost without question.

I clench my jaw hard and squeeze shut my eyes as if that will protect me from the tidal wave of bitterness. I lose the struggle and drown in my anger.

I'll show them somehow. I'll figure out a way to come out on top, and they'll all be sorry they ever obeyed a single command from Dr. Christiansen's lips.

I fold my arms tight and scowl at the ceiling. I may be small, but I've been engineered to be smarter than any one of them and there has to be a way to beat them. I'm not even sure what "beating them" would mean, but I'm determined to figure it out.

CHAPTER 17

ON OUR THIRD DATE, WE loaded into the middle of the crumbling Colosseum. As soon as I figured out where in the world we were, I ran, laughing, to the edge of the floor.

"What's this down here?" The ground ended abruptly, exposing a maze of stone tunnels below.

"I read they kept the gladiators and lions down there in between performances. I guess two thousand years was too much for the floor to take," Jack explained.

I squatted and then hopped down to the lower level. Grass and weeds had long overtaken the stone foundation. Jack joined me, and we walked, palm to palm, through the ancient hallways where men waited to die so long ago.

"Can you imagine what it would be like?" I asked him.

He gave me a wicked grin. "Want to find out?"

"What?!"

"Hang on a sec." His avatar went still, and I knew he had pulled out of the world and was adjusting something. Moments later, he came back to life, and the walls began to grow upward, forming a ceiling above our heads.

"What's going on?" But I needn't have asked because flaming torches soon appeared in rusted holders along the walls. We were standing on a ramp, facing an opened gate.

"Shall we?" Jack led the way up, and then we were standing inside of an empty, reconstructed Colosseum, complete with banners.

"This is terrifying," I said. "Think of how many people died here."

"Bread and circuses," Jack muttered as we walked around the arena. "I guess humanity hasn't changed much."

I wish I could say we had a serious conversation about the nature of modern entertainment, but we were too in awe of the history we were standing in. It seems strange now to remember how free we felt, how we didn't have the slightest inkling I would be on the stage myself someday.

We walked through the halls of the old place, tracing our fingers along the walls, and found the spot where we thought the emperor might have sat to watch the spectacles.

I plopped down onto the seat and waved an imaginary fan. "Oh, Claudius, you simply must *let him live!" I exclaimed in a wretched British accent.*

"Julia, er…" He twirled an imaginary mustache. "We must escape because English aliens have invaded from the future and taken over your mind."

"No, my dear, this is simply how everyone talked long ago." I tried to keep a straight face, but the giggles took over.

He held out his hand for me, even though we both knew I couldn't grab it. "Come, let us…away? And go to the Vatican for to see—gosh, I can't keep this up. Ready to hit the rest of the town?"

I grinned. "Indeed, let us away!"

So we "awayed" to the Sistine Chapel to see Michelangelo's famous artwork. We laid down on the floor and stared up at the ceiling. I kept squirming because it seemed strange to lie down without my wings interfering, but since it wasn't real, I couldn't feel anything anyway.

Jack's shoulder should have been touching mine, but he was pixels and air. I stared at the side of his face, longing for him to truly materialize. He turned his head, his deep brown eyes holding mine.

"What are you thinking?" he asked.

I hesitated. "I wish this was real."

A laugh pulled at the corners of his mouth. "Well, if it was real, then we would be getting trampled by tourists right now."

At any other time, I would have laughed, but my emotions were too close to the surface. "No, I mean, I wish it was all real. I wish 'here' was real, with no one else around. Just us. And all of this art." I traced the outline of God's finger with my eyes. *"Maybe if we prayed hard enough."* But I didn't really believe that.

"I don't think that's how it works."

"Jack?"

"Hmm?"

"Do you ever wish you had different parents? Or that you were born into a different family?"

"I used to. When my dad died, I got really jealous of the other kids I knew. I didn't think it was fair that they still had their dads and mine was gone. When the war ended, it just got worse, especially since everyone was always complaining about how hard things were." He shook his head. *"I would have gone without food for weeks if it meant I got my dad back."*

We were quiet for a moment.

"Can I ask how he died?"

"He was infantry for the Northern Reconstructionists in the Second Civil War. He died a couple of months before they struck the ceasefire agreement. Hit by a grenade."

"I'm sorry. How old were you?"

"Eleven. My mom remarried one year later. That didn't work out real well. He was an abusive loser. After he left, my mom started drinking. I'll never forgive him for that." His face hardened, and I drew away. He had shut me out along with everything else.

I rolled my head to look at the ceiling and waited for him to say something. Moments ticked by in silence, and my mind wandered. I thought about all of the times I'd wished for real parents and siblings. It had never occurred to me that my life might have been even lonelier and harder if I'd gotten my wish. Or, if not more difficult, a different sort of difficult.

Jack's words interrupted my thoughts. *"What are you thinking about?"*

"I prayed for...different parents when I was a kid. Maybe it's better that my prayer wasn't answered."

"Are your mom and dad really that bad?"

I snorted, unsure of how to phrase my situation in a way he would understand. *"Um, they're not really involved in my life at all. I wanted parents like yours were, who were still married and actually cared about me."* My throat began to tighten up. *"At least your dad loved you. You'll always have that."*

"I'm sure they love you in their own way."

"I wouldn't bet on it."

"Okay. I'll take your word for it then."

"I just wanted to be normal," I blurted out. "I wanted a family that celebrated holidays and had big, noisy reunions. I wanted to have dinner every night with them after school."

"I don't think I know anyone who does that, to be honest."

"Dad would say a prayer before dinner. Your dad never did that?"

"Nope. The Lakota don't really do that."

"Do you think God answers prayer?"

"Sometimes. Do you?" He rolled toward me and propped himself up on his elbow.

"I'm not sure." I frowned at the ceiling. "This might sound really stupid, but…" I had to take a moment to re-gather my courage.

"I won't think it's stupid," Jack said.

"Okay. Well, sometimes when I try to pray, I think I sense something. But I'm not sure. Maybe it's my imagination."

"Do you really think it's your imagination?"

I thought about it. "No."

"Then I believe you." His smile warmed me all the way down to the tips of my toes, and that was real enough. "I was really worried about you after our last date. I was so sure it was my fault that you had an asthma attack. In fact, I still think it's my fault. I was positive you were about to cry."

"I did cry." The words left my mouth before I had a chance to think about what I was saying. "I can't believe I just admitted that."

"Why wouldn't you want to tell me?"

"Because. It's a silly thing to cry over. I get asthma attacks all the time." I fiddled with the hem of my shirt.

"Was something else bothering you?" There was that look again. The compassionate, whole-person-seeing look.

I wanted to tell him everything, but I struggled through the words and thoughts in my head. "I'm just… I'm not used to anyone caring how I feel about what happens to me. I'm used to taking whatever gets thrown at me and making the best of it. And I'm good at that. Really good at it. I don't know what to say when you ask me if I'm okay. I know I'll be okay because that's who I am. But *it's like, with you, I don't have to make the best of something bad because you really care about keeping the bad from ever happening in the first place. And I like it that you do that. I wish the rest of my life was like that, too." The corners of my mouth began to pucker inward as I tried not to cry again. What was with all the crying?*

"I'm sorry," he said. "No one cares how I feel about things either. My mom drinks herself to sleep every day. She never asked me if I wanted to parent my sister and brother and take care of them. So I sort of get how you feel."

I nodded. "I wish I could pray myself into this world." The words taste like relief on my tongue.

He leaned in closer until I could distinctly see the very edges of his lips, the curve of his cheekbones and jaw, and every single one of his eyelashes.

"Do you know what I would do if this was real?" His voice was low, almost a whisper.

I lick my lips. "What?"

"I would kiss you."

My entire face immediately went hot, not to mention every other part of my body. I parted my lips and tried to breathe normally as every inch of me craved his touch.

"I'd start with the tip of your nose, then your cheeks, then your lips."

I was sure I would never breathe again.

"I think my cheeks are on fire," I squeaked when I couldn't look into his eyes any longer without exploding.

He laughed and laid back down with a satisfied expression. "Too bad I can't see them. Your avatar doesn't show when you blush."

"Well, that's one answer to prayer."

CHAPTER 18

TODAY, STANDING INSIDE A MINIATURE replica of the Sistine Chapel with Row waiting for me, I whisper another prayer. This time, I ask for the ability to smile for the cameras. I pray Jack is not watching. I pray he realizes this was not my idea.

I'm wearing a white miniskirt with a light blue tank top. I tried to convince the stylist that a miniskirt is impractical for flying, but she handed me a pair of short bloomers to wear underneath. I tug at the elastic that's digging into my skin and then give my thigh a discreet scratch. A half-dozen camera shutters click, and I turn and scowl at them.

"Can't a girl get a modicum of privacy around here?" I snap at the show runner.

"Sorry, Lina. Everything on set is fair game."

"Seriously?"

He shrugs and resumes barking orders at some hapless assistants standing by the lights.

I kick a pew hard enough to let off some steam without hurting myself.

"Watch it there. You're going to shake down the whole place." Row's voice trails over from the front section. I search for his blond head, but see nothing. Then he sits up and waves.

I fly up over the pews and sit down next to him. One of the grips flips on a light behind us, and hard sunlight bleaches out the nape of Row's neck and his hair, accentuating the shape of his jaw and cheekbones. He gives me his winning smile, and it occurs to me that every unattached teenage girl in the world who watches the show is going to wish she was six inches tall.

"So," he says. "What do you think of our Sistine Chapel?"

"I think 'Styrofoam Chapel' is a better name for it. I bet I could poke a hole in that wall with my little toe."

"Do it!"

I grin. "Nah."

"No, seriously. Do it! I want to see. I'll even make a matching toe hole."

I swivel around to see if anyone is watching us too closely. Most of the crew are wrestling with the lights.

"Okay," I say. "Shoes off."

We wiggle the footwear from our feet and then walk to the wall, pretending to have a deep conversation about art.

"So do you have any idea what sort of paint this is?" Row asks with a very serious expression.

"Dear sir, I do believe this is Melted Crayon Paint. Of the highest quality. Circa 2081."

"Oh, really? I was under the impression it was ochre made from the wings of dead ladybugs."

"That's really gross, Row."

"Sorry." He looks down. "Any success yet?"

I take one final glance backward at the crew, then hold my leg up, pinky toe extended, and ram it into the wall as hard as I can.

"Mother—!" I clamp my mouth shut and sink down onto the pew, holding my foot with both hands. In the wall is a perfect impression of my foot as deep as the wooden frame I didn't know was there.

Row drops down onto the pew next to me. "Are you okay?"

I grit my teeth together. I can't answer him yet because I'm too busy suppressing a scream of pain.

"Well, I can't let you out-do me," Row says. He stands and gets into position to karate kick the wall.

"What the heck are you doing?!"

"Giving myself a matching broken toe." He makes his own mark in the wall right next to mine, hops up and down for a few seconds, and then collapses next to me.

"That was so stupid," I say before giving in to laughter. My pinky toe resembles a swollen grape. Row holds up his own foot to compare.

"Mine is juicier," he says.

"It is not. Besides, I was first. You're only a copycat."

"I can't allow my date to get hurt without sharing in her pain."

I press my lips together as my smile drains away at his words. For a few beautiful minutes, I totally forgot why we are here.

"Hey," he says, concern in his eyes. "This can be fun, Lina. I know it's awkward, but we can enjoy ourselves. You can just be you."

"Yeah, well, 'just me' is crabby at the thought of being on this show," I say.

"That's fine. I totally get it. If you want to take out your frustration on the rest of your toes, I promise to write an individual message on each little toe cast."

"Touché."

"I'm serious. We've got lots of Styrofoam to kick in here."

I extend my leg and study my throbbing toe. It's a victory, albeit a small one. It's enough for today.

"Too bad we didn't kick Adam's finger or something," I mutter.

"There's still time."

But there isn't. The motion behind us has slowed, and the lights are now staying in one place.

"Almost ready!" the show runner shouts. The principal photographer presses to the front of the crew and drops down so his eyes are level with ours.

"Okay," he says. "Let's start with some photos! Hey, how did those holes get there?"

We both play dumb.

"Hey, Richie, can you hand me one of those extra pews?" The photographer gingerly places the pew in front of the holes. "There, all fixed! Can't see a thing now. Okay, if the two of you could walk or fly up to the altar area, I want to take a couple of quick photos."

Small victory indeed.

We pose for several pictures, including a particularly distasteful "proposal" photo. I doubt they'll use that one, though, because I was glaring the entire time. Pretty sure they can't spin my frown into something "romantic."

When we're finally done, the photographer gives us our next instructions. "All right, Lina, you come over here by the entrance. Row, stay up there. We're now going to film the 'beginning' of the date. Look excited to see each other, maybe fly a little bit. Just don't knock over any of the pews. The set designer forgot to glue them down."

I roll my eyes toward Row, and he grins down at me.

"Come on," he says. "Let's give them a show. When's the last time you watched *Casablanca* or something else that's old and classic?"

"Can't remember. I've tried to block out the memory."

He makes a face. "Well, how about we channel our inner Hollywood?"

That's the last thing I feel like doing, but it means I'll get the chance to make fun of this stupid show while doing exactly as I've been asked.

"All right. I'll run through fields of golden flowers for you. But only for today."

"Inner ham activate!"

"Just steer clear of the toe please."

I fly back to the door and settle onto my throbbing foot with a wince. Row does some shadow boxing up front, shakes out his arms and stretches.

"Places please! Quiet on the set!"

I take my mark, sprinter-style. I'm pretty sure I'm giving the entire crew a full view of my bloomers.

"Action!"

Row looks at me with dramatic surprise. "Lina?" he gasps.

"Oh! Row!" I fling my arms out to the sides, almost dislocating my shoulder. I toss my hair for good measure. "Row!"

I take two exaggerated leaps through the air, keeping myself aloft with my wings for a second too long each time, then flutter toward the altar with my hands over my heart.

Row throws his arms open wide before wrapping them around my waist and spinning me in circles until I'm dizzy and begging him to stop.

He sets me down with tremendous care and holds me until the world stops whirling. He's a little too warm and far too close. I stay there as long as I must, then wriggle free, overwhelmed with guilt I'm not quite comfortable owning. I didn't do anything wrong, did I?

"Excellent!" The photographer's voice interrupts my thoughts. "Now, arms around her waist. Look happy to see each other. Talk a little bit."

"Are you all right?" Row studies my face as he slides his hands around my middle. I resist the urge to slap them away.

"I'm fine." It comes out more snippish than I intend. I frown and back away as far as I can without being too obvious. I don't understand why there is so much electricity there between us. I don't have feelings for Row...do I?

"Did I step on your toe?"

"No." It takes all the gumption I have to force a smile onto my face. "Everything's fine."

I can tell he doesn't believe me, but he lets it go.

"So I guess we're supposed to talk now," he says. "How's your toe?"

"Hurts like the dickens," I reply with an unnatural smile. Time to fool them into thinking we're having a blast. "Yours?"

"I need someone to pour a little salt and lemon juice on it to complete the pain cocktail I've got going on."

I raise my eyebrow. "Very witty of you, sir."

"That's me. So what do they have you doing when you're not shooting the show with us?"

"I get locked up in a little room. You?"

"Something like that. We're actually sleeping in the dining hall where they had your birthday party."

"Do they lock you guys in there, too?"

He nods. If I hadn't tried to escape, security would be a bit looser for all of us. I try to feel sorry, but I'm not. The whole thing only fuels my anger toward Dr. Christiansen.

"Enabling microphones now!" the director shouts. Row takes a deep breath. Now the real acting begins. We're supposed to pretend we're having our first real conversation. I'm mentally exhausted already.

"So," Row says. "It's a pleasure to meet you! You can call me Row!" He's speaking in exclamation points again, but I can hear the strain in his voice. He lifts my hand to kiss it, and I stiffen.

I clear my throat. "Likewise. I'm Lina." And now I have no idea what to say. I lick my lips, willing my brain to get into gear and start churning out inspired witticisms.

"It's a beautiful day! How are you doing? Are you ready to check out the chapel?"

I pray a silent thanks Row couched his questions in such a way that I don't have to lie about how I'm doing. "Sure, let's investigate."

"I hear you're a fan of Michelangelo and his paintings," Row prompts me. "You must really love art."

I nod. This is something I can talk about. "Yes, I do. I'm not much of a painter though." I think about the elaborate line drawings Jack would show me from his portfolio, and my heart aches.

"Me either," Row continues on. "I can't draw for the life of me, but I still love beautiful things." He looks at me a bit too pointedly, but I can't find anything in his eyes other than perfect sincerity. It puts me into a fluster, and I wonder if he's still hamming it up for the camera on purpose. If so, I really wish he would stop.

"Well then," I say, "you're in the perfect place. This chapel is full of beautiful *paintings*." I drop a little too much emphasis on that last word, and Row visibly straightens but then smiles.

"I hear Michelangelo was actually a better sculptor than painter," Row says.

I'm nearly positive someone coached him to say this, but I guess I still have to come up with some sort of reply for this pointless conversation.

"That's true," I say. "His sculptures are superior. Most people prefer his *David* sculpture, but my favorite is the *Pieta*."

"Oh, well, I actually have a surprise for you outside." He shifts his weight from one foot to the other, his usual cheeriness curiously subdued.

"Let's go check it out," I say.

"Cut!" shouts the director. "Very nice work. Let's move to the next set."

Confident our mics are safely turned off, I lean over to Row. "Let me guess. It's a reproduction of *David*."

He barely nods, his lips pressed into a tight line. I can't fathom why he looks so discouraged. Guilt over my inability to fake a good mood presses down into my stomach, but I try to ignore it. He can't possibility think this could go somewhere. I can't afford to think about that. I can't hold his hopes or Blue's or Al's or any of the other Toms'. I can't be their happiness.

Row stares at my face as though he's reading my mind. "Would it really be so bad if you ended up with me?" he asks, his words measured. "Or—I can't believe I'm saying this—any of the other guys?"

Well, this is most unexpected. My mouth falls open, but I have nothing to say.

"I guess I don't understand," Row continues. "I don't know what you're thinking, but it's obvious you don't want to give any of us a chance. At first, I tried to shrug it off and be understanding because it was more of a shock for you than it was for us. We knew the plan before coming here. It wasn't fair the way they sprung it on you. But we're all stuck here now, and I'm trying, really trying to make the best of it."

I close my eyes. "Row, I'm sorry. It's not what you think. It has nothing to do with you or any of the other guys."

"What is it then? We're not so bad, and we're the only guys in the world like you."

His blue eyes are completely devoid of bitterness or anger. I want to tell him. I'm so tired of all the lies and the secrecy.

"Can you keep a secret?"

"Yes."

"The sort of secret you can't change your mind about keeping once you've heard it?"

He thinks for a moment. "Yes."

"I'm in love with someone else." As soon as the words leave my mouth, I realize how stupid they sound.

Row sighs. "Lina…"

"Don't lecture me."

"I wasn't going to. I understand how you feel."

"Oh, really? You're in love with one of the scientists or something back at Lilliput II?" I can't squash the sarcasm.

"No," he says quietly. "Do you remember when you asked us about crushes the other day? I said my biggest crush was the landscaper's daughter."

"You made it sound like it was a long time ago."

He rolls his eyes. "Yes, Lina, because I don't want anyone to find out."

"Oh." I've never seen him irritated until now. "Does *she* know?"

"Yes. I told her about six months ago. I would have done anything for her."

"What happened?"

"Her father was fired, and I haven't seen her since."

"I'm sorry."

"It's all right," he says glumly. "It's better this way since I'm not hoping for the impossible anymore." He glances at me. "I'd hate to miss out on something good because I was holding out for a fantasy."

"I don't think it's that simple."

"That's your choice."

"What the heck does that mean? I can't turn off my heart and my feelings and make myself fall in love with you. It doesn't work that way."

"No, but you can decide to make the best of it. You're not the only one here with feelings, Lina."

I stare at him, refusing to believe he's made this so personal, as if this is all my fault. As if I asked for this. His face is pleading, uncompromising.

I clench my teeth together and walk out to the next set.

CHAPTER 19

WE PASS THE REST OF the date talking nonsense about Michelangelo and the glories of human achievement in art and science. Things I couldn't care less about right now. I only barely keep my frustration under wraps until the cameras stop rolling and I'm carted back to my prison cell.

The assistant leaves, and the door closes. I'm all alone.

I've been wanting to be alone all day, but now that I'm here in this empty room, wrapped only in silence and walls that are annoyingly high, I feel like the only person on earth. I just want my old house again. Is that too much to ask? I want to be surrounded by things my own size, things that belong to me. I'm sick of sleeping on this giant pillow, of waiting for other people to bring me food and dress me. There's not even anything for me to kick or punch with any satisfaction.

I fly up to the window and stand on the edge of the sill. A single yellow leaf swirls to the forest floor outside to join its fallen brothers and sisters. The trees have become clusters of dying sticks. Soon the snow will blot out the reds and browns and yellows, and the world will be black and white and blue.

I miss Jack. I miss him so much. I wish I'd never told Row. I'm well-aware of the fact that I'm a fool to love Jack. I don't need to be reminded by someone else. I can't toss him aside like an insignificant childhood crush.

Yet, a part of what Row said does make sense. It's what I've been squirming against all day.

Being with Jack *is* impossible, and there's nothing I can do to change that. Before today, I hadn't realized I could ruin my chances with these guys forever if I blow them all off now. And while I might not be able to get over Jack anytime soon, it's bound to happen someday, and then I'll be all alone. I have a hard time believing that Dr. Christiansen won't eventually find a way to create spouses for the other Toms. I mean, that would be a waste of perfectly good mini men. So, even if the Toms are still single, why would they want to date me later, knowing I see them as a second-best choice? Heck, forget dating. Why would they even want to be friends?

I bang my head against the cold glass several times as the tears come unbidden.

"Why can't love be convenient?" I whisper.

The window and the world outside don't have any answers for me.

The door beeps open and in walks Dr. Christiansen. She's alone.

I shrink back against the window. I have no idea why she's here. Did she hear me tell Row about Jack? Were those microphones on after all? Does she know I was in her office? Maybe there were cameras in there. Why didn't I think about that?

She waits for the door to close behind her before speaking.

"The schedule has been changed. The show has received several new sponsors, so we will now be shooting on location. We'll be leaving in two days."

"For where?"

"I appreciate your cooperation so far, but be aware that we will be tracking your movements while on the road. If you try to leave without permission or go anywhere off the sets, there will be consequences."

"Yeah, I remember. The kind of consequences that hurt an innocent guy who has nothing to do with any of this?"

Dr. Christiansen sighs. "There is more at stake here than your happiness or this young man's. So, yes, if I can save many people by punishing a couple, I will. Because that's what needs to be done."

"What does that even mean?"

"It means that I have a plan and it's your duty to do as you're told. Understood?"

I glare at her. I understand very well, but I won't give her the satisfaction of a reply. She doesn't seem fazed.

"We're going to Hawaii," she says. She doesn't bother to wait for my reaction before leaving.

CHAPTER 20

JACK PUSHED THE STEM OF *a hibiscus bloom into my virtual hair.* "There. A flower for a flower."

I rolled my eyes, but my heart was bursting all the same. "Where did you get that line?"

"Wouldn't you like to know. Also, I think you're blushing," he said with a satisfied smirk.

"Oh, really? And how would you know that?"

"Because your voice gets higher and louder whenever you're embarrassed."

I pressed my hands against my thighs to remind myself not to touch my fiery cheeks.

"Wow, this is some really great scenery up here," I said, turning toward the view from the top of Diamond Head. Waikiki Beach stretched out below us, littered with hotels and long lines of waves racing toward the sand.

"Way to change the subject," he said. "But yes, I love it up here, and I figured we'd skip the hike this time and load right at the top."

"You really like mountaintops, don't you?"

He shrugged. "I guess. I never thought about it before. Technically, this is a volcano though."

"Close enough." I climbed over the barrier and inched my way to the edge.

"You have a thing for edges," he shouted after me while staying at a safe distance.

"What do you think happens if you jump while in a construct? I mean, you can't die."

"I don't know. I just don't think I could do it."

That surprised me. I'd never seen Jack be afraid of anything yet. Yet there he was, hugging the rail like it was his new best friend.

"How about I jump first?" I suggested. "We'll see what happens."

"No," he said, folding his arms. "I can't let you do that."

"Can't? Let me?" I cocked my eyebrow at him. I took another step backward.

"Lina, please," he said, misery edging his voice. "Don't."

The plea tugged at my heart, but so did the expanse of sky and the long way down. I knew I could do it and that it would be okay. Why couldn't he just loosen up? I turned toward the edge and took a deep breath.

I jumped.

I wasn't prepared for the sensation of being out of control midair. My wings struggled in the real world to right my body from its headlong virtual dive. Vomit crept up into my mouth, and my breaths came sharp and fast—too fast to deliver enough oxygen to my burning lungs. An outcropping hurtled toward my head, and at the last moment, I screamed. My virtual body hit the rocks and exploded. I felt no pain, but the screen went blank.

White words flashed onto the black screen: "You have died. Reloading now."

Shaken, I watched as the top of Diamond Head materialized. Jack stood at the edge, staring down at the spot where I'd fallen.

"Jack."

His head whipped in my direction. His face was scrunched into an expression of intense grief that transformed quickly into anger.

"Why the hell did you do that?" he demanded.

His intensity surprised me, but I snapped back quickly. "Because I wanted to. And nothing happened. Here I am. What's the big deal?"

"I had to watch you jump to your death. That's the big deal."

"Except I'm not dead," I said. His irritation was torqueing me off. "It's just a video game."

"Really?" He crossed his arms. "These dates are 'just a video game'?"

"That's not what I meant."

He stared long and hard into my eyes and then turned away to look out at the ocean.

"Jack," I said. He didn't respond, which only irritated me further. "Jack, talk to me."

His voice came out choked and strained. "Why? You don't care about my feelings, so why should I do what you want? I asked you not to jump because I didn't want to see it, but you did it anyway."

He was crying. I swallowed my exasperated sigh and went to stand next to him. When I spoke again, my voice sounded small and whiny to me. "I don't understand why you're so upset…"

"Do you even know what I had to see just now?"

I bit my lip. All I had seen was a lot of red, then nothing. "No."

He shook his head. "Look at that sunset. Does it look real to you? Do I look real to you? We're inside the best simulation software ever created. I had to watch your perfectly simulated death. No one should ever have to see that."

"I'm sorry."

He took a deep, shuddering breath. "Okay."

"I didn't… I didn't think about that part."

He rolled his eyes. "Yeah."

We stood there in silence as the sun was swallowed by the glittering horizon. I was still confused about what I should have done differently. I wasn't used to others being hurt by my decisions, hurt by watching me hurt. The only person who came close was George, but he was still fine with watching me being chased by a giant, hungry falcon. I shifted uncomfortably next to Jack. I felt restricted somehow, but I couldn't decide whether I liked it or not.

Jack's ragged breaths slowly steadied as the last embers of the sun were snuffed out. Muted oranges, reds, and pinks melted into indigo, and the stars began to press through the darkness.

"This is beautiful," I said through my fear.

He nodded and inhaled deeply. "Just promise me you won't force me to watch something that painful ever again."

"Well, technically I didn't force you."

He turned to face me. "You know what I mean."

"Jack, I'd hate to promise and then break my word later on unintentionally."

He sighed and pressed his lips into a firm line.

"And no, I'm not trying to avoid your wishes here. I don't want to make promises I might not be able to keep. But I can promise I won't intentionally make you watch something that will hurt you unless it's for a very good reason. That's the best I can do."

He shrugged, clearly not happy with this concession. "All right."

"I'm sorry if it's not good enough."

"No," he said, staring thoughtfully at the horizon. "I can respect that."

"All right then."

He gave me a weak smile. "Are you ready for the next part of the date?"

Relief washed over me, and my shoulders drooped from their tensed posture. I hadn't even noticed how tight I was. "There's more?"

His eyes sparkled, and I knew he felt like his normal self again. "I figured we could stay up all night and then conduct a sunrise service to celebrate your resurrection."

I reached forward to playfully slap his arm, completely forgetting I couldn't touch him in this world.

"Here," he said, holding up his hand with his palm facing me. "Hold your hand up to mine."

I matched my fingers to his. We were pressing our hands together, and although I couldn't feel the warmth of his skin, the sight still made me smile.

"For now, we'll pretend we're really touching," he said.

I imagined what it would feel like to actually feel his fingers, his hands, and I started blushing again.

"Are you ready for the next part?"

I nodded.

"Give me a moment and I'll reload us."

The mountain vanished, and the beach floated up from below until we were standing on the sand. The sun was peeking up from the east, washing the foaming wave crests with the colors of sunrise. Two surfboards rested on a stand.

I laughed. "Surfing? In our clothes?"

He winked at me. "Why not? Are you afraid to try it?"

"Oh, heck no." I ran over to the boards and snagged the bright blue one before sprinting toward the ocean. I plunged in and waited to feel the coolness of the water and the weight of my wet clothes, but there was no sensation. I fought back my disappointment. Of course I couldn't feel it. But oh, how I wanted to.

A towering wave rushed toward me, picking me up and tossing me below the surface. When I came up, Jack was pushing the nose of his surfboard deep into the heart of the next wave. The swell picked me up, flailing, and I watched him pop out the other side. He whipped his hair to the side and smiled at me.

"Where did you learn to surf?" I asked as I paddled furiously to catch up.

"We lived in Florida for a couple of years because my step-dad got a job down there right after the war. There wasn't a lot of work, so he had to take it. I skipped school a lot and went to the beach with friends. They taught me how to surf."

I sat up on my board and stared at him. "You skipped school? That surprises me."

"Why's that?"

"Well, you're...smart."

"I'm not sure what being smart has to do with it. Anyway, I only did it for a couple of months at the beginning of high school, and then my step-dad found out and threatened to kick me out if I did it again. That was that."

"Did you not like school?"

"No, I did. I always got good grades. I just had a lot more fun at the beach. Does it bother you?"

A turmoil of emotion whipped through my stomach. I couldn't figure out why it felt like a big deal to me because it didn't seem like it should be. "I don't know."

"It didn't hurt me, Lina. I did just fine in high school."

"So you've already graduated then?"

"Sort of. I took the passage test last year so I could work and help my mom."

"What's a 'passage test'?"

"It's kind of like a final exam. The reservation offers them to kids who want to get out of high school early. I took a summer to study for it. Watch out for that wave."

I turned in time to see a swell as tall as Jack headed in our direction. We'd drifted toward the beach while we talked, and now we were going to have to paddle hard to make up for the lost ground.

Jack went ahead and pushed himself and his board down below the wave. I followed suit in a mechanical fashion, my mind still chewing on the information he'd just shared. The skipping school bothered me for some reason I couldn't quite pinpoint. *Why was it such a big deal? I'd always imagined myself ending up with a guy who played by the rules when it came to education, and here was a guy who was intelligent in his own right and helping to take care of his family. I'd never had to make a single decision about my education. It was all planned for me, and I'd never given it a second thought. Should I have questioned things more?*

I shook my head when I reemerged, sending both pixel water drops and pesky thoughts flying into the air.

Jack's firm hand grabbed my board and pulled me toward him.

"You have a worried look on your face, Thumbelina."

"We're just so different," I blurted out. "And sometimes I'm not sure what to think."

He cocked his head to the side. "What to think about what?"

"How we fit together. I mean, even as friends. I've never considered skipping class. It's one of those things you don't do." I shook my head, trying in vain to gather my thoughts into something cohesive. "I don't know what how it feels to lose a parent or be in a war. When you talk about that stuff, I don't know how to relate to you at all. I don't know what to say."

He straddled his board, and I couldn't help but notice his wet shirt stuck firmly to his chest. "Lina, you're doing fine. I think you relate by telling me what you're thinking and you're doing that right now. Do you enjoy hanging out with me?"

"Yes." I swallowed hard. The morning sun was growing in strength and pouring its light around Jack's silhouette. The cool blues and grays of the ocean were clipped with highlights here and there. It was nothing like my forest, nothing close to Denmark. The entire setting was strange and new to me, but wonderful all the same. It was that way every time I met with Jack. "More than anybody else," I added.

"And I'm not leading you astray or encouraging you to do anything bad, am I?"

"No."

"All right then. I'll just be me, and you can be you. Cool?"

I sighed with relief. "Okay."

"Just don't go jumping off any cliffs again please."

I laughed. "But you said I could be myself! It's not fair if you make rules!"

"It's not a rule," he said with a grin. He tugged my board closer to him. "Only a request."

It took all my self-control to not tear my eyes away from the overwhelming intensity of his gaze.

"Now," he said. "Are you ready to learn how to surf?"

CHAPTER 21

"ARE YOU READY TO LEARN how to surf?" Al leans in closer to me, a goofy grin stretching from ear to ear across his midnight face.

"I already know how," I say, turning toward the airplane window to look at the endless stretch of turquoise blue below us. Last week's episode featuring me and Row in the fake Sistine Chapel met with mixed reviews. Apparently several critics pointed out how artificial and cheap it looked, so from here on out we'll be going to real locations. At the moment, one of the tech staff is sorting through dozens of upgraded drones in the rear of the cargo plane. If I try to make a break, I won't make it very far. Not that I would anyway since Dr. Christiansen continues to remind me that Jack's happiness depends on my cooperation.

Al's elbow gently jabs against my arm. "How did you learn?"

"To surf? Online."

"Ah." He returns to his chair and settles in. "Well, nothing's as good as the real thing."

I suppose he's right. The other guys are lounging on our own personal flight deck. It's a small cabin built right up against one of the windows. Instead of the uncomfortable plane seats everyone else is subjected to, we have bean bags. I even have a tiny bedroom with my old bed.

Shrike and Blue are arguing about something over in the corner—about what, I couldn't care less. Al has been hovering around me ever since I woke up this morning. I've gathered he considers surfing to be his territory, and he's waiting to get a head start on the other guys on our upcoming group date by showing me the ropes himself.

I rest my arms on the bottom of the window casing and press my forehead against the warm glass. It's nearly noon in this new time zone, and the sun is fluttering her veil of glitter over the surface of the water. I've never seen such an expansive, limitless sky. In fact, I've never been out from under Lilliput's dome before. For a moment, I imagined how it would feel to somehow get out of the plane and fly, completely free, through the piles of clouds in the distance.

Then, as if on cue, the ceiling of our miniature seating area begins to roll into place and the captain's voice crackles through the intercom. "Please return to your seats. We are about twenty minutes away from Honolulu, Hawaii, and we'll begin our descent shortly."

Hawaii. The name still gives my stomach a little flip. I sit down in my bean bag chair and fasten my miniature seatbelt, then lean back and close my eyes. Soon, when I remember the flower Jack pressed into my hair, I'll have a scent to go with that memory. I'll know the feel of the salt and water on my skin and the weight of wet clothes and the heat of the sand beneath my feet.

The plane noses gently downward, and soon enough my ears are full enough to pop. We touch down with an unsettling bounce.

"I'm glad I didn't eat much for lunch," Perry grumbles.

"I can't wait to get some chocolate-covered macadamia nuts!" Row says with his customary exuberance. I can't help but smile at him. This whole ordeal would be much worse without his cheeriness.

When the flight attendant opens the door, a breeze, heavy with the scent of fresh blooms, wafts through the cabin.

"Wow," I whisper, inhaling deeply. It's not too hot, not too cool. Like Goldilocks' porridge, this place is just right. If this is how their airport smells, maybe this trip won't be so bad after all.

Several of the Lilliput II assistants get us tiny people loaded into our new carriers. Mine is considerably more posh than the cat-carrier-with-pillow I'd been riding in before. This one is on wheels and rides low to the ground. Inside I have a bunk bed, mini-kitchen, desk, couch, and bathroom. I even have windows instead of slits, although they're far too narrow to allow me to climb out. I open them all up to get some air inside and flop down on the couch. The plastic door looks out the back and I can see everything we're passing inside of the airport terminal.

I don't think I've ever seen this much carpet. The Lilliput Project doesn't have any carpet, probably because this place used all of it up. I sit there, staring at the miles of lint materializing from under the carrier wheels. We go through some doors, and I start noticing people bending down to get a look at me. A little girl about six years old (it's my best guess, but I'm not sure since I never see kids) drags her younger brother over and points at me.

Then we're through another set of doors, and screams surround me. I panic and fly up into the bunk bed as the carrier swings around.

Hundreds of writhing bodies press against a guardrail, screaming and waving at us. Some are waving signs with slogans like "Lina and Row Forever" and "I Love Little Boy Blue."

I get down from my bed, walk over to the door, and fan out my wings. Dozens of fingers point at me, and the crowd goes wild.

I'm a freaking rock star.

***

"Are you sure this isn't going to kill me?" I ask as I watch the hover plane's wings slice through the clouds. We're flying high above Waikiki, and the Toms and I are getting ready for skydiving.

I'm wearing goggles and a hot pink bodysuit a la Barbie, with the brand name "Apollo" marked in clear white letters down my side. Mercifully, Tina the hair demon did her best to slick my mane down as much as possible so it will hopefully look a tiny bit less wild after it's experienced the high winds and a several thousand foot drop. My wings have been painted with some mysterious coating that is supposed to make them less susceptible to tearing. Right now they feel heavy and sticky.

The Toms are suited up in different colors, all with the same branding. Row is in red, Blue in…blue, Al in neon green, Perry in purple, Shrike in yellow, and Crane in an unfortunate shade of orange that transforms him into a limp carrot. Our entourage hovers, fixing makeup, adjusting suits to make sure we're perfect specimens of product placement.

We break through the clouds into clear sky and begin to slow down. There's Diamond Head to the East. Several helicopters hover off to the sides of us, probably waiting for some cameraman to get his parachute in a tangle.

"All right, kids, let's review our instructions!" It's our "ride," the world-famous Cameron Kelso, champion skydiver. He's covered from neck to toe in ads. I wonder if his curly mop of hair is an advertisement for some sort of hair product. I can just picture the commercial: "This gel keeps my hair smooth and shiny jump after jump!"

"Before we open the door," Cameron continues, "we'll get each of you strapped onto my belt here." He taps a strap fitted with us-sized harnesses positioned right across his stomach. "Once my parachute opens and we're slowed down enough so your wings won't tear, I'll release you to fly on your own. Remember to tuck in and dive first so you're well below me before you start flying, otherwise you might get stuck in the parachute. Any questions?"

Nope.

"All right then. Lina, let's strap you in first."

I flick my sticky wings and then fly over to him and land in his hand. It doesn't have as much "squish" as I'm used to; it's made up of lean muscle and skin. He lowers it so I'm standing right in front of the harness, and I strap myself in so I'm facing outward. My wings are pressed flat against his stomach. I can't even move them and that makes me nervous.

As the Toms get harnessed in, I notice that an assistant is switching on the drones one by one. Dr. Christiansen already informed me the drones will be released right after we make our dive, but they won't be put into "seek" mode unless we wander off course—i.e., decide to get the hell out of there.

Other than the bounty hunter bee drones, there are also several camera drones. Those will follow us after we separate from Cameron. We're supposed to fly in formation and do a few tricks. Then we land on the speedboat that will be tracking our movements.

That's it. Simple enough. Why is my heart beating so fast?

"Hey." Blue offers me his hand. "You look a little nervous."

"Oh! I'm fine! Hey, how about we all hold hands? That way we can dive together when we're released." Blue nods, and I take his hand as well as Shrike's. The rest of them grudgingly link up.

The door opens, and a rush of wind pins my hair to Cameron's stomach. I can hardly get a full breath through the pressure. So much air and I can't seem to find any oxygen in it.

Cameron holds a thumbs up for us to see, and we all nod. Yes, we're as ready as we're going to be.

He lumbers to the edge and throws himself overboard. My lips are flapping in the wind, and it takes me a few seconds to keep my wings from struggling to take over.

Blue. Everything is so vividly blue. From the water to the sky. Cameron turns us around so we can see the island itself. There's the ribbon of beach and Diamond Head.

Cameron pulls a cord, and the sudden jolt knocks the wind out of me. I nearly let go of Blue and Shrike, but they are both holding my hand in an iron grip. We've slowed down to floating. Cameron holds up another thumbs up for us, and my harness gives way.

Stomach lurching, I dive forward with the Toms. Straight as arrows, we shoot down toward the ocean. Blue squeezes my hand before both he and Shrike let go. All seven of us unfurl our wings at the same time and level out into a "V" formation as we practiced. I'm leading the way. I duck my head down to make sure they're all there, and Row gives me a little wave.

Up ahead, one of the camera drones is getting into position.

It's flower time.

I take a deep breath and wish we'd gotten more than one day to practice this before I fan out my wings, pull myself into a ball and stop flying. The guys pivot around me like petals. They slowly fly in pinwheel formation before tucking in close. Then we all explode out from the center and zoom in different directions. I nearly crash into Perry, but we both recover just in time.

We open our wings and snap out of freefall. The strain of the sudden slowdown almost makes me lose my breakfast.

After doing a few more easy formation exercises, we coast down to the waiting speedboat and land on one of the seats. There's barely anyone on board—only a driver and a young woman who I assume is only here to set up the food. The rest of the crew is supposed to meet us here.

I'm panting. After a few weeks of being cooped up in a little room, I'm in the worst athletic shape of my life. Sweat beads up from my skin, but the cool Pacific breeze dries it instantly. My lungs begin to tighten, and I pat down my suit, looking for my medicine. I tug it out of a Velcroed pocket and inhale the contents of one of the capsules.

Shrike nods at the tin in my hand. "How often do you have to use that?"

"Only sometimes when I exercise. It's unpredictable."

He grins mischievously. "Does it slow you down?"

"Not usually. Why?"

He shrugs and runs his hand through his dark brown hair. "We'll have to race sometime. Are you fast?"

"Faster than a butterfly."

He scowls but then laughs. "I guess I did ask for that."

"Well, you were the only one who picked the name of a butterfly-eating bird. A little hard to forget if you ask me."

"I was trying to make an impression. It's hard to do with Blue around."

"Yeah, well, usually you want to make a *good* impression." I slide the tin into my pocket. The other Toms are scarfing down food from the craft services table on the floor. Looks like a lot of tropical fruits.

"Okay, I get your point. But I'm not a bad guy. Really."

I fold my arms and study his face. He looks earnest enough, but I can't quite figure him out. He seemed so intent on turning me off the first time I met him, but now he's actually trying. Like he's had a change of heart somewhere.

I don't get it, and I'm not really in a trusting sort of mood lately.

"Okay, well, how about you tell me how awesome you are over some lunch?" I brush past him.

"Forget it then."

"Suit yourself."

I was right about the tropical fruits. The "fruit bar" is half of a pineapple cut open and filled with bits of melon, strawberry, blueberry, pineapple, and banana. Beside it is a halved coconut full of fruit dip.

It reminds me of the tzatziki sauce George makes, and I wonder how he's doing. Dr. Christiansen didn't bring him along for the trip because she knows his sympathies lie more with me than with his job. I miss him.

Row's laughter grabs my attention, and I look up to see him run and dive toward the dip, only to pull back at the last second and flutter to the ground. He catches me watching him, and a grin breaks out across his face.

A blueberry fight has started between Al and Perry. I dodge one stray, juicy bullet and grab a walnut shell bowl full of pineapple and strawberries before walking over to Blue, who is leaning against the side of the boat.

"Hey. Can I join you?"

"Of course." He tilts his head against the wall and breathes in the ocean air.

"I bet this reminds you of home."

"It does. This is your first time seeing the ocean, right?"

"Yep. Want a bite?"

"No, I'm not very hungry. Thank you though." He shifts his wings into a more comfortable position and folds his arms. "Was Shrike trying to make nice?"

"How'd you figure that out?"

"That's his way. He's a bull in a china shop. Breaks everything and then wishes he hadn't."

I consider that for a moment. "He said he's not a bad guy."

Blue snorts out a laugh. "Maybe. But being 'not bad' is nowhere close to being a 'good' guy. I don't trust him anymore. I never know what he's going to do. But Row—"

"There you go again."

"What?"

"Why are you always bringing up Row? You keep shoving me at him." I make a pushing motion with my hands and accidentally flick a blob of pineapple on the ground. Blue retrieves it, flies up to the edge of the boat, and pitches it overboard.

"I'm not trying to push you toward him," he says. "I just want to see you end up with a great guy."

"So," I say, feeling brave, "why not yourself? I'm curious."

"I think you're more his type."

I burst out laughing. "Oh, really? How many girls our size are there who are *your* type? I didn't know you had so many choices."

He stares straight ahead. "I don't. But you do."

I sigh in disgust and lean against the wall. "You're impossible."

That, at least, gets a grin from him.

"Sorry, gotta move!" the driver shouts as he throws the throttle down. The floor beneath me jerks forward. Both Blue and I lose our footing and tumble backward into the seat. Chunks of fruit bump and roll around us. A girl—I imagine she's an assistant—falls to the floor in the center aisle and nearly crushes Al under her knees.

Foaming saltwater crashes over the bow and spatters across the windshield. Several drops make it all the way to me and soak me to the skin. The driver looks frantically over his shoulder and accelerates even more. We hit a large wave, and I'm suddenly airborne.

My wings snap into motion right before I slam into the chest in the rear of the boat. I crawl into a cup holder and loop my arms through the plastic openings inside.

What on earth is going on? I peer over the top. Row and Shrike had a similar idea—they're inside the long mesh pocket lining the side of the boat. The fallen assistant has picked up Al and is dusting him off like he's a doll. I can't see Blue or Perry, and my heart starts beating harder. Where are they? Is it possible they were tossed overboard? Even with our wings, it would be hard to recover and reorient after being punted into the water.

Apparently the assistant is wondering the same thing because she drops Al into the same mesh pocket with Row and Shrike and walks to the edge where I can't see her.

We're still riding fast over the water and I have no idea why. Where are the others? We were supposed to meet Dr. Christiansen and all her cronies before heading toward land.

Then I see it: a long speedboat with more power than ours coming up along the left side of us. While our boat flops over the waves like a belly-flopping kid learning to dive, this boat slices through with barely a bump. And it's full of people with cameras. Big cameras, little cameras—they're part of one never-ending firework of flashes.

The boat sidles dangerously close to ours, and our driver waves at it to go away. I count at least twenty people clustered together along the edge. Several of them are leaning over, pointing and searching, cameras at the ready in case they spot us.

Faint voices pull my attention to the guys in the mesh pocket. They're on the wall facing away from the other boat, so the cameras can't catch a glimpse of them. Row yells and points right down below me. I hesitate to look and expose myself to those cameras. It feels like stepping out into public with no clothes on, but I do it anyway.

It's Blue. He's squatting at the corner of the table and a seat. Perry lies unconscious behind him, a huge welt on his forehead, completely obscured by the plastic table. They have nothing to hang on to, so if there's another bump or abrupt change in speed, they're going to hit something and hit it hard.

Blue looks up at me and motions toward Perry, then toward the cameras. We need to get him to safety in such a way that doesn't expose him.

I glare over at Row. He's going to get an earful for this later. Why isn't he flying over to help?

Then the lights come on. If he flies over, they'll know something is wrong. That is, unless we distract them somehow.

I vault over the edge of the cup holder and flash out my wings. The wind nearly drowns out the resulting shouts from the press boat, but I can still hear them.

I fly to Blue and pull him up to a standing position before linking my arm through his.

"What are you doing?"

I turn us around and wave at the cameras. "Distracting them. Come with me."

"What about Perry?"

"Trust me," I say through my smile of clenched teeth. Row and Shrike are already climbing out of the pocket.

I drag Blue out into the open, taking care to stay behind the windshields so we don't get gusted off the boat. We fly to the passenger's side and sit on the top of the seat back, offering the cameras a perfect view of us. I give Blue what I hope is a convincingly flirtatious smile, and we both wave. The crowd on the press boat crushes against the railing, and one poor woman looks as though she's about to be smooshed in half.

Hurry up, Row. I turn my head to the side, pretending to let the wind draw my hair out of my face. The guys have crept around the edge and are now air-lifting Perry to the pocket. Just need to buy them a few more seconds.

I scoot closer to Blue, then allow my wings to pick me up and flutter me right into his lap. His eyes fill with surprise, but he wraps his arm around my waist anyway. When I wave to the cameras this time, he doesn't join me. Icky-stained guilt oozes through my veins. I feel like I'm using him— using *us*—and, even though it's for a good purpose, it bothers me. I look down into his eyes, and I find a gentle rebuke there.

He stands, picking me up in his arms easily, but he holds me as far from himself as possible. Several people on the press boat cheer pump the air with their fists before returning to their photography.

"I'm sorry," I say, although I'm not quite sure why.

"You're doing your best." The words have the sting of an insult. "Is Perry safe?"

I give my hair a toss into the wind and glance over at the pocket. All four of them are inside. "We're good."

He suddenly pulls me tightly to him and kisses me hard on the cheek before spinning me off to the side. My wings recover before my heart does, and I hover above the seat back, my hand still in Blue's. I remember to smile right before the cameras capture my stunned expression. Where will all of those pictures end up?

My stomach bottoms out. Jack will see them. He'll see me in the arms of another guy, flirting and getting a kiss on the cheek.

I give Blue a nod and return to my cup holder. The driver begins a slow turn toward the spot where we will meet the others. The press boat pulls away and gives ours more room. I guess we gave them what we wanted. We bought some personal space for ourselves with me and Blue's show.

Is this what my life would have been if I had gone to college? Escaping the cameras in between classes? How would I have ever made any friends?

My entire body feels heavy and I sink down into the cup holder. Blue joins the guys in the pocket. Once again, I'm all by myself. The loneliness closes in like so many bars on a cage, and the cameras are my prison wardens.

I squat down so no one can see me, and I wait.

CHAPTER 22

WE FIND THE REST OF the crew waiting on a yacht. After an assistant takes Perry away to get fixed up, the rest of the Toms and I waste no time getting inside where we are shielded by the tinted windows. I watch the poor speedboat driver melt into a puddle when Dr. Christiansen stomps onto his boat and gives him a scolding. Even though I can't hear anything she's saying, I cringe anyway.

The inside of the yacht cabin is a bustling production center. The Toms and I find a corner with couches our size and settle in.

"I hope Perry's okay," Row says.

"He'll be fine," says Shrike. "That guy is tough as nails."

We all fall quiet because we know that's not true of any of us. A bow-tied waitress stops by and takes a small tray off of her regular one and sets it down on the coffee table in the middle of our circle.

"Virgin daiquiris. Enjoy!" She moves along to distribute the rest of her load.

"Old enough to get married on television but not old enough to drink." Shrike lifts a toast with a sardonic grin.

"If you had real alcohol, you'd be passed out in seconds," Blue says, leaning into the cushions and sipping his daiquiri.

"At least I wouldn't be bored to death."

Al clears his throat. I'd almost forgotten him. "I think we're going surfing next," he says and nods toward an open plastic case with seven neon surfboards in the colors of our bodysuits.

"How are we going to do that with paparazzi boats chasing us?" I ask, shaking my head. "I don't feel like getting chopped up by a propeller."

Al shrugs. "Something else is happening, otherwise they would be taking us to the resort."

He has a point. I really wouldn't mind going back to the resort right now. I'm tired and damp and sick of playing to the camera. I'm sharing a room with Susanna, which is the first truly pleasant thing to happen to me since this show started. We actually stayed up late last night, talking. She told me it reminded her of the sleepovers she had when she was in high school. I was tempted to say it reminded me of playing with the paper cutouts of Hansel and Gretel in my pop-up books, but I kept that to myself.

Our room even has a me-sized bed, supplied by a doll furniture company. It has the softest mattress I've ever slept on and sheer white curtains that wrap around the wooden canopy like a cloud. When I woke up this morning, I actually felt happy. So far, Hawaii isn't treating me too shabby. Well, except for the constant presence of the paparazzi.

When we drove to the helipad for our skydiving extravaganza, we were followed by eleven different cars. As soon as we stopped, they nearly ran over each other to get close enough to snap a picture.

Each of the guys looks tired now. The pace of the last few days has been exhausting. The day after Dr. Christiansen informed me we were leaving for Hawaii, we practiced our aerial formations from morning until night so we would be ready. The next day after was an all-day plane ride. And now today.

Blue sets his empty glass on the table and leans back, closes his eyes.

Row slides closer to me and points to my drink. "Hey, what do you think?"

"Oh." I take my first sip. "It's okay." The sugar rush nearly makes my hair stand on end. "A bit too sweet."

He gives me a sly grin. "I'll take it if you don't want it."

"Aha! I should have known you had an agenda. You were trying to part me from my sugar water!"

"Yep. So can I have it?"

I hand it to him, and he gulps it down.

"Doesn't that give you a headache? I get a nasty cold headache whenever I do that."

He squeezes his eyes shut and presses his fingers against the bridge of his nose. "Nope. I'm perfectly fine. Give me a minute."

The director squats down and puts his elbows on the tabletop holding our seating area. "Hey everyone! Hope you all had a great flight down. We got some awesome footage. Nice tricks. They looked fantastic."

None of us says anything.

"Just letting you know we're going to be turning the mics on now. Curtis is going to give you new mic packs real quick, and then we'll get started."

"What's going on?" Shrike asks.

"Well, you're in for a real treat," the director says, his tone dripping with sincerity.

Oh, goodie.

"The local police are blocking off a section of the water for us. You all are going surfing."

I glance over at Blue. His eyes are wide open now.

A gangly young man with spiked brown hair and a too-tight shirt comes over, and the director claps him on the shoulders. "This is Curtis. He'll take care of you guys." He turns to Curtis. "Oh, and when you're done, make sure they get another round here and maybe some snacks. Whatever they want. See you guys!"

Al slides off his chair and slips onto the seat next to me as Curtis examines Shrike's microphone pack. "So, surfing!"

"Yep."

Al's teeth are bright white inside his chocolate smile. "Can I teach you?"

"Sure." I really wish he wouldn't. I don't want anything to replace the lessons I got from Jack. I'd rather try to get the hang of it on my own, without any help, even if it means making an utter fool of myself. But I can't tell him that. He's so clearly excited, and this is his chance to show me what he's got.

"What's wrong?"

"Nothing." I fake a smile.

"You sighed."

"I think I'm just tired. But I'm fine."

"Your turn, Lina!" Curtis beckons me over. Yay, a diversion. He hands me a nearly flat black box the size of my palm. There's no cord.

"What do I do with it? I ask.

He taps a pocket on my thigh. "It goes in there."

"Oh. Where's the mic?"

"That's it. Brand-new technology. It picks up sound and filters out any noise. The battery's in there, too. You're all set."

"And now it's my turn," says Susanna, armed with her makeup kit. "Over here, Miss Lina."

I follow her through the crush of panicked assistants putting together lenses and lighting sets, down a few steps and into a cabin bedroom. The bed takes up almost the entire room. Unfortunately, Tina the Terrible is also waiting for me, but she's looking a bit green. I guess the gentle bobbing of the yacht doesn't agree with her.

"What happened to your face?" Susanna asks as she attacks me a powder puff.

"I got hit by a drop of water, and I meeeellllted. MELLLLLTED." I do my best Wicked Witch of the West impression of sinking into a puddle on the bedspread. "Anyway, I'm going to be in the water, so I don't think makeup will matter."

"It will matter to Dr. Christiansen."

"Pfffft."

"You know there's going to be pictures beforehand. And lots of footage of you and the Toms gazing off at the ocean."

"I've already had my picture taken too many times today."

"I bet." She holds up her magnifying glass and carefully lines my eyes with white.

Tina begins working my hair into loose curls. When they're done, I've been transformed into a genuine surfer girl.

"I could get used to this," I say as I admire myself in the mirror. "But I need a coconut bra."

Tina gives me a weak smile and then races from the room, slamming the door on her way out.

"She's already thrown up twice," Susanna says. "I feel bad for her."

"Yeah, well, it's nice and quiet now."

"Lina!" But her tanned shoulders are shaking with laughter.

"Are they really going to make me surf in this bodysuit?"

"As far as I know. I haven't heard anything different." She pokes the giant logo on my side. "It would be hard to fit that on a swimsuit. No one would be able to read it."

"And it's all about the money."

She purses her lips but says nothing. Curtis pokes his head through the door. "You're up, Lina. Time to shine!"

"Another hour, another million photos," I grumble.

***

I'm not sure what I pictured when the director told us the police were reserving a section of water for us, but I certainly didn't imagine there would be dozens of boats and two helicopters waiting for us. All of this fuss over a little bit of surfing.

We're right off Waimea Bay, prime surfing waters. Today the waves are reaching heights of six feet, which means the front of the wave is actually closer to twelve feet. Why they don't say the waves are twelve feet is beyond me. Apparently it's some old Hawaiian measuring system, but it makes no sense.

Perry has rejoined us, although he's looking a little drunk and squinty-eyed. Shrike keeps putting one hand on his friend's shoulder to return him to a fully upright position.

After posing with our surfboards for an obscene number of photos on the railing of the yacht, we're now finally getting ready to jump in.

Al jostles me gently with his shoulder. "Ready, Lina?"

"Yep."

"Follow me. I'll show you the best tricks."

147

"Right. After you."

The other guys see what's going on and take off without us, whooping and zooming through the air. They're right at home out here. Al checks to make sure I'm still waiting on him, and I nod. All ready. Let's go.

We fly over the cresting waves, and Al stops and hovers.

"We'll wait for a good one."

Blue suddenly stops and dives, sliding his board under his feet right before he reaches the face of the wave. He keeps using his wings to propel himself down the towering wall of water. The spray tickles my toes as the wave passes beneath us.

"Is that the trick?!" I shout to Al.

"No, that is not it. All right, let's take that one."

"What?"

But he's already jetting toward the tippy top of the next wave, so I fly hard to catch up. The wave is still building its height; the top edge is reaching, reaching for the sky and has yet to crest. Al flies in perfect pace with it and beckons to me even though I'm right there with him.

"Lie down on your stomach. Like this!" He presses his board to his chest and dives over the edge.

"Oh my gosh."

I follow his instructions and "sled" over the teetering ledge of water. I'm one wrong move from free-falling down the vertical face. I scream, half out of fear and half out of pure glee. My teeth chatter as the board skitters across the rapidly changing water. I know when the wave crests because I pick up speed, and now I'm squealing uncontrollably. I turn my head and see a mass of roiling foam coming my way, so I get my wings going and skip out in front of the wave.

"Lina! Come up here!" It's Row, and he's waving at me from above. His strawberry blond hair is on fire with sunlight. Two black camera drones zoom behind him—the first reminder I'm being filmed since Al and I rode our wave together. I'd completely forgotten I was miked until now, and it bothers me that I'm getting used to this.

I barely escape the pummeling wave as I fly to join Row. He's hovering with his board tucked under his arm.

"Want to try some double-boarding?"

"How does that work?"

"You ride with me, of course. In front." He flashes me his signature smile. "My noble steed is here, at the ready."

"Do I have to ride side-saddle?"

"Only if it pleases her ladyship."

"No thanks. What do I do with my board if I'm riding yours?"

"Blue!" Row waves him over.

"What's up?"

"Can you hold Lina's board for a minute? We're going to do some double-boarding."

"Absolutely." Blue barely even looks at me as he takes my board. He's ignoring me, and that's annoying. I'm not sure if he's offended that I pretended to be into him or if he's wishing it was real. Or maybe it's something else entirely. *Not everything is about you*, I remind myself.

Row holds his hand out to me, and I take it. We fly hand-in-hand to the spot where the waves are cresting.

"All right, this is how it works. We're actually going to start in the water and surf this the old-fashioned way."

"And what's the old-fashioned way?"

"We both lie on the board—same as you did with Al's technique—in the water, and we wait for the wave to pick us up. I'll stand first and then I'll help you and we'll be surfing!"

"What if I can't get up? It'll be hard to get my balance with my wings if you're right behind me."

"That's why it's the old-fashioned way," he says with a sly grin. "Just try not to flap me right off the board."

Right. So basically we're going to be surfing like regular people. The way Jack taught me. But this time I have to do it with Row.

"Let's get set up down there," Row continues, pointing at a trough between the swells. "We'll have to be quick."

Once Row positions the board in the water, I climb up on my stomach, and he follows suit. He's basically on top of me, and I squirm under his weight.

"Sorry, I'm kind of heavy. I'll be off you in a sec." He presses his hands into the board right near my shoulders and pushes himself slightly away from me. I'm surprised at how muscular his forearms are. He's rolled his bodysuit sleeves to the elbow, and he's all lean muscle. That's when it occurs to me how *close* he is, and shivers run over my whole body.

"Are you cold?" he asks.

"Nope, just dandy."

"Sorry, I thought I saw you shiver." I feel him twist around to check out the next wave, and then he starts pushing us forward with his wings. "This is a good one, but we need some more speed."

At first, I don't feel the same surge I did with the other waves—we're going only a little faster—and then I notice we're going up the wall of water backward.

"Lean forward!"

"I'm leaning!"

We shoot forward like a cannonball on the water, and Row stands in one fluid move. This is it. I know how to do this. I did it dozens of times with Jack. I slide onto my knees, and Row's hands are suddenly under my armpits, guiding me. I wish he wouldn't help me. I wish he would let me succeed or fail on my own, but I guess that's not his style.

Right after Jack demonstrated how to get up on my board, he went off on his own for fifteen minutes to let me work it out on my own. When he returned, I was still flailing like a drunken spider, but I was standing.

Look at me! Look at me! I screamed at Jack right before I tumbled off into the wave. When I came back up, sputtering but happy, he only winked at me and pointed at the incoming waves.

Together? he asked with a grin.

Definitely.

He never showed off. He didn't congratulate himself for being such an amazing teacher that I got up in less than five tries. As far as he was concerned, we were on a level playing field. Teammates on surfboards, conquering the waves!

I loved it.

Now, here with Row gently pulling me by my arms, I'm more of a helpless doll than a fearless Amazon. Not a very sexy feeling.

Not that I'm trying to feel sexy right now. No, definitely not. Not with Row.

I lose my balance and fall into his chest. More annoying shivers and that quickening feeling deep in my stomach.

Stop it, Lina! This is Row!

I gather all of my focus and get myself to an independently upright position.

"You've got it!" Row shouts. "Way to go!"

If it was anyone else, I would feel patronized. I can't see Row's face, but I can imagine his guileless smile.

As we hurtle through the spray, I wonder how it's possible to think so highly of Row but feel so completely unlike my best self when he's around. It's not that he's doing anything wrong either.

Maybe it's just me.

CHAPTER 23

LATER THAT DAY, WHILE THE sun sinks into the molten fire of the orange ocean, I sit with the Toms around a sputtering bonfire of tightly rolled paper.

Today was the first time I've gotten to really spread my wings since the show began, and my muscles are already aching. I've got that sleepy-contented feeling you have after a long day spent playing in the sunshine. After I took a long, hot bath in rosewater (of all things), Susanna said I was positively glowing. She only gave me some lip gloss and the slightest dusting of powder. Even Tina went easy on me. When they handed me a mirror to survey the results, I was surprised to see my old self staring back. I'm even wearing a yellow-and-blue-striped sundress that resembles something I would make myself.

One of the "logs" wheezes and spits out a spark toward the darkening sky. Our group date is almost over and we're still wearing our microphones, but no one talks. It's a comfortable silence.

Comfortable. I never thought I would feel that way with any of these guys. The only one who looks uneasy is Perry, and I'm pretty sure that's because he has a roaring headache. The poor guy looks like he's going to either puke or fall asleep. Maybe both. At once.

I go to sit next to him. He's staring hard at the fire as if he's trying to force his eyes to focus.

"Hey, how are you feeling?"

He winces at my voice. "I've been better."

"I got a concussion once, and I slept for, like, an entire day afterward."

"Isn't that the opposite of what you're supposed to do? I asked if I could go and lie down, but Dr. C. and company won't let me."

"Yeah, well, mine was before the show. I hope you feel better soon. I bet you'll sleep like a baby tonight."

"Yeah. Thanks." He rubs the bridge of his nose and squeezes his eyes shut.

"Can I get you anything?"

"I'd really love a drink of water."

"Sure thing." I've only taken two steps toward the beverage table before Row and Al are on their feet, asking me what I need. "I'm fine, guys. Just chill out for a bit."

When I return with Perry's water, Row is going on and on about how amazing I am at surfing. I got up on my first try! I barely needed any help at all! I'm such a natural!

"Well, she already knew how," Al interjects into Row's series of exclamation marks.

Row's exuberance fades into confusion. "What?"

"She told me on the plane that she already learned."

"But how?" All eyes are on me now. I guess Al never made the connection that, in order for me to learn online, I must have broken a few rules. The other guys, however, have definitely clued in on that by the looks on their faces.

"I learned in a construct," I say. "A friend taught me." There's no use hiding it since Dr. Christiansen already knows. And I'm sure she's going to edit this part out anyway.

"Isn't that…against policy?" asks Blue.

"So what if it is?" I lift my chin, challenging him to look down on me.

Shrike laughs. "I love it." He stands and applauds.

Row studies my face. He's already made the connection between my online love and my surfing instructor. I find I like him better when he's been brought down to earth. He seems more…reachable. Like someone who might have a shot at understanding me.

"What sort of friend?" asks Crane.

I roll my eyes and try to brush it off. "A…friend. I didn't grow up the way you guys did. I never got to have anyone around my own age or size. If you were me, you would have done the same thing."

I don't dare look at Blue. I can feel his piercing stare anyway, and I don't need to get skewered through my eyeballs. My cheeks grow hot despite my best efforts to look calm and collected, and I'm afraid to say anything else because my throat's run dry.

Perry's staring down into his empty glass, and Al and Shrike are giving each other raised eyebrows.

"I can't believe this is such a big deal," I sputter. "I met a friend online. Why do any of you care?" As soon as the words are out of my mouth, guilt washes over me. They *should* care. They should care very much that they're competing for my affections while I'm in love with someone else.

Row clears his throat. "You're right. It's not our place to judge." He stands and offers me his arm. "Let's go get some ice cream."

"Yes, please." I link my arm through his and, as we walk to the giant ice cream cone and hot fudge fountain, I give his hand a squeeze of thanks.

"Remember what I said," he whispers. "You can still make the best of this."

Numbly, I nod, but something clicks into place inside my heart. I glance at the rest of the Toms sitting in uncomfortable silence around the fire. Only moments earlier, the mood was completely different. All it took was one revelation from me to change everything. I've never had that sort of power before. I've never even wanted it. But now, like it or not, the happiness of six guys hinges on how I handle myself from here on out.

I can't choose one of them just to keep Jack safe. The one I choose will know it's an act, that my heart's not in it. He might not be able to articulate why he thinks that, but there will always be a distance, that question between us. None of these guys deserve that.

Each one of the Toms deserves a girl's whole heart, all her love. Jack has already laid claim to mine, but I wonder what will happen if I give in to the tug I feel toward Row. What will happen if I…let go?

Tears surge into my eyes, and I almost drop the scoop of ice cream I'm ferrying toward my bowl. A sob pushes against my throat, but I force it down. I follow Row to the bonfire, but all I can see in my mind's eye is Jack.

The conversation turns to easy talk about the surf, the view, the crazy paparazzi, but I am unable to smile. My face feels as though it's been frozen.

And in my heart, I'm wrapping my arms tightly around all I know about Jack. I'm tying him to me so I can't let him go.

***

Susanna is already asleep when I slip out of bed and flutter to the open window. The screen is the only thing separating me from the outside world. I sit cross-legged inside the window frame and watch the moths zip and zap against the lanterns illuminating the pool. I squeeze my toes around the metal guide piece at the bottom of the window so the cold can soothe my tired, aching feet. The photo sessions are starting to really wear on me because I'm not used to spending so much time standing in one place

I'm not sure why Dr. Christiansen has relaxed her security code where I'm concerned, but it's a welcome relief, even while it makes me somewhat nervous. Is she so confident in my continued cooperation?

I press my forehead to my knees and groan. For once, I'm happy that my voice is too small to wake anyone up. I could ramble out loud and Susanna's snores would continue on unabated.

I wonder if Mr. Coxworth has found any new information about the other Thumbelinas. I didn't get a chance to talk to him before we left for Hawaii. I casually asked Susanna earlier if she had any idea why there is only one of me while there are six of the Toms and she brushed off the question, but I could tell she knows something. She's just not telling me. Mr. Coxworth did say he found out through the papers, but I have no access to the Internet. No one will let me get within a foot of a tablet in order to read the news. Right after the group date, I saw one of the production assistants showing off his brand-new Bexter 4000 tablet with holographic keyboard. When I flew over to see what the fuss was all about, he immediately turned it off.

I was hoping Susanna would have one so I could use it when she was asleep, but she dutifully turned hers in to Dr. Christiansen before we were locked in for the night.

My hand presses against the screen. It wouldn't be so hard to cut a slit into it and slip outside. But where would I go?

A flitter of orange wings inside the hibiscus hedge outside my window catches my eye. Row peeks his head around a wilting bloom. He grins at me and waves before flying over. I tug my sweater around me. I'm only wearing white pajama shorts, a tank top and the sweater, and I'm feeling a little self-conscious.

"What are you doing?" I hiss at him when he flies over.

"It's just me. I wasn't sure if you'd be up, but I thought I would check."

"How did you get out?"

He brandishes a razor blade. "They forgot to remove the courtesy razors from the bathroom in our suite. And it's a beautiful night. May I?" He points to the screen.

I bite my lip but nod. He slices an opening barely long enough for me to slide through and holds my elbow as I twist out into the cool night air.

The moonlight glitters off of the puddles remaining from the light shower earlier in the evening, and the air still carries the faint veil of humidity.

"Check out the stars," Row says, pointing upward.

Indeed, the sky is so clear now I can even see the haziness of the Milky Way.

"This way. I know a spot where we'll be able to see better."

I follow him out to the pool but hesitate by the fence. "They'll see us if we go out there."

"Everyone's asleep, Lina. Just trust me."

"Well, obviously not *everyone* is sleeping. We're not."

"I know, but no one will be looking for us on the lily pads."

I peek around him and notice the plastic green lily pads floating in the pool. They have raised, scalloped rims and votive candles burning in the centers. It's a perfect hiding place.

We lie as flat on our backs as our wings will allow on top of the centermost lily pad. The candle sputters in its glass lantern near our feet as we watch the stars in silence. Our vantage point gives us an almost unobstructed view of the sky, save for the black outlines of the palm fronds. Row's put a respectable distance between the two us so I don't feel that same heat I do every time he touches me. Thank goodness for that—I don't need any more confusion right now.

A meteorite streaks across the sky before blinking out right above us, and Row's breath quickens.

I have never seen the Milky Way like this before. It's so clear I can imagine flying through its filmy layers of glitter. The stars don't even blink; they're solid points of brilliant light pouring down on us. I can even see faint hints of red and orange and blue surrounding them. It's all so vividly real. And I thought the Hawaiian sky in the construct was beautiful.

A light breeze waves over the fragrance of the magnolia trees. This is what was missing from my date with Jack: the smells, the sensations, the vividness. The thought has the taste of blasphemy, as though I'm growing out of something precious and well-loved, like a beloved stuffed animal from childhood. Jack himself is beginning to fade a little in my memories. I can't recall his face as clearly as I once did no matter how hard I try to trace out his dark lashes and high cheekbones inside my mind. I can't even remember the sound of his voice. And no matter how hard I try to ignore it, the fact that our date would have been completely different if it had happened in person keeps popping up like an unwelcome guest. At least Row knows Daphne loves him as he is, six inches and all.

"Row?"

"Lina?" He rolls onto his side, smile solidly in place.

"Do you miss Daphne?"

"Yes, but I don't think about it as often anymore. It's been months since I saw or heard from her."

"Does that bother you? I mean, that you don't think about it as much?"

"It did at first, but I guess it's for the best. It never would have worked out. I'd hate to miss out on something because I was thinking about her." He doesn't meet my eyes. "She wouldn't have wanted that. And I don't want that for her either."

I squeeze my eyes shut. "I can't think of Jack being with someone else yet."

"No, I don't blame you." He pauses, gives a little cough, and continues tentatively. "But has it occurred to you maybe he has moved on? I mean, how long has he known by now? A month?"

A horrible churning sensation takes over my gut, and goose bumps sprout all over my body. I haven't considered that possibility until now, although I think some part of me always knew it could happen. I can't believe Jack would shut me out so quickly.

"I'm sorry, Lina," Row says, his voice gentle. "I wouldn't ever ask you to forget about him."

"I couldn't even if I tried," I whisper, pretending to rub something out of my eye. "But I'm so tired of knowing I can't have him." A shaky laugh burbles out of me. "And I'm really sick of crying about it. I've never been such a big baby before."

"You're not a baby."

My breathing is returning to normal, my tears under control. "I thought it was so real. Even though it was all online, it was so…alive. But now that I'm here, in all of this…" I wave my hand up at the sky. "I was only getting half of the real thing. I don't even know what he's like in person, and I thought I knew him so well. I never even got to kiss him."

"Well," he says carefully, "that would have been a little bit awkward."

"Are you speaking from experience?"

"Nope!"

"Ha."

We descend into silence again. I move my feet closer to the candle for warmth.

And then, out of the blue, Row asks, "Can I hold your hand?"

I'm startled but surprised to discover the answer is, "Yes."

His warm fingers weave themselves through my own, and he gives my hand a squeeze. The electricity races up my arm, through my head, and down to my groin. My heart beats so hard I'm afraid to speak.

"Did you feel that?" he whispers.

"Yeah," I breathe, suddenly shy. There are goose bumps all over my head. Guilt and elation swirl together until I cannot tell one from the other.

Row scoots closer and leans over me. Then, looking straight into my eyes, he raises my hand to his lips and kisses it.

A shock travels through me, and suddenly the world seems to have more color. I *see* Row for the first time. His ever-ready smile is still there in his eyes, but it's mixed with hunger now. I've never noticed before how perfectly his neck is shaped, how its muscles intertwine with those of his shoulders and his chest. The candlelight flickers off of his finely sculpted features, turning into flakes of fire in his eyes. And his lips. I can't take my eyes off of his lips. Even as they slowly sink ever closer to my own and I worry about when I should breathe—as if I could—and how I taste. But I close my eyes as his face draws so near that all the world is Row and nothing else.

His lips only graze my own, soft as a feather, and I groan as my mouth parts to ask for more. But he's pulling away from me, his eyes startled like he did something wrong. I reach out with my other hand and wrap it around his neck to gently coax him back. *Oh, don't stop now. I'm all on fire. Help me block everything out.*

"I'm sorry," he says, sitting up. "I shouldn't have done that."

I let go of him and press my lips together. He drops my hand and stands.

"I should get you back to your room."

"What the heck just happened?"

"I'm sorry—I'm not..." His face contorts in misery. "I'll escort you."

"Don't bother." I hop up and fly off by myself.

"Lina!" he calls after me. But I don't turn around, and he doesn't chase me.

CHAPTER 24

MY DATE WITH AL IS an exercise in misery. We're taken to Diamond Head's peak by helicopter and spend an awkward several hours attempting to get a conversation flowing. I can't stop thinking about how much the scenery reminds me of Jack, even though the real-life version trumps the construct any day. And that thought rips open the scab that's been slowly covering the wounds from last night with Row.

I couldn't sleep after our barely-there kiss. I can't figure out why he would act that way. Did he feel guilty because he thought Daphne would be watching? Or because I'd just been confessing how much I still care for Jack? And here I was thinking I was finally moving forward in some fashion.

The director shouts "It's a wrap!" and I give Al an awkward hug.

"Thanks for coming," he says, as if I had a choice.

"You too! See you later."

The grips and assistants wrestle with their gear, forcing it into hard plastic cases. One pulls a diffuser away from a light, and I blink hard in the suddenly overpowering whiteness.

But when I open my eyes, I see it: a lonely tablet on top of the director's chair.

I glance around, but everyone is too busy with their individual tasks. The assistant assigned to supervise me is stuffing her face at the craft services table. It's now or never.

With shaking hands, I tap the screen. The screensaver blinks off, and there's no login required. It's my lucky day. About time.

I type and tap my way to the Internet and search for "Christiansen." I furtively check again to see if anyone is watching me, then look at the results.

Hundreds of articles pop up with crazy headlines: "Quack scientist called to account for dead Thumbelinas," and "Tiny new television star the only survivor?" I tap on the first entry and skim it until I come to:

Dr. Julia Christiansen is expected to appear before a judge in December. A prosecutor will determine what charges she will receive at that time. A panel of scientists is convening to determine whether or not the Thumbelinas can be classified as humans so Christiansen can be charged with manslaughter. If not, she may get off with an animal cruelty charge, which carries a maximum sentence of two years in prison and a fine of 20 grams of gold. No evidence against Dr. Christiansen has been released to the public at this time.

So that's it. I scan the rest of the article, looking for information I don't already know, but the only thing I find is that Dr. Christiansen was turned in by an unnamed source and the Lilliput Project never revealed how many Thumbelinas were born. They didn't even announce my birth until I was six months old. So the other girls must have died between birth and six months.

It's enough for now. I click off of the news article and join my assistant, who has salad dressing dribbling down her chin.

"Ah waf wooking awww ovuh for you," she says through a mouth full of salad.

"Well, here I am. Can we go now?"

She swallows. "Sure, but let me finish. You don't want any?"

"No, I'll get room service later."

"They have tiny cupcakes."

"Really?"

She points at a giant cupcake tree on the dessert table. The topmost tier is lined with mini versions of my Achilles' heel—the chocolate cupcake.

I excuse myself and launch over to the tower of sugar. There are several different kinds of icing on them—mint, cherry, strawberry, and peach. I pick a strawberry one and pull away the foil wrapper on the bottom.

"Hey, Lina."

It's Row, and he's looking apologetic and awkward.

"How did you get here?"

"We all came along," he says. "We had to stay in the trailer while you were shooting. Look, I'm sorry."

I don't even know what to say.

"I'm really sorry. I felt bad after…everything we had talked about."

"What does that even mean? You've been telling me over and over again to 'make the best of it, Lina, blah blah blah.' Then I go ahead and follow your advice and suddenly you're freaking out and apologizing. What were you sorry for—that you stopped kissing me or that you ever started in the first place?"

"Kind of both?"

I cross my arms and glare at him. "Well, that's real helpful."

"Listen," he says, an odd mix of dejection and panic in his downcast expression, "it was a reaction. I don't know exactly where it came from. It was kind of an intense moment there, and I was having a really hard time thinking clearly." A bashful smile chases away the gloom. "You have that effect on me."

I keep my arms folded, but I'm melting on the inside.

"Give me another chance?"

I chew on the inside of my lip. I'm not sure how "another chance" will look, but I don't have it in me to hold a grudge against him for this. All of the cameras, all of the photos, the constant primping and virtual imprisonment—it's taken a toll on us all. I can't blame him for feeling confused. "Confused" has been my middle name since this all began.

"Okay," I say, even though a thread of doubt winds around my heart.

A sunbeam smile bursts from his face. "Thanks." He sweeps me into a hug, and electricity zigzags through me again, leaving me breathless. "I'll make it up to you, I promise."

A flush creeps to my hairline. I'm not sure I'm ready for him to make anything up, but I nod anyway.

"Well, aren't you cute," says a derisive voice.

Row lets go of me, and I turn to see Shrike wearing his disgust on his face.

"Hi, Shrike," I say.

"I guess you've already made your choice."

"Shrike, it's not like that."

"Sure it's not." He nods curtly. "I get it. I'll leave you two alone."

I make a loud raspberry noise and drop my head into my hands.

"Is he your next date?" Row asks.

"Yep."

"Sorry."

Me too.

CHAPTER 25

"SO, I FIGURED I WOULD take you some place a little less exotic this time," Jack said after I'd booted up my halojector. "And all you need for this one is your monitor and camera."

I switched off the halojector, puzzled. "Where are we going?"

He grinned into the two-way camera as he tugged it off its stand. "How would you like to meet my family and see where I live?"

"Oh! Wow. Sure!" I ran my fingers through my hair and smoothed it down, and then I knotted my hands together in my lap. I hadn't seen this one coming.

"Awesome. I'll try not to jiggle this around too much." Then he dropped the camera. "Oops, sorry about that. Hope you don't get motion sickness."

"Yeah, me too."

"Okay, here's my room. You've probably seen my wall already since it's behind my computer chair, but here's the rest." He panned the camera around, and what I saw sobered me. A twin bed with a sagging mattress sat against the wall. The sheets and blanket were clean but fraying around the edges. The floor was water-stained, bare plywood. He panned to the ceiling. "That's my leak. It lets me be one with nature all the time!"

There was a small bookcase crammed full of shabby paperbacks. A broken dresser stood in the corner, one of its drawers hanging out halfway.

Jack walked over to the bed. I could hear him breathing. "And this is where my little brother Matt sleeps." He pulled out a trundle from underneath his own bed. It was neatly made with faded cartoon sheets.

"It's not much, but it's pretty comfortable. Matt likes to play outside when he's not in school, so it feels like it's my own room most of the time." He turned the camera around so I could see his face again. His brown eyes were full of joy. "And if he's in here when I'm talking to you, I can kick him out since I'm the boss!"

"It's lovely, Jack," I said with a smile. "It's very homey."

Behind him, the door swung open, and Matt burst inside.

"Raaaaaawrrr!" he shouted as he ran full-speed to Jack and disappeared from my view. The sudden lurch in the camera told me Matt had made contact.

"What's up, buddy?"

"Can you come and play with me?"

"I will in a minute. How about you say hi to my friend first? Here, can you see her?" Jack knelt down, and Matt peered into the camera. He was only about six or seven years old, and he looked like a younger, smaller version of his older brother.

"What's her name?"

"Lina. Go ahead and introduce yourself."

"Hi, Lina. I'm Matt! When are you coming over?"

"Not for a while, Matt. I live a long way away. But it's nice to meet you!"

"Why can't she come over?"

"Because she lives across the ocean."

"Oh."

Jack's face again. "And that's Matt! There he goes." The door slammed behind the tiny black-haired whirlwind as he ran out to play. "Ready for the rest of the family?"

"Um, yep! Bring it on."

He opened the door into a living room crammed with tattered old furniture. A gleaming cherry wood coffee table stood out as the only nice piece in the room. The floor was unfinished particle board with several rugs thrown down here and there.

Next to the living room was the dinette and kitchen. A small table that would only comfortably seat three people at most sat against the wall. A chubby girl with ill-fitting clothes and carefully curled hair sat coloring a map.

"Say hi, Kendall."

She set down her marker, tossed her head, and glared at him. She was about twelve years old and full of attitude.

"I'm not a baby, Jack."

"I didn't say you were. I want you to say hello to a friend of mine."

"Are you recording?"

"Yep. She's watching right now."

"Seriously?"

"How many times do I have to say it?"

And with that, she cowed a little. Her confidence receded when she realized she was being watched by an unfamiliar face.

"Who is it?"

He walked closer, held the camera so she could see who I was. I waved and smiled.

"Hi Kendall, I'm Lina! Nice to meet you."

"Hi."

"Lina lives in Denmark. That's in Europe."

"I know where it is. I know where all the states are in Europe."

"That's because you study hard." And to me, he said, "She really likes geography. She's always color-coding different maps."

"I don't color-code them," she said and rolled her eyes dramatically.

"Anyway, moving on! This is Mom."

I'd expected a short, heavy-set woman. What I saw was a lithe creature with beautiful, haunted eyes. She kept her hair in a single, long braid, and if I didn't know better, I would have thought she was Jack's older sister.

She flipped a pancake and waved at the camera. "Hello, friend of Jack's."

He stepped closer and she peered at me.

"She's very pretty," she said. "You're welcome any time, Lina. I can tell you make him happy." And then she smiled her faraway smile and went back to her cooking.

"Okay, now for the outside."

I held onto my lunch as he shaky-cammed his way out through the weeds and several rusted-out cars to the stable.

"And this here is my pride and joy, Sampson." The pinto snorted and stamped as if he knew someone was talking about him. Jack held an apple slice *in his open palm and the horse ran his thick lips over it and snatched it with another snort as if to say, "Do better next time."*

Jack laughed and turned the camera on himself once more. "So what do you think?"

"I really wish I could meet your family in person. They seem like such interesting people. I love your little brother."

"Yeah, he's a handful. But fun. You really should come here sometime."

My breath caught in my throat. "Jack, you know I would love to, but I don't know how that would happen."

"I know." His smile stayed put. "But a guy can dream, can't he? It's what keeps me going. Anyway, want to see the Badlands?"

"From horseback?"

"From horseback."

"Oh, yes please!"

CHAPTER 26

I THOUGHT THEY WOULD TAKE us to the Badlands next, but I was wrong. I stare out the airplane window, filled with both relief and disappointment. I could have been so close to Jack—only miles away from his home. Maybe that's why Dr. Christiansen decided the next date would take place back in Denmark.

Dr. Christiansen is definitely relaxing her icy grip, although I'm not sure why. I still have the tracking device implanted somewhere in my skin and the drones are tuned and readied each time we go outside, but she herself is more distant. We've barely spoken since we left Copenhagen for Hawaii. I'm sure she's somewhat preoccupied with the hearing, but normally she gets even stricter when she's stressed out. Maybe she's "rewarding" my good behavior like she would a dog.

An arm brushes mine. Row sets his elbows on the window sill and leans against me. "Ready to go home?"

"Only if I get to sleep in my own bed." I remember sitting on the living room floor, crumpled and broken with my computer in my arms. "But I don't think it will be the same as before."

"I hear you'll be coming to New Zealand after you, you know, make your choice."

"Who told you that?"

He shrugs. "People. It's a rumor that's been floating around. I heard some of the assistants saying Lilliput I will be closed after the show wraps."

I frown and gaze out the window. That means I'll never get to fly through my forest again. My treehouse will be no more. And what about George and Mr. Coxworth? I can't imagine them moving to New Zealand.

"Hey," Row says, nudging me. "Don't look so depressed. New Zealand is gorgeous, and we're right on the beach."

"I bet it is, but it's not my home."

"I think you, of all people, could make a home anywhere. You've got this way of bending everything and everyone toward you."

"Pssh. I do not."

"Lina, look around. You've got six guys after you and an entire show about your love life."

"Yeah, well, it's not like you have any other choices."

"Maybe not, but that doesn't change the fact you're in the center of our world."

I squirm under the weight of those words. The only reason there's any truth to what he says is because of Dr. Christiansen, not me.

But, now that I think about it, hasn't it always been that way? The entire Lilliput Project I Compound exists to protect and care for me. Sure, Dr. Christiansen has always continued her own research, but she didn't need a forest with a dome fence to do it. I am the reason for all of the fuss.

My cheeks flush as I realize I've always been at the center of attention. I took it for granted, expected it. Even Mr. Coxworth's work revolves around finding natural medicines for me. I've never even thanked him.

"Hey, are you okay?"

I shake my head. "Yeah. I'm fine." But the world has shifted slightly in my mind, and I'm seeing everything through a different facet now. When my eyes meet Row's again, he looks older. He still wears his sunny smile, but there's something more beneath the familiar exterior: a depth of soul I never guessed at before.

"You're looking at me funny."

"Sorry. You seem different somehow."

He laughs. "I was going to say the same thing about you."

I shake my head. "There must be something in the Hawaiian water."

"Something good, I hope."

We watch as the islands disappear into the horizon. In fifteen hours, we'll be in Copenhagen.

***

The crowd outside the Copenhagen airport is almost identical to the one that waited for us in Honolulu, with one important difference—this one looks angry. Instead of holding signs having to do with my love life, they're waving slogans like, "1% Human is Still Human," and "Free the Fairies." I'm surprised I'm not more encouraged by their presence. I mean, I'm happy the public here is rallying behind my cause, but I doubt it will have any real impact on my life.

We're escorted off the airport grounds by the politiet. My carrier sits next to Dr. Christiansen in the back of the limo, and I can't see anything but the seat in front of me. She says nothing other than to give terse directions to the driver.

I curl up in the bunk bed and snap the guardrails into place. I try to nap, but sleep evades me. We've been gone less than a week, but it seems like much longer. I feel as though I'm years older.

And I'm tired.

The limo stops outside the gate to the compound, and the driver lets us out. A golf cruiser waits for us inside. Jane hops out and helps to unload our bags into the trunk of the cruiser. She grabs my carrier a little more roughly than I think is really necessary and sets it down on the backseat.

"Let her out," says Dr. Christiansen.

Say what? I press my ear closer to one of the slits in the carrier. She flips open her suitcase and pulls out a drone, powers it up. If I run, I'll be chased down. Yeah, yeah, I know the drill.

Jane opens the door and I step outside.

"Lina, you are free to travel about the grounds once again. Your treehouse has been prepared for you. I am sure you understand what the consequences will be if you decide not to cooperate."

I do.

She raises her eyebrows as if to ask me why I'm still there.

"I guess I'll go then."

Jane gives me her creepily sincere smile, and I head toward home. It's a clear day, but the light seems dimmer in the compound. It must be the dome. Strange I've never noticed it before.

I slide under the door to Mr. Coxworth's house, but he's not there. In fact, the entire compound seems unusually quiet. Where is everyone?

When I check for George at the aviary, it's empty. There are no birds in the roosts. The entire thing has been cleaned out.

"George!" I check every single inch for any sign of him, hoping against hope he left something for me that will tell me where he is and how to contact him.

Nothing.

I race off to his dormitory on the far side of the living area. When I get there, a housekeeper I've never seen before is sweeping the wood floors. All of his things are gone.

"Where is he?" I ask her. "Where's George?"

"I do not know," she says in a thick German accent. "I was hired and told clean the empty rooms."

The urge to cry tugs down the corners of my mouth. I have to find someone who will explain this. I need to know where and why he has gone. How can there be a Lilliput Project without George?

A hand waves at me from behind a tree. It's Mr. Coxworth. He's scraping bits of bark off of the tree into a plastic bag, but he stops and lifts his sunglasses when I fly up to him.

"Where's George? What happened?"

"Ah. I knew it wouldn't take you long to notice. The white witch thought you'd be slower on the uptake. George received his notice two days after you left for Hawaii."

"But why?"

Mr. Coxworth sighs and raises his eyebrows at me. And then I know. It was George who turned in Dr. Christiansen and she found out. She got rid of him before he would have a chance to tell me anything more.

"Did you find anything out from him?" I ask.

Mr. Coxworth nods slowly. "Why don't we have a chat at my house? You can meet me there in a few minutes. Go ahead and stop by your place and make sure everything is in order and then come on over."

I nod numbly.

My treehouse looks the same as it did when it left, except my garden is one giant weed patch. I try not to look at it as I fly to the front door and step inside my home.

The ceiling and window have been repaired, which is good. The wallpaper has been painted over with a boring beige color to hide the water stains, and the desk is organized. There are no signs of my old computer. A felt-bound journal now sits where the keyboard used to be. I open it and run my finger along the binding. There are only six stitches holding the entire thing together. George would never buy me something so poorly made.

I suddenly don't want to be in here anymore. Every single piece of furniture, every decoration, was a gift from George. I run back onto the porch and see Jane lugging a huge bag toward me.

"No, don't!" But it's too late. She's already dropped the bag right on top of whatever's left of my garden.

"Here are your fan letters! Dr. Christiansen decided you should be able to have these. It's good have you back! Did you have fun in Hawaii?"

"Yeah, it was super fun, Jane," I say with as much sarcasm as I can manage.

"I'm so jealous. I wish I could have gone. Oh well! Let me know when you're done, and I can put them somewhere else so they don't get rained on." She nods with a satisfied smile and then tromps through the woods.

Incredulous, I shake my head and wait for her to disappear. I'll check out the letters later. I really want to hear what Mr. Coxworth has to say.

He's sitting on his rotten dining room chair and sipping tea when I slip under his door. He waves me over, sets his mug between his knees. I settle onto my pincushion as he formulates his thoughts.

"I thought it would be easier to tell you here," he says with uncharacteristic carefulness. "George turned himself in."

"What? No."

He continues. "Apparently he was so guilt-ridden after you were forced to do the show that he went to the politiet and confessed he accidentally caused the deaths of the Thumbelinas. But, of course, Dr. Christiansen is still responsible. After all, she covered it up all this time, and this was her project."

I stand up. "I don't believe you. He wouldn't do that."

With a sigh, he gestures for me to sit back down. "Lina, I know you were very close, but you need to face the facts."

"You're telling me George killed six girls by accident and then lied about it, and you expect me to believe it? No one has protected me the way he has. Not even you."

His face turns to stone. "That is what happened."

"I have to go."

"Suit yourself. I'm sorry to be the one to tell you."

It doesn't make any sense. That isn't the George I know. Nope, not buying it for one second.

With my heart enclosed in steely resolve, I leave Mr. Coxworth's cottage and shake its dust off my feet.

CHAPTER 27

I SIT CROSS-LEGGED ON MY porch, glaring at nothing in particular and shaking head to toe. I don't believe him. There would have been something about George in the article I read in Hawaii if Mr. Coxworth is telling the truth. He has to be mistaken somehow. Maybe he needs to get his hearing checked again.

I fold my hands together and press them between my calves to keep them from trembling. I imagine George handling tiny baby girls, dropping them. Or would he have squeezed them too hard? I shake the horrifying images from my head. There is no way he could ever kill another person. Not even by accident.

No. I don't believe it. I won't.

"Hey, Lina!" It's Al, leading the rest of the Toms to my house.

I fight down a surge of annoyance. Can't I get a few minutes to myself? I have no desire to play the part of the gracious hostess right now.

A camera drone snaps off a brittle branch as it flies into the clearing. So that's why they're here—this is being filmed.

With a sigh, I unwrap my feet and wave.

"I hear we have fan letters!" Row exclaims as all six of them descend on the bag. I should have known they weren't all for me. Shrike and Al work on untying the knot while Blue hovers, arms folded, off to the side. The other three come to the porch, and I stand to greet them.

"Hi. Welcome to my house."

"Thanks!" Row stuffs his hands in his pockets, and my heart beats faster at the sight of him. He has dark circles under his eyes and I'm pretty sure he wore those clothes all last night, but he looks adorable in his sleepiness.

Crane and Perry give each other a look. "I guess we'll wait down there," Perry says with a grimace. Before I can stop them, they're gone.

"Do you want to come in?"

"Yeah, but I can't. We're under strict orders to stay where the camera can see us."

"You look like you didn't sleep a wink."

He grins. "That's because I didn't. I had a certain blonde-haired beauty on my mind." He blushes when he says "beauty."

"Are they letting you guys stay somewhere less prison-like now?"

"I'm not sure yet. I think they're preparing something for us in the old aviary? I don't know where that is. All of our stuff is in the dining hall for now." He rubs his hand up and down his arm and blinks as if he just woke up.

"I wonder how long we'll be here before we get shipped off to the next place."

"I'm not sure if we're going anywhere. You didn't see Dr. Christiansen almost get denied entry in customs?"

"What? No, I didn't."

"Yeah, I didn't hear everything, but I got the impression that the only reason they allowed her in is because she's a permanent resident. Something about a court case. I wonder if she'll have the same trouble if she tries to go to another country."

He still doesn't know about the Thumbelinas, and I wonder if I should tell him. A dark shadow passes over us—a drone drawing in for a closer shot.

Yeah, now's not the time.

"I can't wait to show you my house!" I exclaim as dramatically as I can. "But let's go look at our fan mail first!"

Row follows my lead down to the mail pile that the other Toms are already swimming in. Blue sits on the edge, taking it all in, but everyone else is buried to their waists in letters and cards.

"Most of it is for Row and Blue," Shrike whines. "And Lina."

"You have one here," says Perry, handing it to him. "And here's one for 'Pixie.' Geez, our fans can't even read."

I hold out my hand. "I'm pretty sure that's for me. Unless you think anyone would address you guys as 'pixies.' No? I didn't think so."

I stand on the edge and examine the envelope, my hands shaking. There's no return address and no name, but only one person in the whole world is allowed to call me "Pixie." I glance up at the camera drones. One is circling around my house and the others are in front of me and won't be able to see what I'm reading. I breathe a sigh of relief and slide my hand into the flap to tear it open. Inside, I find a single postcard with a picture of a falcon that is the spitting image of Petunia. Only three words are written on the other side in a scrawl I would recognize anywhere.

Don't trust anyone.

I lick my lips to force some life into them. My blood's run cold.

Row sees my terrified face and gently takes the postcard out of my hands. "Hey, what's wrong?"

"Nothing. I think it's…a stupid prank."

He flips the card over, and his jaw tightens as he reads the inscription. "That's a bit creepy." He takes my hand. "Lina, I'm sure it will be fine. No one can get into this place—it's got better security than a prison."

Yeah, that's what I'm afraid of.

I grab the card, kneel down, and stuff it into the bag.

"What are you doing?"

"Protecting the few freedoms we have left," I whisper.

"We should tell someone."

"Over my dead body. I do not want to be locked in that room again just because Dr. Christiansen is paranoid."

He clamps his mouth shut, but the frown remains. He won't tell. I'm counting on his silence.

We sit in silence as the other guys tear through the letters. Row doesn't open a single one of the cards addressed to him. When Shrike tries to pressure him into reading them, he only shrugs and says he doesn't care. Blue seems to have the same level of interest.

I can't stop thinking about George. Clearly he was the one who turned in Dr. Christiansen, and no one wants me to know why. And now Mr. Coxworth… Why does he have to be involved in this? Why is he trying to turn me against George? I spent hours playing in his cottage, making friends with his mice and the cutout paper dolls of the pop-up books. He paid me in illegal tobacco for my help in his research. How could he possibly be on Dr. Christiansen's side?

Is anyone who I think they are? I poke at my kneecap. Am I still my old self or have I changed beyond recognition since I've started this show? I thought I was doing this to ensure Jack's safety, but I'm not sure anymore. Is it right to trade my own free will for the safety of someone else if it allows a perpetrator to keep on victimizing even more people?

I don't know. I have no idea what I can be sure of anymore.

A hand on my shoulder. "Lina? Are you listening?"

"What?"

"She's asking what you want for dinner," says Blue.

"She" is a young woman in catering get-up, holding a tablet at the ready. I would much rather eat food cooked in my own kitchen, but I imagine I don't have much of a choice here.

"What are my options?"

"Vegetarian or vegan?"

I should have guessed. "Vegetarian."

"Thank you. And what will you have?" She collects the Toms' preferences before heading off to the kitchen.

"What was that for anyway?" I ask.

"She said something about a banquet."

Huh. Banquets are infrequent around here. Yet again, nothing is normal lately. I shrug it off and excuse myself to get ready. I need a long, hot bath and some room to think.

With both hands, I crank the wheel above my tub that opens the faucet. Hot water pours down, filling the bath almost instantly. I turn the wheel back to "off" and slip out of my clothes before sinking into the tub. I didn't bother to light the votive stub in the corner. Instead, all of the lights are off. The last of the sunlight leaks through the crack in the curtains and spills onto the floor in a weak line of orange.

I slide down until my wing joints hit the top of the tub. I wish I could go all the way down until my chin touches the water like I've seen women do in movies, but that's a physical impossibility. I lean forward and submerge my face and head instead. The heat eddies across my skin in delicious little currents. When my skin feels as though it will start melting off, I pull my head out of the water and breathe deep.

I hold up my hand and count the things I've discovered on my fingers.

I know Dr. Christiansen has a court appearance in just under a month.

I know she had something to do with the deaths of six girls.

I know George turned her in and Mr. Coxworth is trying to keep me from finding out any more information about the case.

And I know Dr. Christiansen is working on something else, something new, and she needs money. Is it another sort of human mutant? Maybe something with accelerated growth so the other Toms can have girlfriends their own size.

I shake my head. That can't be it. She wouldn't put so much time and energy into something so six teenaged guys won't be lonely. That's not who she is.

My arms and legs are starting to look pruney, so I hop out of the tub with questions still on my mind. Where is George now? And what exactly did he mean by not trusting anyone? Is there *no one* at all in the entire compound who is honest?

Row's face pops out of the background of my confused thoughts, and the relief is instant. Blue is another possibility, but he's always so cryptic and distant. I'd hardly think of him as reliable. But Row I can trust.

I nod my head emphatically at no one in particular and then laugh at my own antics. I towel myself off and throw on a bathrobe.

Someone knocks on the front door and nearly knocks it in.

"Lina?" asks a muffled voice. I open it slowly in case it's a man, but it's Susanna. "I'm supposed to get you for hair and makeup. Oh good, you had a chance to take a bath and relax. I was worried you might not."

"Yeah, I'm all clean now and sort of relaxed. What time is it?"

"5:30. The banquet is in an hour, so we need to hurry."

"All right, I'll be out in a minute." To myself, I grumble, *Geez, what's the rush? Couldn't they have waited until everyone's not so jet-lagged and exhausted?* I comb my hair and throw on a button-up dress. I'm still damp and sweaty from my bath and my hair is soaked, but I'm ready.

Back in my former cell, Susanna, Tina, and the rest of the fashion minions transform me into a painted doll. As Susanna puts the final touches on my makeup, I glance up through her looking glass at her distorted face.

"What's this banquet for anyway?"

"I heard it's for some employee's anniversary."

I frown. "Who?"

"I'm not sure. I didn't really care enough to pay attention. Everybody blends together after a while here." She flicks her brush across the apples of my cheeks and smiles. "Everyone except you and a few other people."

"Why thanks. It's so comforting to know I stand out from boring people."

She purses her lips but says nothing. Her brusque brush movements are enough to clue me in that something is wrong.

"What?"

She raises an eyebrow as if to ask me "what?" right back.

"You look upset."

A muscle twitches near her mouth, but she stays quiet for an uncomfortable minute.

"You don't know how to take a compliment, Lina. You're so...prickly sometimes."

I'm taken aback, but her words ring true. "I'm sorry."

She shrugs and says it's okay, but she still looks annoyed. Susanna holds a mirror so I can inspect my makeup. "You look beautiful."

My heart feels too heavy now to accept I am attractive as a human being, but keeping her comment in mind, I say nothing except, "Thank you. You did a great job."

She smiles in reply, but her eyes remain flat and listless. "Off you go. Get some clothes on."

My stylist takes over and dresses me in a light blue wrap dress with silver accents. I swivel side to side, and the skirt swishes along with me.

"I like it," I say, pleasantly surprised. As I twirl around, I catch Susanna watching me with serious eyes.

"You look nice," she says with little enthusiasm. "You'd better get going. Eat lots of good food for me."

I hesitate, but after searching her tanned face for some sign that the tension has dissipated and finding nothing, I head off for the banquet. Tonight, the door to my old bedroom is wide open. The hallway is fully illuminated, and I fly out of the building without the slightest trouble.

I rub my arms to chase away the chill from the autumn night. It's not even 6:30, but darkness has already fallen and the road to the dining hall is far too quiet. One lonely lamppost illuminates my frosty breaths. Winter will be here soon.

The warmth and light of the dining hall draws me closer, breaking through the barren trees and falling full on my face as I approach. A banner hangs above the front doors, proclaiming, "Congratulations, Dr. Coxworth!"

So that's who this is all for.

Wait a minute. *Doctor?* Since when?!

A couple of waiting photographers see me and start snapping pictures. I wave and pose, then they open the doors for me and I find my place next to the Toms at the head table. Row's saved a seat for me, and I slide in next to him. He's looking dapper in a dark green button-up shirt and khaki pants. Blue, as usual, keeps his title of "Sexiest Tom" with a wide-cuffed cerulean blue shirt. He's got one extra button unbuttoned, and his hair is a tousled mop of bluish black. Al's dark skin looks even richer against his bright white shirt. The other guys are looking pretty standard, but handsome.

"Hey, gorgeous," Row says, draping his arm around my shoulders.

I exhale for what seems like the first time today. He seems to carry a bubble of "safe" around him wherever he goes, and it would be nice to stay inside it for a while.

Shrike clears his throat and glares into his water glass, but I ignore him.

"You're looking great," I say to Row. "Everyone does." He gives me a squeeze, and I melt against him.

"Are you feeling better?"

"A little. Thanks. I think I could sleep forever."

He laughs. "You and me both."

He rubs my shoulder with his thumb, and I'm momentarily tongue-tied. I scan the room to see who is here, but I only see Lilliput employees and a couple of people from the film crew. It's a small gathering. I catch Dr. Christiansen's eye. She's watching me with a smug expression on her face. I whip my head away and lean forward so I'm no longer in her line of sight.

Dinner is served. As the last bits of food are scraped from our plates and napkins are folded, Dr. Christiansen takes the stage.

"Welcome and thank you for being here to honor an employee who has outlasted all of the others. Dr. Coxworth has graciously lent us his mind and scientific prowess for these past twenty years. He was one of Lilliput's first researchers, and it was his breakthrough findings that allowed us to create Lina and the Toms. We hope to have him with us for many more years. Please welcome Dr. Coxworth."

I'm frozen in my seat, a boa constrictor of panic wrapping around my throat. Twenty years?

I started working here when you were three years old…

He lied to me. He's been lying all along.

CHAPTER 28

DR. COXWORTH TAKES THE STAGE, thanks Dr. Christiansen for her kind introduction, and begins his speech, but I can't focus on anything he is saying. How could I believe a word of it anyway?

Shrike leans across the table with a devilish grin. "I've heard he's a real crackpot. Is it true?"

"Shut up, Shrike," Crane whispers.

Shame seeps through my heart. A crackpot? I've never thought of him that way before. He was always just eccentric old Mr. Coxworth to me—someone I loved and respected. I already knew he was lying about George, but some part of me still wanted to believe he was doing it out of a desire to protect me. Now I know he's been deliberately deceiving me.

Tears prickle at the corners of my eyes, and I angrily wipe them away. I have never experienced humiliation and betrayal on this level before. I want to stand and scream "I *trusted* you!" Instead, I fumble around under the table for Row's hand and grasp it like a drowning woman would a life preserver.

"I need to talk to you," I whisper into his ear.

He frowns. "Now?"

"After the speeches are done."

"Okay. Is everything all right?"

My breaths are coming so fast I feel as if I'm going to have an asthma attack. "No," I croak.

His green eyes are full of questions, but he says nothing more. He squeezes my hand and turns his gaze to the stage.

The rest of the speech goes by in a whirl. I don't hear anything Dr. Coxworth says, and he never once makes eye contact with me. I'm holding Row's hand so tight my grip is getting slippery from sweat.

When the applause has faded and Dr. Coxworth has stepped down with his framed certificate, I give Row's hand a tug.

"Let's wait until a few others get up," he whispers.

An eternity passes, but eventually some of the staff scoot their chairs back from the tables and begin to mingle. Row stands and, still holding my hand, leads me outside.

"Over here," I say and fly around the corner of the building and onto the roof where we can't be seen. The musty stench of damp, rotten leaves floats up from the gutter, but we sit down anyway on the tiles. The cold penetrates my skirt, and I shift around, trying to get comfortable.

"What's all this about?" Row asks.

"I need to tell somebody," I begin. So I spill everything, from the deformed cat to the threats against Jack if I don't cooperate. I tell him how Dr. Coxworth deceived me into believing he was on my side and the court case against Dr. Christiansen. His brows furrowed, Row listens without interrupting. When I'm finished, I exhale in relief and laugh.

"What are you laughing at?"

"It just feels so good to tell someone. It's like a huge weight has been pulled off of me."

He smiles, but his eyes look troubled.

"You don't believe me?"

"I didn't say that. It's a lot to, you know, absorb all at once. I need a minute." He falls into silence, and I pick at my fingernails as I wait for him to finish thinking.

"Lina, did you ever find out what they were doing to that cat?"

"No. I couldn't find any clues."

He nods. His whole body looks stiff and uneasy. "Where was it?"

"In the research building. We could try to sneak in later."

"No, I don't want to do that," he says hastily.

"Why not? Maybe we could get some answers, and it would be easier with two people. One of us could keep watch and—"

"I just don't want to."

"Seriously? That's it?"

He bristles. "You're acting like I owe you some sort of explanation. I don't. This is your crackpot idea. You go ahead if you want."

Speechless, I lean back against my hands. The grit from the roof digs into my palms, but I don't move. He's never talked to me like this before. I didn't even know this side of him existed.

I swallow my irritation and shock and manage to speak evenly. "I'm surprised that the guy who snuck out of his hotel room in Hawaii is too chicken to go investigate a situation that could hurt other people."

"Think about it, Lina. If they're experimenting on animals or even people... Do you really want to see that?"

"Wow, is that how you stay so cheerful? Do you ignore anything that's evil or ugly?"

He stands and shakes off his pants. "Yeah, okay, I'm done here. I'll see you inside."

He's actually leaving. What a coward. "That's right. Just walk away and keep on smiling!" I shout after him.

Without so much as a reply or backward glance, he launches himself off the roof and disappears.

"Coward," I hiss. "Freaking coward." I smack my fist against the roof.

Well, if he won't come with me, I'll go by myself. I'll wait until everyone is sleeping, and then I'll investigate. My pulse quickens as I make my decision, and I smile maniacally into the darkness. The last time I went to the research building, I ended up having to escape. Now I'm going to break in.

***

I lie on my couch with my feet toward the window. It's hard to believe I came crashing through that glass only a month ago, but I found a shard of it in the cushions when I first laid down. I nearly skewered my arm on it but luckily came away with only a small cut.

I hold the glittering shard to the candlelight and turn it around and around, remembering my broken computer. Ages have passed since I last spoke with Jack. Will I ever get to talk to him again? The familiar emptiness yawns open in my gut, stretching itself ever wider until I'm breathless from the ache. My desk looks so very empty without my monitor, without Jack's face smiling at me from the screen. I didn't realize how lonely I was before I met him, but now that I'm lying in this silent room, my aloneness is hard to ignore. It presses in on me from all sides.

About three months ago, while training with George, one of the other falcons (not Petunia—she was injured at the time) managed to grab hold of my right foot. He whipped me around so hard I almost blacked out. George caught up and hooded him just as I saw that horrible blunted beak aiming at my head. I looked that bird square in the eye, and I thought that maybe if I was brave and sure enough, I could win, I could scare him off. I thought I was still invincible.

But I was wrong. The only thing that could reign in the creature was force, and if George hadn't gotten there in time… A broken ankle and lots of cuts and bruises were the extent of my injuries, but it could have been much, much worse.

That night, I was so shaken I couldn't sleep. It wasn't the pain that kept me awake or even the danger I'd avoided. It was the fact that I knew there was nothing I could have done to escape. Even with all my training and all of my education, my best simply wasn't good enough. It was the first time I'd ever experienced hopelessness.

Jack had known something was wrong when I talked to him later, but I couldn't articulate what was going on inside me without revealing my secret. I told him I was bitten by a dog and broke my ankle when I ran away, but my explanation didn't cover why I was so profoundly affected by the whole incident. That night, he insisted he would stay by his computer and watch over me while I slept on the sofa.

"But that's ridiculous," I said. "Even if something happened, what would you do?"

He held up his phone. "I've got the Danish police on speed dial right now."

"Which address will you send them to?"

"I'll have them look up your IP address."

I had to give it to him. It was actually a clever plan, and it didn't involve me divulging where I lived, which was something I refused to do. So I told him to wait a moment and I snapped the lens cover onto the camera. After I'd changed into my pajamas and cloaked my wings with my blanket, I uncovered the lens and curled into a ball on the couch. He leaned back against his chair and pulled out one of his well-worn paperbacks and began to read.

"What—you're not going to watch me?" I asked.

He raised an eyebrow. "I thought that would be a little creepy."

"I'm kidding."

"I'm Jack NO stalk, remember?"

I smiled and snuggled down into the cushions without ever taking my gaze off of him. He checked on me now and again, then went back to his book. I fell asleep imagining he was really right there in the room with me. It was such a comforting thought that I dozed right off.

Tonight, the ache subsides as I remember how it felt to fall asleep knowing someone was watching out for me. I cling to that small, slippery bit of happiness and slip into sleep.

I dream of strange things. Bears with bat wings and crocodile tails who have the souls of humans. I am one of them, and I keep screaming to Jack that it's me! It's really me! But everything I say comes out as a deafening roar and he runs away. I chase him and chase him, but then I realize he will never stop running. He will never love me this way. But I can't stop trying. I have to get him to *see* it's me.

So I follow him pell-mell down a path by a creek. The rushing water drowns out all of my roars, but finally, I'm able to corner him and I'm so full of joy that now he has to listen to me. He has no choice. I open my mouth to speak, but he covers his ears and screams. It's such a strange sound. Muffled and small, as though it's coming from a long way away. But he's right here in front of me. He screams again, and something doesn't seem quite right. I listen harder. Another cry.

I awake into darkness. It takes me a moment to figure out where I am because the candle has long since blinked out. I lie there, motionless and covered in sweat. My dress sticks to my legs and back, so I peel it away to let the cool night air from the open window work its magic.

There it is again. I wasn't dreaming the scream. The sound of an animal crying in pain raises all the hair on my body.

I bolt off the couch and fumble around on the desk for the old watch face I use as a clock. 12:42 AM. It's time to go and investigate.

My heart thuds against my ribs as I change into darker clothes. I'm not even sure if it makes sense to wear black to go search in a laboratory, but it's the most logical choice and I can't think of anything else to wear. I hold a white shirt against my skin and check myself out in the mirror. Maybe white really would be a better camouflage.

And then it strikes me how utterly absurd it is that I'm debating what to wear at *this* moment. Of all times. I toss the white shirt on the bed and head out the door.

I fly through the branches of the trees, mimicking the flight of a bird. No one would ever guess it was me, even if they were looking hard. Every so often I pause and listen, but I don't hear the cries of agony anymore.

The research building is too well-lit for me fly in from the side without being spotted, so I climb high into the sky and cut over to land on the roof. Once I'm there, I crouch down and hold my wings flat. There's no disguising their iridescent blue, so if anyone spots me, it's going to be because of them. I run around the edge, taking care not to kick any loose bits of dirt into the gutter.

I don't see anyone. I don't hear anyone either. The silence seems too absolute. Almost eerie. The hair on the back of my neck prickles, and I get the distinct feeling I'm being watched. Slowly, I turn around.

Along the ridge of the roof, a pair of wings flick up and then flash out of sight, but I can still see the silhouette of their owner against the moonlit sky. The person's build could belong to Row or maybe Shrike even. Whoever it is, they know I've seen them.

What to do? Try to sneak around and figure out who it is first or take the direct approach?

Well, I've never been a subtle sort of girl. I crouch down and then sprint forward, all muscles engaged for maximum speed. My target is slow to react, but he doesn't even try to fly. He stands and steps tentatively away.

It's Row.

I glare at him. "What are you doing here?"

"I heard the screams, and I changed my mind," he says sheepishly.

"And you didn't even bother to come and get me. How long have you been here?"

"I've already scouted it. There's no way in and all the lights are off."

"You checked all the windows, all the doors?"

He rolls his eyes. "Yes, Lina. I'm not an idiot."

"Good. I'm glad to hear it. I was having doubts about that earlier." He winces at the low blow, but it feels so good to deliver it. "I'm going to have a look myself if you don't mind."

"I'll come with you."

It's a long shot, but I'm hoping the mouse hole I used to escape last time is still there.

And…no, it's not. The underside of the porch is even swept clean of the mouse droppings I fell into.

"Shoot," I whisper. "Wait, I have an idea. This way."

On the other side is the women's bathroom, and as it happens, Jane has a tendency to leave it open. She's got the worst stomach problems in the compound, and she gets really embarrassed about it, so she cracks the window to air the place out.

We're in luck. It'll be a tight squeeze, but it's open all right.

"I don't know how I missed that," Row says with a nervous laugh.

I have a theory that he didn't actually want to see it because then he wouldn't have to go inside, but it's probably best I don't tell him that.

I grab hold of the inside ledge and hoist myself through the crack. Halfway through, something snags, and I hear a sound like the tearing of paper accompanied by a pain so sharp I can feel it all along my spine. I hold my breath, my heart pounding.

"Row," I whisper through clenched teeth. "I'm stuck. My wings are caught." I bite my lip and squeeze the tears out of my eyes. "I think I tore one."

I feel him next to me, investigating the situation, and I hope with all my being it's not a bad tear. A small hole isn't a big deal, although I won't fly as fast, but a big one… That could ground me until I get medical attention.

Which means asking Dr. Christiansen for help and she'll want to know how I did it. I sigh and hang on tighter. My arms are burning from holding myself so still.

"Did you find it?"

"Yeah." His voice is grim. "Hang on, let me get you unsnagged. Don't let go."

I wince as he fumbles some more, and then the pulling sensation goes away. Most of the pain leaves, too, and I let out a breath I didn't realize I was holding.

"How bad is it?"

"About an inch. I'll have to carry you."

I groan. "Seriously?"

"Yeah. You're lucky you didn't rip one of the major veins."

"Lucky" isn't a word I would use right now.

"I'll carry you down to the ground, and you can try to fly if you want. Maybe you still can."

He holds my waist as I slide through the crack.

"Easy," he says. "I don't want you to fall."

"That makes two of us."

He chuckles softly, and I wrap my arm around his neck once I'm all the way through. He holds me tightly to himself, and even though I try to look casual by turning my head away, I can still feel the heat from his muscular body through my clothes. My cheeks flush so hot I am almost certain he can see me blushing even though it's dark.

"Hang on," he says as he squeezes me even tighter and pushes off the wall. He sets me down on the ground and backs away.

I extend my wings and check for the tear. One section flaps like a flag in the wind. I flutter as hard as I can, but I can't get enough oomph to get off the ground. It's not going to happen.

"Well," Row says. "It's a good thing I decided to come tonight after all."

I imagine myself hanging from the window all night, unable to get down or to crawl inside, and I shudder. "Yeah, I'm really glad you did."

"Shall I take you home?"

"I suppose."

He cocks his head to the side. "Why are you upset? There's nothing else we can do here now."

"I really wanted to look around because I thought it was the right thing to do. I know there's nothing I can do about it now, but I reserve the right to be disappointed anyway."

"Or you could decide to look on the bright side, even though it's hard. It's up to you how much you allow ugly, evil things to affect how you feel."

"Okay, I'm sorry about earlier. I shouldn't have said those things."

"Well, you were sort of right and that's why I came."

"Thanks."

He holds out his arms, and I wrap my arm around his neck again. He hoists me up princess-style and carries me toward home.

It's so strange to allow him to do the flying for me, knowing I will fall to my death if he lets go. I lay my head against his shoulder and try to relax, but I can't stop thinking about my wings. The last thing I want to do is ask Dr. Christiansen for help. She'll want to know how I tore it, and I'm a rotten liar. I could ask George to fix it. He's repaired the wings of several birds...

George is gone. The realization is a punch in the gut. I don't know how I'll ever be able to get used to his absence. That yawning ache opens again in my stomach, and I hold my breath, waiting for the pain to ease.

"Ouch. You've got some strong fingers."

"What? Oh." I've been unwittingly digging my fingers into the side of his neck. "I'm sorry."

"Anything on your mind?"

Tears spring into my eyes, and I swallow down the sob pushing its way against my throat. "Yeah," I say, my voice hoarse. "I'm tired of losing people. And I'm trying so hard to be brave, but I'm nothing more than a chicken most of the time. A very small chicken."

He laughs just as another muffled scream comes from the buildings behind us. It wails into the night and then suddenly stops midway through as though someone cut away its owner's life.

"Row," I whisper.

"I know." He turns around and flies back but stops short of the building and lands high in the branches of a tree.

"Why are we stop—" He clamps a hand over my mouth, and then I see her. Dr. Christiansen walks toward us still dressed in her pajamas, but with a coat thrown on. Apparently we weren't the only ones to hear the noise. She presses her thumb to the lock reader, opens the door, and goes inside. Lights turn on throughout the building. The silhouette of another person—I can't tell who—runs toward her. The other person gestures wildly and I can hear faint hints of their conversation, but Dr. Christiansen is her usual icy self. They walk off and disappear from our view.

"Can we get closer?" I ask.

"All right." He picks me up again and flies to the roof. Here, at least, I can run. I sprint across the ridge to the other side and stop at the edge to listen. Low voices leak through the walls, but I can't decipher what they're saying. They drift into silence as they move into the heart of the building.

A cricket chirps into the night. He must be the only one left—all of his brothers and sisters have succumbed to the frosts. He sings his solo into the silent night.

The front door opens and clanks shut with a bang. We run noiselessly and get to the gutter in time to see Jane turning around in confused circles, her trembling hands wrapped around some unmoving thing inside a piece of cloth.

Another bang. Dr. Christiansen walks out into the yard.

"But...but what do I do with it?" Jane asks.

"Incinerate it."

CHAPTER 29

JANE STANDS IN THE CLEARING, staring after Dr. Christiansen's retreating figure. Her coat hangs loosely around her shoulders, several sizes too big, and for the first time, I notice huge dark circles under her eyes.

"But I…I don't know how to do that," she says in a small voice to no one in particular. The doctor is already out of earshot.

She lifts one shoulder and wipes her eyes against it as the strangled cry of a wounded animal escapes her lips.

"…can't…I can't…" is all I can make out. She opens her hands, but her fingers are in my way. I can't see what she's holding. Whatever it is, she's talking to it in between burbled sobs.

I press my fingers to my lips. I can't seem to register what I'm seeing. My mind can't process what could possibly make Jane so upset. Jane who happily experimented on a cat. Jane who tried to catch me as though I were nothing more than an escaped bird.

It has to be a person. All the facts scream that it's a tiny person, but I can't seem to feel anything in response. Shouldn't I be screaming? Or at least crying? I pinch my arm, trying to force some feeling through my stupor. I glance at Row; his face has gone white in the moonlight. He meets my eyes, and that's when the full tidal wave of emotion hits me.

I sink to my knees and clutch my hand over my mouth as I my throat tightens and convulses. Over and over again, I gag, and it's all I can do to keep my dinner down.

"Lina," Row whispers. He points at Jane who is walking off into the forest.

I don't have to ask him to follow her. He holds out his arms, and I grasp his neck and we're off, flying through the branches. Jane stops near a large tree trunk and kneels down in the frost-covered leaves. Gently, she places her bundle next to her, taking care to ensure it stays wrapped up. Then she digs with her bare hands.

Every so often, she stops, glances around, and wipes her nose before continuing her grave-digging. When she finishes, she places the bundle inside and buries it.

Jane stands, crosses herself with unsure movements, and bows her head for a few moments before shuffling through the forest toward her dormitory.

I grasp Row's ice-cold hand. His jaw is locked tight, and his nostrils are flared.

"We should go look," I whisper when I'm certain Jane can't hear me.

"No!" he shouts. I jump as he flings away my hand. "Heck no, I am not going to go and dig up that body to see who it is and how exactly they died. We both know *what* it is already. It's a person. I don't need to see the gruesome evidence. It's bad enough imagining it in my head."

"But Row, what if there are more? What if that's one of the Thumbelinas?"

"So what if there are? Digging up a dead body isn't going to help them. We'll…think of some way to help them."

"Yeah, but—"

"Look, Lina, you may get your way most of the time, but this isn't one of those times. You're not going to manipulate me into doing this." He folds his arms as indignant fire burns in his eyes.

I raise my eyebrows. "I get my way most of the time? Oh really? That's definitely news to me." I'm losing it. Tears run down my face, their heat evaporating into the chilly night air. I can't stop my lower lip from trembling. He thinks I'm *manipulative*? That is just too much.

He exhales loudly and covers his face with his hands.

I brush past him and begin making my way down the tree trunk by stuffing my hands and feet into cracks in the bark.

"Hold on a minute. What are you doing?"

"What does it look like?"

"You could fall. Come on, let me take you home." He extends his wings and flies behind me. I can feel his hands at my sides, and the urge to kick backward into his stomach overwhelms me.

"Don't touch me, Row. Go home. You don't want to be here, remember? I can do this myself." And I can. I'm good at climbing as long as there are enough footholds, and this tree has plenty.

"All right, I won't touch you. But I'm not leaving until you're safely down."

Much to my annoyance and relief, he flies behind me the whole way down and then scoots out of my way when I stomp toward the grave. I claw at the frozen dirt, and it's a lot harder than I thought.

"That will take forever," Row says.

"Then why don't you stop ogling and help me?"

"Lina, it's almost three o'clock in the morning. I haven't slept since...I don't even know when. We were on a plane all night. Don't you think it would be a better idea to come back here in two nights after your date with Shrike? You can get your wings fixed and bring digging tools and go to town."

I keep digging, but I'm not listening to him anymore. There might be another way to get the information that I want straight from Dr. Christiansen herself, but it means compromising Jack's safety.

My fingers touch something soft, and I scream and scramble away.

"What?! What did you find?!" Row is at my side, holding my shaking shoulders.

I catch my breath and wait for my heart to slow its panicked beating, then I crawl to inspect what my fingers just found. A corner of the death shroud pokes through the dirt. It was cloth that I touched.

"Grief, Lina. You almost killed me," Row says, his hand over his heart. I stare at him, his words striking my heart. He reminds me so much of Jack right now with the shadows masking the color of his hair. His frame is so similar.

"If I don't do something," I say, measuring each word, "you actually might die. We all could die from her experiments."

He nods, but barely.

I swallow down the rising panic and begin digging again around the exposed cloth. After a few minutes, Row joins me.

"I...I feel something," he says before leaping to his feet and running to vomit under a nearby leaf. I can smell my own bile rising in my throat as I tug the cloth away.

"You might want to stay over there," I choke out. A moon-white arm the size of my own, broken in several places, disappears into the rest of the still-buried cloth. Whoever it was painted her fingernails a brilliant shade of purple before she died.

Breathe in, breathe out. A tsunami of tears breaks through my flimsy courage dam. How could anyone do this to another human being? Who was this girl, and why did she believe them? How could they utterly destroy her and then cover it up?

"You're right," I manage to say in between sobs. "I wish I hadn't seen this." I carefully wrap the arm back up and begin the process of reburying her.

Row helps me, but at a slower pace, as though he's struggling with his thoughts.

"Did you see what she looked like?" he asks.

"No. Just her arm. That was enough."

"What do we do now?"

"I have to stop Dr. Christiansen somehow."

I shove the dirt into place, and Row helps me cover the grave with leaves. Then he carries me home with a promise to come and get me in a few hours for lunch.

I know what I have to do now. I just have to figure out how.

CHAPTER 30

SPEARS OF SUNLIGHT STAB AT my eyes long before I plan to wake up. I forgot to shut my curtains again. I could get up and close them, but my body thinks otherwise. So instead I bury my face against the pillow and try to fall asleep again, but now that the events of last night are replaying inside my mind, sleep is impossible.

It was only a few hours ago, but I'm so jetlagged my sense of time is all jacked up. What day is my date with Shrike again? Today or tomorrow?

I stumble out of bed, still wearing the same clothes from yesterday, and remember my torn wing. Crap. And I don't have any food in the kitchen either. Still, I bang through all the cupboards anyway. All I find is a single half of a walnut. That's not really my idea of a balanced breakfast, but now's not the time to be picky. So I chop it up, dump it in a bowl, and sit on the couch to eat and think.

The old watch on the wall tells me it's seven in the morning. If this was a date day, Susanna would already be here, so that means I'm not expected to show my face until 9:00 for the production meeting. And since I'm not going to walk half a mile to the main buildings, I won't be showing. So I can expect a visit from Dr. Christiansen at approximately 9:20. I have two hours to figure out what I'm going to say.

I wait on my porch. The morning frost still clings to the remnants of my garden and the leaves scattered along the ground. I pull my blanket coat tighter around my shoulders to shut out the chill. An unexpected peace has

197

settled into my soul, even though my heart is pounding hard. For the first time since this whole show started, I am no longer crushed by helplessness.

Snapping twigs and the crunch of boots against frozen earth tell me Dr. Christiansen is coming long before she walks around the hedge. I take a deep breath and stand up.

Her usual confidence melts off her face when she realizes I'm expecting and prepared for her arrival.

"You are late, Lina."

"I'm not coming."

Her mouth twitches. "You realize—"

"I heard the screaming last night, so I went to see what was going on, and I saw you and Jane come out with something…something dead. And it wasn't an animal. I'm not going on any more dates until you tell me what is going on."

She says nothing, and that's a little unnerving, so I continue. "And I know about the Thumbelinas. Is that who you killed last night? One of them? Have you been hiding them somewhere else like you did with the Toms?"

A smirk cracks her icy expression. "It would behoove you to keep your nose out of matters you clearly know nothing about. Especially considering the consequences could be severe."

"I think you're bluffing. And I'm not going to be your pawn any longer." I hold my chin up and try to look more confident than I'm feeling.

She straightens her posture and smoothes her coat. "Very well then. We will simply take the show in a new direction."

"What does that mean?"

Her smile horrifies me. "You will find out soon enough."

***

Hours later, she reappears with Jane. I'm wading into my blackberry plants to try and find one that's still good to eat when they close in on me. I can't fly, but it wouldn't make a difference anyway since they've brought the drones with them. Jane scoops me up and tosses me into my carrier. It seems she used up all her gentleness last night because I hit the plastic back pretty hard.

When they let me loose inside my old prison cell, the hair and makeup team is already waiting. This time, Dr. Christiansen stays and watches the whole process.

"It doesn't matter how you dress me or what you put on my face! I'm not going on your show!"

She only stares at me with condescending eyes as Tina tugs at my hair.

"Doctor, there's a rip in her wing," Susanna says.

"She will not be needing it."

Panic sets fire to my veins when I hear those words. What will she do with me now?

CHAPTER 31

AS SOON AS THE DOORS of my carrier are opened, bright lights shine directly into my eyes. Someone's hand reaches through the white and plucks me out while I'm still blinking.

When my eyes adjust to the light, I find myself standing on a table in one of the conference rooms with a green screen behind me. A monitor is rolled out and positioned in front of me.

"Let's test the sound," says an engineer behind a laptop.

"Sure," I say. "How about I say something like, 'I'm not doing this?'"

Dr. Christiansen steps in front, arms folded and blonde hair glowing in the light. "Tell us exactly what you think, Lina."

"Wow, I think this is the first time you've ever asked me what *I* think, how I feel. Well, here it is. I think you're a control freak, and you disgust me. Do you even have a soul in there? You've destroyed my life, and who knows how many other people you've ruined as well? I don't want to have anything to do with you anymore. Ever." I take a deep breath, still shaking with fury.

Dr. Christiansen shows no change in emotion. It's as if nothing I said affected her at all. I want to kick in those pearly white teeth of hers to see her suffer as her victims have suffered. Still, she smirks at me, and inside I'm a frustrated five-year-old again, screaming at the top of lungs to get her attention.

"Are you quite finished?" she asks, but she doesn't wait for an answer. "Good. Put him on the screen."

The monitor flickers to life, and the image of Jack sitting in a studio fills the screen. My heart plummets into my shoes and I open my mouth, but nothing comes out. He looks perfectly fine, although they must not be broadcasting my image back to him yet because he's looking around the room he's in with a hopeful expression on his face The contours of his face are sharper than I remember. Funny how a simple change of lighting can make someone look so different.

"We have decided to give you a choice, Lina." Dr. Christiansen speaks her well-rehearsed lines with cold precision. "Jack has agreed to undergo our new, groundbreaking procedure to become your size."

No, this can't be happening. So that's what they've been doing—testing out their shrink ray gun on people. They'll kill him. Maybe they even intend for him to die.

"If you choose him, we will fly him here to Denmark with all expenses paid, and it will take about a month for the process to be complete. His family will receive a brand-new home, and they will never have to worry about a thing for the rest of their lives."

No.

"A celebrity wedding planner will assist you in putting together the wedding of your dreams, and you will spend a week honeymooning in each of the following places: Egypt, Italy, and Hawaii. Now, let's get Jack on the line. Jack, can you see Lina? She's right here."

His whole face lights up. Oh, how I have missed this man.

"Hey there, Thumbelina!"

Oh God, this can't be happening. I need to force some measure of happiness onto my face before he thinks I'm not happy to see him.

"Hi, Jack." I manage a weak smile. "I can't believe it's you." *I love you. I've missed you. How are you doing?* I want to say all of these things, but it's not the time. Not yet.

"I know," he says. "Um, I really thought I would never get to talk to you again."

It feels like someone is stepping on my chest. "Yeah, I...I didn't think we would either."

"Did they tell you they contacted me?"

I lick my lips. "No, they didn't."

Uncertainty flashes across his face. "Oh, I thought maybe this was your idea. Did they already tell you what they can do for us?"

"Yeah…"

"I can't believe this is possible. Man, I was so worried about you after the last time we talked and you vanished, but when I saw the news the next day, it just all came together." He laughs. "I can't believe you actually used 'Thumbelina' as part of your screen name. I should have guessed. You had so many weird pieces of furniture in your living room."

This is all too surreal. Is this really happening? Isn't he mad?

"I'm sorry, Jack. I should have told you."

He sobers a little, but the happy look remains. "Probably, but it's okay. I was upset about it for a couple of days, but I get it. I know why you did it. Anyway, it's all in the past, and I'm really excited that I can be with you now. They're going to take care of my family and everything, so there's nothing to worry about."

"No." I bite down on my lip until I taste blood.

"What?" He sits back, glances side to side.

"The procedure can kill you, Jack. I can't let you do it. They've killed people already—I don't even know how many!"

But the connection shorts out as I speak and Jack freezes on the screen. When he starts moving again, he looks confused.

I know what they're doing. They'll never let me tell him about the risks. The only way I can keep him from doing this is to break his heart. Permanently.

Dr. Christiansen watches me, waits for me to acknowledge that I understand what she is forcing me to do. Either choose Jack and let him do this or choose one of the Toms. I nod, hating her with every fiber of my being.

"I've already made my choice, Jack," I say. "I'm so sorry. I never wanted to have to do this."

Embarrassment flickers across his face. "What…what are you trying to tell me, Lina?"

"I told you I loved you, but I don't. I didn't know what I was saying, but I've fallen in love for real this time. I'm sorry."

Something in me dies as I watch humiliation transform into anger in his eyes. He shakes his head and blurts out a humorless laugh.

"So this is how it ends," he says. "You know, the way they described you to me, I thought they only made you tiny physically, but your heart is even smaller. Like a..." He stops to regain his composure before he spits out the words that slay me. "Like a germ."

His words knock the wind out of me. I clutch my belly and gasp for air as the monitor flicks off. Jack vanishes along with any shred of hope I still had.

***

After the studio lights have been turned off and I'm left in the dull sheen of the fluorescent bulbs, after I've caught my breath and regained my composure, I have a few fleeting moments to make a decision. Dr. Christiansen can no longer hurt Jack. He will never wish to be involved with her organization ever again.

And I have one card left to play.

"All right," I say. "I'll give you one more episode, and that's it. I've decided who I want to pick and I won't go through any more dates, so you can run your...I don't know what you would call it...final ceremony? I'll make my decision on camera. But that's it. I'm not dragging this out so you can make more money for your sick experiments. We both know your 'procedure' doesn't work."

She presses her lips together. She's thinking it over.

"You will cooperate for one final episode," she says. It's a statement, not a question.

"Yes."

She nods. "In one week, then."

It's done.

CHAPTER 32

THIS IS MY TRUE TALE now:

I live a cotton candy life on the ocean's shore. On my wedding day, I carried a bouquet of lollipops hand-selected by the man who loves me. I wore a short, white dress, and we danced on flower petals while our guests blew dandelion fluff into the air.

We are playing by the sea today. I stretch my toes down into heated sand while a smaller person with shimmering wings plays at my feet. His hair is blond, his eyes green like his father's. Row returns to us carrying ice cream cones. The little one squeals and leaps into the air, sending sand and laughter flying in every direction.

Row smiles his sparkling smile. He is kindness through and through.

I am happy that he is happy. I am proud that I have become a woman who loves well. It is what I like best about myself.

I fold my story inside of myself as I carefully chase a tear away from my eyeliner.

I'm inside of a freaking plastic tulip. Seriously, it's 2081 and they couldn't think of something better? I tuck my wings to the side and take a seat on the stool to wait.

My tulip is one of many inside the "Garden of Love"—a room full of artificial flowers, all tightly closed into buds. When Dr. Christiansen brought me here an hour ago, I was informed all of the Toms were already in their own tulips. I was sealed inside of mine for the ceremony.

The deal is they will announce the names of the Toms one by one and open their tulips. I have to wait until they call the Tom I want to pick, then I press the camouflaged button under the stool that triggers my tulip's opening mechanism. I will "bloom" for everyone to see, and it will be oh-so-romantic.

Right.

Someone sneezes nearby. "Bless you," I whisper.

I take a deep breath and knot my fingers together. My stomach has become home to a three-ring circus and the tumblers are performing. *Please don't let Jack be watching this,* I pray. *Please.* Not that it really matters.

I've made my decision. I think I can live with it, but I'm not sure. At least one person will be happy as a result. Maybe I can be happy by proxy.

I smooth out my long, pink silk gown. It's one of the least offensive of all of the outfits they've forced me to wear. It's a halter-top, and the neck is lined with purple sapphires. It actually looks sort of pretty next to my blue wings. I wouldn't have thought of the color combination myself, but it's not bad.

I lift my chin even though no one is here to see. I'm ready.

"And...we're live!" a production assistant calls. All rustling within the tulips stops. The show's theme song plays over the speakers.

Hurry it up please. Let's get this over with. I resist the urge to twist my skirt into a wrinkled mass. I settle for bouncing my knee instead.

"Ready in the garden!" the assistant shouts.

My heart beats so hard I can feel it moving the bobby pins in my hair.

The host's voice booms over the speakers, "Tom1!"

Crane. I can't see him, but I can picture his tulip opening into the silent loneliness. I bite my lip and pick at my fingernail.

Get ready.

"Tom2!"

It's Row. I fumble around under the stool for the button and press it. This is it. There's no going back now. I stand as fast as I can without tearing my dress, and the tulip begins to open. The stool is pulled through the trap door below.

The petals slowly press outward, and I catch my first glimpse of Row. His tulip is already fully bloomed, and his red-blond hair is afire in the studio lighting. My breath catches in my chest. His tux fits his muscular frame perfectly. His face breaks into a dazzling smile, and a glimmer of happiness ignites in my heart.

I manage a small step forward. Maybe if I just keep my eyes on him, I'll be okay and I can get through this. But something catches his eye off to the side, and a shocked expression replaces his trademark happy face. He glances at me and mouths three unmistakable words: "I'm so sorry."

I don't understand, so I follow his gaze, and as I turn my head, a blur of long brown hair and blue dress runs past me toward him. The hair is attached to a *girl*. A girl who is a head shorter than Row. A girl with no wings. She skips across a plastic pathway of leaves and runs straight into his arms. His shock transforms into joy, and he lets out a cry of amazement.

Daphne.

I stare at them. Row pulls her close, then holds her out to look at her before crushing her against himself again with unrestrained joy. I have never seen him like this before—this open and happy. His previous cheerfulness was but a shadow of this ecstasy. Did I ever even know him?

Nothing within me can make sense of what has happened. Each camera slowly turns toward the weeping couple until not a single one watches me anymore.

Stunned, I barely hear the production assistant bend down and ask me to exit stage right. Numb, I follow her direction and fly toward the door. I turn around before I walk out of the room, but all eyes are on Row and Daphne. I am invisible.

This show is no longer about me. It's someone else's fairytale.

CHAPTER 33

I'M ALL ALONE. I NEVER imagined it would end this way.

The door closes behind me, clicking shut with a finality I'm not quite ready for. I struggle to make sense of it all. Row's stories about the gardener's daughter come rushing back from my memory.

I had such a crush on her. I would have done anything for her.

Anything. Laughter rips out of me, beyond my control. I'm bending over at the waist, clutching my ribs, screaming in laughter. Tears run down my face. How could he do that to me? But of course he would. He loves her. He would do anything for her, including leading me on. I never would have guessed Dr. Christiansen gave him the same choice she offered me. Except Row probably didn't know about the failed animal testing. But the real question is: *When* did Dr. Christiansen offer to shrink his girlfriend?

I remember my conversation with Blue and him telling me I should get to know Row because he deserved to be happy. Blue said he would get his own chance later.

He knew. Even then, before any of the dates, he knew.

I was a pawn all along.

Sobs overtake me, and I sink to my knees. How could I have been so dumb? And why on earth am I crying? Wasn't this what I wanted—for Row to be happy? Well, now he's happy. Stop crying, stupid girl. You're a fool. Are you sorry you don't get to be the martyr now? Now things will go back to normal, and no one needs your epic sacrifice.

Don't you feel stupid? Stop crying. Shut up.

The tears only fall faster, a rain of loneliness, guilt, anger, and shame. I hold my hand over my mouth to try to hold it all in.

The sound of laughter draws my head up. Two production assistants joke and talk over cups of coffee on the far side of the room. The assistant who guided me into this room has already returned to the "Garden of Love." A drab gray sofa squats in the middle, facing a TV projection featuring a live feed of the show.

I wipe off my cheeks and fly to the arm of the sofa where I sit down to watch. I haven't seen any of the show since it started; Dr. Christiansen forbade me to watch it.

"Well, the feedback from our viewers is already pouring in on the results of the show," says the host. I recognize his voice. His hair is as immovable as his tone. "We have a few tweets to share with you now.

"First one is from Alienna8050 who says, 'So glad this turned out well and Row didn't end up with the cold witch.'"

My blood drains from my face. She can't possibly be referring to me...can she?

"And here we have another from pinkducttape saying, 'serves her right after how she turned down that other guy.'

"Some very strong opinions here, folks. We now have a recap for you from last week where Lina breaks Jack's heart in front of the world. Here it is."

And there I am on the screen, telling Jack I've chosen someone else, but wait! Now I'm spewing some truly venomous words at him. Words that were never meant for him. Words I had directed solely at Dr. Christiansen.

Wow, I think this is the first time you've ever asked me what I think, how I feel. Well, here it is. I think you're a control freak and you disgust me. Do you even have a soul in there? You've destroyed my life and who knows how many other people you've ruined as well? I don't want to have anything to do with you anymore. Ever.

I stare at the screen, openmouthed. I see Jack's hurt reaction all over again, and his cutting goodbye stings almost as much as it did a week ago.

I gave Dr. Christiansen the drama she wanted all along. She wasn't interested in seeing me get married because Row was already willing to fully cooperate. He'd already agreed to choose Daphne if he got the chance.

I drop my head into my hands.

The show cuts to the happy couple. Flower petals cascade around them as they cling to one another, wreathed in smiles. A flicker of pain crosses Daphne's face, quick as a lightning strike and gone equally fast. I frown and lean forward. Her body seizes, and she clutches Row's shoulder in agony. His joy evaporates as he asks her if she's all right. The sound cuts out, and the show's theme song blares through.

Her legs buckle and her silent scream raises the hair on the nape of my neck. The scene cuts away to the shocked host who can think of nothing to say for several seconds while the production assistants race into the "Garden of Love," not even bothering to make sure the door closes behind them.

I peer through the crack in the doorway, but I can't see anything. The Garden of Love is a crush of staff, all scrambling to help in some way. The all-too-familiar screams send chills up my spine. I heard those cries of pain the other night with Row. I would recognize that sound anywhere.

An assistant brings her phone up to her ear, but Dr. Christiansen slaps it away. I can't hear what she says, but the girl goes white. There will be no help for Daphne. The whimpers of pain sound tired, but frantic. I cover my ears with my hands because I just can't bear to hear it anymore.

I crawl into a corner under the television and allow the noise of the commercials to drown out the horrible sounds from the other room.

Half an hour later, sirens and flashing lights flood the compound. The politiet burst into the room, scouring everything with their blinding flashlights. Still, they don't see me curled up in my corner. I watch them take Jane away and several of the film crew. Once they've cleared the room, a familiar face bursts in.

George. He knows just where to look.

"Come on, pixie," he whispers, beckoning to me. "It's over. It's time to go."

CHAPTER 34

RED AND BLUE LIGHTS SLASH through the falling snow as I follow George into the parking lot of the politiet station. The cold leaves me breathless after the too-warm station that smelled of burnt coffee, old furniture, and broken hearts.

I keep seeing Daphne *breaking*. Slipping through Row's arms, her body no longer her own to control. And the other dead girl's moonlit arm with the purple fingernails that were the exact shade of the dye I put in my hair on my birthday. I see them over and over again.

They questioned me for several hours in the dingy station, with officers cycling in and out to get more and more information out of me. I saw the Toms waiting their turn in the lobby, but I didn't get a chance to speak with them. I'm not sure if I would have wanted to anyway. It became clear pretty quickly that Daphne was the one I heard screaming late at night. There were several other test subjects—all girls who wanted to compete for the hearts of the Toms who weren't spoken for at the end. All but Daphne died within weeks.

And Row knew they were doing this to Daphne. I suppose he didn't know about the failed testing on the cats before. Maybe they fooled him the way they did Jack. Maybe he couldn't deal with knowing the truth when we heard the screaming that night. He couldn't handle seeing the girl he loved in pain or dying.

I still don't completely understand. If I had been him, I would have busted down the door. I guess, in the end, it didn't matter. She's gone now. I saw Row crumple onto the floor when the officer took him aside. I couldn't hear what was said, but I didn't need to. The look on Row's face—that look of complete devastation—was all too familiar to me.

George hasn't let me out of his sight since he found me in the corner of that room. He held me a little too tight when we passed by a handcuffed Dr. Christiansen in the driveway of the Lilliput Project. All of the staff were taken into custody—everyone but Dr. Coxworth. He was nowhere to be found.

The officer in charge wasn't sure what to do with me when they were done, but George insisted he would bring me home and give me a place to stay until everything was sorted out. After all, where else could they keep me?

George leads the way to the car, an old rustbucket. I dodge a few large snowflakes. Another turns bright red as I approach it, and I scream before realizing it's just reflecting the color of the flashing police lights. George watches my freak out with concern, but says nothing as he opens the door for me.

"Just ten minutes," he says. "Then we'll be home."

I manage a smile for him, even though the cold has paralyzed my face muscles. Everything seems frozen, like the world moves in slow motion but with the intensity of a wildfire. Fire and ice. That phrase makes sense to me now.

And the snow… How fitting. The white witch, the snow queen, has beaten me.

The vinyl car seat feels like ice against my thighs, so I pace along the armrest as George drives. I want to scrub the images of Daphne and the dead girl out of my head, but I can't find anything to replace them. They have seared themselves into the fabric of my mind.

George pulls into the parking lot of an apartment complex and sits back, staring blankly ahead. We are both lost. The cold air seeps into the car, overcoming the heat, until George's breath starts turning into evanescent clouds.

"Shall we go inside?" he asks, breaking the silence.

"I guess."

He offers his hand. His palm is sweaty and smells of car leather, but I sit down in his protective grip anyway.

Inside the house, he flips on the kitchen light and sets me down on the table. The flat has the feel of a place time forgot, where devilish gnomes used every appliance, every piece of furniture day in and day out. It's worn out and badly in need of redecorating.

"Tea?"

"Yes, please.'"

He sets the kettle on the stove, but it takes several tries for the gas to ignite. I didn't even know you could have a gas stove.

"It's propane," he says as though reading my mind. "It's the only cheap fuel we've got nowadays." He pulls out a matchbook and lights the pillar candle at the center of the table before turning off the overhead light. Outside the window, it's pure white. The snowfall is so thick I can't even see the road.

George disappears into the next room while we wait for the water to boil. I can hear him rummaging around, and then he returns carrying a handful of doll clothes.

"I got these for you. I'm sorry they aren't very nice, but I wanted you to have something to wear until they let you get your things. And this here is a sewing kit. I cut off the needle for you and sharpened it." He places them into my arms and sits down again, his hands cupping his empty mug as though he's forgotten the tea isn't ready yet. "I set up a room for you, too. It's in the living room, and there's a curtain."

"Thank you, George. For everything."

We both stare at the flickering candle flame. The teapot's whistle interrupts the silence and George pours the tea. I get a thimble-full from his mug once it's finished brewing.

"I'm sorry," he says. "I should have done something a long time ago. I was afraid...oh, but that is so cowardly. Still, it's the truth. I was afraid they would fire me and you would have no one there to look after you. I couldn't put you in that position, not after everything that took place."

"What *did* happen?"

"There were seven of you to begin with. Actually, let me start at the very beginning. After the European Republic formed and the Greek revolution failed, the part I lived in was very poor. We had no services, no sewage or even good drinking water. I was married then and I had a brand-new daughter, but the delivery was hard on my wife and she was very weak. My daughter was also not in good health because my wife's nutrition was so bad while she was pregnant. They both became very sick. My wife died first from pneumonia, and my daughter died two weeks later."

I've never heard this story before. "Oh, George, I'm so sorry."

"After this happened, I had nothing left for me in Greece. The rest of my family died in the war. So when I received a job offer from the Lilliput Project several months later, I accepted. They had seen some of my published research on birds, and they took me on. I didn't know the scope of the project, and I was under contract to keep their experiments a closely guarded secret.

"I never saw any of the Toms. They were born in England and taken to New Zealand after it happened."

"After what happened?"

"There were seven of you. You were all born at once, and I've never seen anything so tiny. You were all kept together so you could get human contact from one another, but you were the only one with asthma and you came down with a bad respiratory infection a couple of months after you were born. Dr. Christiansen had you quarantined and told us no one could touch you. But you would lie there and scream and cry, and all I could think about was my own baby girl, so I would go in and hold you for hours when no one was around.

"You started to get better, but the other girls were declining and no one knew why. They were…listless. They stopped crying or trying to get anyone's attention. Then they stopped eating, and they were too small to be fed by a tube. They were only six months old, and they'd never even rolled over.

"They died one by one, almost all within a week. Only one, number five, held out another month."

I wipe the back of my hand across my eyes to chase away the tears. "But why did they die? And why am I the only one who made it?"

He bites his lip and looks down at the table. "Dr. Christiansen said they died due to mental conditions, but I think that was only partly correct. I think they died from a lack of affection. While they were always lying close to one another, no one ever held them. They never received the slightest bit of love. I will never forgive myself for that."

"So…my asthma saved my life."

"In a way. I suppose you could say that."

"But only because of you."

He sighs and nods, uncomfortable with taking credit for my continued existence.

"Why did the Toms survive then?"

"They very nearly didn't, but after one of them died, I emailed their director—Dr. Lee—and told him about your survival and how you had been held every single day. So they implemented the practice at Lilliput II and sick Toms got better."

I stare down into my tea, absorbing everything he's told me. This isn't what I'd imagined. I'd pictured horrible experiments, torture, etc. I never guessed the Thumbelinas died because they weren't loved enough. I didn't even know that was possible.

Yet, somehow this information isn't a surprise. It seems to explain and validate this yearning I have that never quite goes away. I've almost gotten used to it. It was there even when I was talking to Jack every day, although it wasn't quite as pronounced then. I crave human touch, and I rarely ever get it.

"Will you forgive me, pixie?"

"For what?"

"I could have done better, and if I had, you wouldn't have grown up so lonely. None of this would have happened to you. You didn't deserve this."

"Well, Dr. Christiansen would still be just as wacko, so I'm not sure about that."

"Maybe not. She changed after that. She's never been a warm woman, but she got worse. I think she truly thought she was doing a good thing when she created all of you." He shrugs. "Most people think they're doing the right thing."

"Yeah."

"Well, are you through with your tea?"

I hand him the thimble.

"You should get some sleep. We have things to discuss tomorrow."

"What kinds of things?"

"Many news agencies are asking for your story. You can right your reputation if you wish. But we'll talk about it tomorrow after you've rested."

He carries me to my makeshift bedroom, lights a tea candle near my bed, and carries his own light away with him. I wait until his door closes before changing into the cotton nightgown with massive Velcro strips that I have to leave open in order to make room for my wings. I'll cut off the Velcro tomorrow and add a tie. The nightgown is too big, but it's warm and comfortable, a welcome change from the evening gown I've been wearing all day.

My bed is a shoebox full of stacked washcloths, and I sink into it with a contented sigh. I remember what George said about righting my reputation. What would it take for that to happen? A pulse of excitement at the possibility of vindication wakes me a little, but not enough. I fall asleep with the candle flame still flickering in the darkness.

CHAPTER 35

"YOU'RE ON SOON. ARE YOU ready? Know your cue?" The assistant pulls out his earpiece and leans toward me.

"Yeah, I've got it," I say. "You put my name up in huge letters on that screen and then I fly out."

"Right. Good!" He gives me a thumbs up, totally oblivious to my sarcasm. "Break a wing!" He chuckles at his own joke.

Haha. Very funny. My wing finished healing a couple of days ago, and I can finally fly at full speed. George helped stitch me up, but it took longer to heal than usual because it was such a large tear. Then it took us a week to find a publicist who would work pro bono until my trust money is released. That won't be for a while since Dr. Christiansen is now in custody and awaiting trial and my lawyer can't get the money until a verdict is reached. Still, everyone considers it to be a slam-dunk. I'm still bitter she wasn't arrested until she killed a "real" human on international television, but I'm happy she's in a place where she can't hurt anyone else.

Now I'm waiting in the wings of a British television studio, about to appear on *The Tani Ellis Show* to share my side of the story with the world. It was strange to have someone new fix my hair and makeup, but I'm pleased with the results. The hairdresser pulled out the world's smallest flatiron and gave me the first smooth hair-do I've ever had. And my makeup isn't over the top. Best of all, I'm wearing my own clothes—a sari patchwork skirt, leggings, and a black tank top. And scrunched socks. My feet are pretty happy that they're no longer stuffed into plastic doll shoes.

My name flashes on the monitor in neon yellow letters: LENA CHRISTIANSEN. They've managed to misspell my name, and it throws me off a little bit. Also, I definitely want to see about changing my last name.

Deep breath. Adrenaline floods my veins as I burst through the curtain and wave at the audience. A cacophony of boos and cheers greets me, but I focus on my instructions.

Fly out to the dais, wait for the host to come and shake my hand. Tani is a pretty dark-skinned woman with blindingly white teeth. She smiles and her lips move as she makes a show of holding my hand, but I'm concentrating so hard on my next step I don't hear what she says.

Go to the desk, sit on the doll sofa. I'm careful to make sure Tani reaches her chair first before I seat myself on the rock-hard cushion.

Answer questions. Be charming. This will be a lot harder.

"So, Lina. Welcome! We're so excited to have you on the show with us."

"Thank you. It's an honor to be here."

"Now, usually we have folks on to promote their new movie or book, but you're here for a different reason. I'm sure I don't need to recap for our audience because you've become a household name all over the world, but just in case anyone's been hiding under a rock for the past two months, Lina Christiansen recently starred in a reality dating show featuring six contestants who are as unique as she is. Her six Toms were also about six inches tall. However, she shocked the world when her online boyfriend Jack offered to undergo a transformation procedure to bring him down to her size and she turned him down in favor of a young man named Row or Tom 2. In an even more unexpected turn of events, Row was reunited with his former girlfriend, Daphne Livingston, who underwent the shrinking procedure. Unfortunately, Miss Livingston passed away due to complications from the transformation, with viewers worldwide witnessing some of the horror. Truly shocking.

"Now, Lina, you've received a lot of flak for turning down Jack and choosing Row, and you're here to clear the air, so to speak. Would you like to tell us what happened?"

"Yes, thank you." I lick my lips, longing for a sip of water. My mouth has gone completely dry.

"Dr. Christiansen is now in custody for the wrongful death of Daphne Livingston. Did you have some idea the procedure was harmful?"

"I did. Before the show even started, I caught one of the assistants doing some sort of testing on a cat. And right before the episode with Jack—where I told him I'd picked someone else—I found out someone had died from Dr. Christiansen's experiments. I didn't know then that she was trying to shrink full-sized people."

"So when Jack told you what he was willing to do for your relationship, you knew he could die if he went through with it."

"Yes. I tried to tell him, but they kept freezing the…the transmission whenever I said something about the risks. So I knew the only way to keep him from going through with it was if I…if I got him to stay away from me."

"You tried to protect him." Tani's face is full of manufactured compassion, and I'm suddenly uncomfortable with revealing the inner workings of my heart to her on this stage. But Jack has to know, and this is the only way I can tell him.

The audience "awwws," and Tani nods at them meaningfully.

"That was all I wanted," I say, looking directly into the camera. "I promised him once that I would never make him watch something painful unless I had a good reason, and I've never broken my word on that."

"Tell us more about the show itself. Were you given a choice about whether or not you would participate?"

"I was told I could either cooperate, or they would hurt Jack."

"And how did they know about him or where to find him?"

"I'd been talking to him online for a year, and Dr. Christiansen took my computer and watched all my video files. Without my permission."

Tani shakes her head. "That's horrible. And from what I understand, you don't enjoy all the rights and privileges we regular-sized people do here in the European Union."

"No. Technically, I'm not a human."

"Unbelievable. Well, is there anything you would tell Jack if you had the chance?"

Not on your show, not because you asked. But I've committed to this thing, so I clear my throat and say, "Yes. I'd like—"

"I'm so glad you said that," she says, "because I have a surprise for you. Please welcome Lina's online love—Jack!"

I whirl around as Jack bursts onto the stage to deafening applause and cheering. I stand awkwardly as Tani rushes over to shake his hand and lead him to the chair. I'm not sure what to do. Should I go over to him? Stay here? Smile and wave? No one prepared me for this.

I stand rooted in place as he sits and waves at the audience. He's looking unbelievably hot in his dark chocolate suit, with his hair all casual. But there's a hardness in his eyes I've never seen before.

"Hello, Lina."

"Hi, Jack," I squeak.

"This is the first time you two have ever been in the same room, isn't it?" Tani asks. Thank you, Captain Obvious.

"It is," he says with far more composure than I can muster right now.

"Now, Jack," she says. "I'm sure you heard Lina's explanation. What do you think about that?"

"I think I'm not quite sure what I believe right now."

"And you didn't know she was the world's first Thumbelina while you were dating if I understand correctly."

"I wouldn't say we were dating. We talked online. None of our dates were real."

Those words sting even deeper than his last goodbye.

"But you cared for her," Tani presses.

He squirms in his seat. "Obviously. I offered to let a quack doctor cut me down to size for her."

"Hm. Well, Lina has something to say to you. Lina?"

This is not how this is supposed to happen. In all my fantasies of meeting Jack, I never dreamed of being put on the spot in front of an international audience in order to say my piece. And I never imagined I would see his face so hard and set against me. My words cannot crack his shell. He has no reason to believe I did it all because I love him.

"I'm sorry," I say as the tears shove their way out, humiliating me in front of everyone. "I can't do this." And then, escorted with gasps of disbelief, I fly offstage.

CHAPTER 36

"GO BACK OUT!" THE ASSISTANT screams when I burst through the curtain. He looks past me, and his eyes widen even more. "You too!"

I whirl around in my teary haze and come face-to-face with Jack. He followed me?

"Can we… I don't know how to do this. Can we talk?" he asks.

"Okay."

The assistant inserts himself between us and goes off on Jack. "Get back on the stage! What are you doing?!"

"Out of my face, please," Jack says. "This is no longer any of your business." His voice is so commanding that the assistant backs off. Jack jerks his head toward the dressing rooms, and I follow him into the one marked with his name.

He closes the door behind us with a muffled click that dies in the silence and stuffiness of the room.

We stare at each other. Finally we're alone and together, and we have nothing to say. Now that we're up close and I don't have an audience watching, I notice the edges of his suit are frayed, and it's a bit old-fashioned. The legs are a little short, too.

"It was my dad's," he says. "I could never afford to buy one right now. That's why I agreed to come on the show. I didn't do it to embarrass you." He sighs and runs his hand through his hair. "I should have known better."

I bite down on the inside of my lip.

He continues, his voice tired. "They didn't tell me you would be here. If they had, I wouldn't have done this. Although I'm sure it would have been hard to say no. On some level."

"You're still angry with me."

"Yeah, I am."

"Even though you heard everything I said out there? About why I had to turn you down? And those nasty comments weren't even meant for you in the first place. Dr. Christiansen asked me to tell her exactly what I thought of her. They recorded it."

He folds his arms. "It wasn't your choice to make. Did it ever occur to you I might be intelligent enough to ask about the risks? That I might be smart enough to decide on my own whether or not I wanted to take the chance?"

I open my mouth, but he doesn't give me opportunity to speak.

"Apparently you didn't because you thought it was all up to you, that you were the only one who could be the hero. Seriously, Lina, I don't think you could have been more of a martyr." He shakes his head in disgust.

"Jack, if you'd been in my shoes, you would have done the same thing. I knew you didn't have the whole story. They lied to me all along. Right before that day when they told me you could be shrunk, I found out someone I'd trusted all my life had been deceiving me from day one. Even if they did tell you there were risks, they didn't tell you all of them. I watched them bury some poor girl they killed. Did they tell you that part?

"If these people were ordinary, honest scientists, it would have been very different. But they're not—they're liars and manipulators! I've lived with Dr. Christiansen and her little band of hack jobs all my life. Give me a little credit!"

He smirks at me. "Liars and manipulators, eh? Seems like you are related to them after all. I guess you couldn't find it in your heart to tell me for the past *year* that you're six inches tall and have wings. Care to explain that one?"

I take a deep breath. There is no good answer. There's no reason he should believe me now. Still, if I'm going to win back his trust, I'd better start being honest. "I didn't want to lose you."

He shakes his head and runs his hands through his hair. "So you let me believe a lie so you could get what you wanted. Did you ever think about what I wanted? Maybe I would have liked the opportunity to choose for myself whether or not I dated a tiny girl? But I guess you didn't really care about me that much. You just cared about yourself."

Every word hits its mark at the center of my heart. Every word is true. It feels more complicated to me than he's described, but he isn't wrong either.

I struggle against the words I need to say but manage to force them out. "You're right. I'm sorry."

"Are you really?"

"Well, I'm not sorry I got to have you in my life for a longer period of time. But you're right that it was selfish, so I'm sorry."

The balloon of his anger appears to be deflating. He chews on his lip.

"Jack?"

"What?"

"Why did you accept Dr. Christiansen's offer to be shrunk if you were so mad at me for misleading you?"

He stares hard at the wall behind me. "Because I kept thinking about what you said the last time we talked. Right before you pulled the plug on your computer." His eyes meet mine. "And I missed you. But now I don't know what to think."

"Jack, I decided to love Row because choosing him kept you safe. At least, I thought it would. Can you understand that?" I throw up my hands in frustration. "I gave up on ever being happy. I remember you telling me about how you felt when you realized you could never stop working and supporting your siblings. You said it felt like a crushing weight that would never go away no matter how hard you wished, no matter how hard you worked. When you told me, I didn't understand how that felt. Well, now I do. Now I know that not everything has a happy ending."

I flutter close to his face. Even though we're inches away from each other, I don't feel any butterflies. I just feel him, who he is, how we are connected. "I can't make you forgive me, and I won't try to twist your arm. But I'm asking you."

He lifts his hand so I can stand on his palm. "I don't know, Lina. What would that even mean now? Look at us. So, say I forgive you—do we shake hands and go our separate ways?"

My heart is a worn-out punching bag, but I have to ask anyway. "Do we have to?"

As soon as the words leave my mouth, I realize I'm assuming a lot. He's never told me he loves me, although his actions have said as much in the past.

He searches my heart through my eyes, and I hold my breath.

"Lina, there are six guys—"

"But none of them are you." And there I go again, showing too much of my hand when he hasn't revealed his. "Jack, can I ask you something?"

"Go for it."

"The last night we talked, when I told you…when I told you that I love you… What did you say afterward? Did you say anything at all?"

His voice is firm and confident. "I said I loved you, too."

Loved. Past tense. My heart drops.

"I still do."

We stare at each other, both unwilling to break the sudden spell that binds us. I can hear my own heartbeat, and my entire body has gone warm.

He loves me.

"I love you, too," I say. "I never stopped. It's not perfect, but it's love."

He nods. I'm not sure how much he believes me, but it feels like we're careening over the crest of the wave here and this will either be the ride of our lives or an epic wipeout.

He draws me closer to his face. "What am I going to do with you?" He smiles for the first time.

"Take me with you."

"You really want that? You'd want to leave your home and come to South Dakota?"

Do I? I've been living in George's flat, but Denmark has always been my home. Until right now, I've assumed I would eventually return to my treehouse and figure out what to do from there. But what if I could start over again with someone who loves me?

"Yes," I say. "I do."

CHAPTER 37

I SWING MY FEET BACK and forth, back and forth from my perch on the stable window and rub my arms to chase away the winter morning chill. The dawn light cuts yellow beams through the dust erupting under Sampson's stomping hooves. He snorts out frosty clouds as Jack adjusts his bridle. The saddle hangs in the tack room, unused. Jack still prefers riding bareback, but today he will have to wear shoes.

"We're lucky it didn't snow last night." He gives Sampson a pat. "Are you ready?"

I nod, then say "yes" as loud as I can. He's not accustomed to my tiny gestures and facial expressions, so I have to speak up more often than I normally would. We're still getting used to each other. I imagine we will be breaking one another in for a while.

He leads Sampson out into the yard, then swings his legs over the pinto's back.

"Come on, pixie!" He unzips his jacket and pats his shirt pocket. I climb inside, and he presses his hand against me to make sure I'm safe, just as he always does. I've told him a million times it doesn't matter if I fall out because obviously I have wings, but he still does the pre-ride pat.

I wiggle inside the pocket until I'm comfortable and my wings aren't bent in odd places, and then I shout, "Ready!"

An hour later, we reach the edge of the Badlands. The orange sun bleeds into the last of the morning shadows, and an icy wind whips around the stony pillars, plastering my hair to Jack's chest. Strange rocky shapes rise from the desert floor as far as I can see. There is definitely nothing like this in Denmark.

I am still getting used to the poverty on the reservation. It's been even harder for George, although Jack's mom seems to be helping him to keep his mind off of anything negative lately. I'm sure he's honing his flirting skills in the kitchen while he makes tzatziki sauce right now. He's a bit out of practice. Then again, so is Jack's mom. They're an odd couple, those two.

I look up at the underside of Jack's chin. Who am I to accuse anyone else of being an odd couple?

But maybe we won't be for long. He hasn't told me about the letter yet, but I read it. It was from some Native American doctor who has developed a similar procedure to the one Dr. Christiansen came up with. Now that it's fully ready, he's offered to let Jack be the first human test subject.

Unease creeps into this new peace I have, but I fight it down. I still want to know how they reproduced Dr. Christiansen's technology so fast and why. But this decision has to be Jack's alone. When he wants to hear my thoughts, I will offer them.

I lean against his chest, absorbing his warmth. He smiles and wraps his hand around me, gently touching my face with his fingertip. Whatever happens, we'll get through it.

For now, this is enough.

EPILOGUE

Lilliput II: Present Time

Row folds and unfolds his arms across his chest. Clears his throat, tries to smile. It won't come.

This is a mistake. He stares down at the pile of flower petals on Daphne's white dress, the one that had been his favorite. The other Toms stand at the ready, each holding a corner, waiting for him to give the word.

It had seemed like a romantic way to remember her when he'd first thought of it. They would scatter the petals and her ashes over the ocean so that she would always be there with him. But now it seemed too simple, too childish. A stupid fairytale.

This was all his fault. Her family wouldn't speak to him, called him a killer. He winced at the thought. The only reason he'd gotten her ashes was because she'd signed herself over to the Lilliput Project before she underwent the procedure. Even then, he'd had to wait until after the trial to recover her remains, and by that time, there was nothing to say goodbye to that resembled the girl he loved.

Oh God. He covers his mouth with his hand, his body wracked in sobs. Blue rests his hand on Row's back, but the gesture does little to comfort him.

"This is for you," Blue says, "not Daphne. Just remember that. She would want you to forgive yourself."

Row blinks back the tears and nods because that is what is expected. But he can't forgive himself—not for what he did to Daphne. Not for what he did to Lina.

He clears his throat. "All right, let's do this." When he smiles, his heart isn't in it.

Lilliput I: One week before the final selection episode.

"Sure! I'll be right there to let you in. Hold tight!" Jane clicked off the intercom button and nervously straightened her lab coat as she checked to make sure the presentation was ready.

Projector set up? Check.

Coffee and creamer set out on the table? Check.

Serums packaged tightly in their case and ready for sale? Jane opened the refrigerator and lifted the lid of the plastic case. It held over a dozen vials placed in neat lines. She counted them under her breath. Thirteen, fourteen, fifteen, six— Where was sixteen?

"Oh, no, where are you, sixteen? Are you hiding?" She dug her fingers down beneath the other vials in case number sixteen had fallen down. It wasn't there. Where could it be? She pulled everything out of the fridge, checked every nook and cranny. It was nowhere to be found.

The intercom beeped to life. "Hello, is someone coming to let us in?"

Shaking all over, Jane hastily put everything back into the fridge before running to the intercom on the wall. But before she could push the button, she heard Dr. Christiansen's voice coming through the speaker.

"Certainly, I am not sure where my assistant is, but I will be right there myself."

Jane pulled her hand away from the button and clamped it against her mouth. "Oh crap, oh crap. Where did I put it? I have to find it!"

But it wasn't there.

One week before the funeral

Dr. Coxworth thrummed his fingers against his briefcase and leaned against the plush couch cushions as he waited. A young woman sat a couple of seats down from him, then wrinkled her nose and left. He discreetly ducked his head down to give his armpits another sniff. Sure enough, they were especially pungent. Perfect. He was guaranteed to be left to himself. No one would get close enough to notice frost was forming around the cracks in his briefcase.

A disinterested bottle blonde girl walked out into the lobby. "Dr. Two Oaks?"

"That's me," said Dr. Coxworth in a perfect American accent. He held the briefcase to his chest as he walked over to her.

She frowned slightly as if she was trying to figure out where the smell was coming from, but then she pressed her lips together and jerked her head toward the door. "This way."

He followed her down the hall and stifled a yawn. Two months ago, he'd left the Lilliput Compound for his daily stroll, except instead of going on his usual walk through the forest, he got into a taxi and went straight to the airport. It had been far too easy. He'd disappeared from their radar with his new identification…and as much of Lilliput's money as possible.

He shook his head. For all her smarts, Dr. Christiansen really was quite terrible at reading other people. That particular fault of hers had served him well.

He'd kept careful tabs on her experiments, identifying all her mistakes so he could correct them later. And Jane… Oh, Jane had only been useful in her carelessness. She was just always misplacing things, even when she had never touched them. It had been far too easy to take everything he had needed from the lab.

When he'd discovered Dr. Christiansen's plans to sell her discovery to a different lab with better technology and funding, he knew it was time to act or his opportunity would be lost. So he'd convinced George to turn her in. She came up with the idea for the reality show in order to raise money, and that was most unexpected. But too late.

Serum #16 was going to make him a very rich man.

The blonde opened a heavy wooden office door for him. Her eyebrows rose when she saw how many men were in the room, but she only said, "Dr. Two Oaks is here." Then she left.

Dr. Coxworth cleared his throat and stepped inside. "Good morning, gentlemen. I can't think of the last time I had the shortest hair in a room full of well-dressed men."

There were eight of them, all in suits and sporting long black ponytails.

One man stood from behind his massive desk. He had a pronounced potbelly and a long scar running along his jawline. "Welcome to the Red Crow Casino, Doctor. Please have a seat. We spoke over the internet—I'm John Little Crow, the manager. This here is Tom Running Deer, the President of Pine Ridge Reservation, and these are several of our council members. How was your flight?"

"Excellent, excellent. Thank you for asking. Thank you for having me here." Dr. Coxworth thrummed his briefcase again and cleared his throat. "I suppose I should start from the beginning, just in case some of you haven't gotten all of the info. But what I have here could give your tribe some real leverage with the Dakotan government."

"The Dakotan government is flat broke," said Tom Running Deer.

"Truer words have never been spoken," Dr. Coxworth said with a little finger wag at the president. "But where do governments continue to spend even when they have nothing left?"

He paused for good measure. "Weapons."

One of the council members laughed incredulously. "What sort of 'weapons' are we talking about here?"

Dr. Coxworth opened his briefcase and drew out vial #16.

"Human weapons."

The council member drew in his breath. "I assume that's untested."

"Never assume, my dear friend." Dr. Coxworth dug around inside his briefcase again before drawing out a small, padded box. He set it on the conference table and opened the lid. A tiny ape climbed out and unfolded its wings—the soft, gray wings of a dove.

"He's a bit groggy. I had to sedate him for the trip." He glanced at the council's open-mouthed stares. "The serum shrinks the mammal, but the wings have to be surgically added afterward."

"How do you know this works on humans?" a council member scoffed. "The entire world is well-aware of what happened to that poor girl."

"This serum," said Dr. Coxworth, "is an improved version of the last one. The first set of researchers made the mistake of testing it only on smaller animals such as mice and cats before making the transition to human testing because mice are genetically closest to humans. Their error was they should have tested it on an animal with a similar mass to a human's. Once I did that, we were able to correct the little problem of…repeatedly broken bones."

"It's such an extreme process," Little Crow observed as the winged ape began flying in lopsided circles. "Who would volunteer for it?"

"As it turns out, a willing young man has stepped forward, and he's right here on your reservation," said Dr. Coxworth.

"Who?"

"His name is Jack Thunderbird."

ACKNOWLEDGMENTS

Many thanks to my agent, Steve Axelrod, for believing in DAMSELFLY and me and also knowing when it was the right time to self-publish. Thanks to Rebecca Weston, the best copy editor and the finder of missing commas.

I owe a tremendous debt to the community at Agent Query Connect and everyone there who critiqued various sections of this book. MarcyKate Connelly, Cat Woods, and the rest of the Kid Crits group - you were all invaluable contributors to my novel!

Thanks to all my beta readers - Derrick Camardo, Sean Jenan, Riley Redgate, Maggen Stone and Caterina Torres. This book would not be the same without your incredible feedback.

Finally, this book wouldn't exist without my husband, Dejan. Your encouragement has meant the world to me.

www.ingramcontent.com/pod-product-compliance
Lightning Source LLC
Chambersburg PA
CBHW031723170626
46808CB00005B/1859